'SPYSKI'

BY
TERRY CAVENDER

*'Bad men need nothing more to compass their ends,
than that good men should look on and do nothing'*
(John Stuart Mill)

ACKNOWLEDGMENTS:

Mags, Sara & Ian Langthorne, Harry & Nicky Clacy, Donna Grant, Tony Brown.

The Bureau d'Information de Villefranche-sur-Mer (Office de Tourisme Métropolitain, Nice, Côte d'Azur).

Every effort has been made to contact copyright holders of any material reproduced in this book. If any have been inadvertently overlooked that will be rectified at the earliest opportunity.

This book is a work of fiction. Names, characters, businesses, organisations, places and events are either the product of the author's imagination or are used fictitiously. Any resemblance to actual persons, living or dead, or events or locales is entirely coincidental.

No part of this publication may be reproduced, stored in or introduced into a retrieval system, or transmitted, in any form or by any means, without the prior permission in writing of the author, nor be otherwise circulated in any form of binding or cover other than that which it is published and without a similar condition including this condition being imposed on the subsequent purchaser.

Copyright © 2019 Terry Cavender
(The moral right of the author has been asserted)
All rights reserved.

Also by Terry Cavender:

A BOY FROM NOWHERE.
THREE TALL TALES.
THREE MORE TALL TALES.
EVEN MORE TALL TALES.
ANOTHER THREE TALL TALES.
BREAKING THE 4TH DIMENSION.
TINKERING WITH TIME.

(With Harry (Brian) Clacy)

TELL IT LIKE IT WASN'T (PART 1).
And
TELL IT LIKE IT WASN'T (PART 2).

(With Steve King)

AS LONG AS I KNOW –
IT'LL BE QUITE ALRIGHT.

SPYSKI - 'SPOOK' LEGEND'

(United of Soviet Socialist Republics from 1922 to 1991): (then The Russian Federation)

FSB - Federal Security Services of the Russian Federation.

The Principal Security Agency of Russia (successor to the KGB and FSK).

KGB - Komitet Gosudarstvennoy Bezopasnosti. *(Committee for State Security).*

FSK - Federal Counter-Intelligence Service.

GRU - Glaznoje Rasvedyvatel'noje Upravlenijie. *(Soviet Military Intelligence Directorate).*

(United States of America):

CIA - Central Intelligence Agency.

FBI - Federal Bureau of Investigation.

(United Kingdom):

Domestic Intelligence	Security Service (MI5)
	Office for Security and Counter-Terrorism (OSCT)
	National Domestic Extremism and Disorder Intelligence Unit (NDEDIU)
	National Crime Agency (NCA)
	National Ballistics Intelligence Service (NBIS)
	National Fraud Intelligence Bureau (NFIB)
Foreign Intelligence	Secret Intelligence Service (SIS/MI6)
	Defence Intelligence (DI)
Signals Intelligence	Government Communications Headquarters (GCHQ)
Joint Intelligence	Joint Intelligence Organisation (JIO)

CHAPTERS:

ONE - SUMMONED TO NUMBER 10.

TWO - PRISONER 887.

THREE - GAME ON!

FOUR - A NEW TASK.

FIVE - PENKOVSKY CAPTURED.

SIX - FLASH TO BANG.

SEVEN - NUMBER 10 DOWNING STREET.

EIGHT - VILLEFRANCHE-SUR-MER.

NINE - THE TIME-TRAVEL HOLIDAY STORE - KINGSTON-UPON-HULL.

TEN - THE AQUARIUM.

ELEVEN - PRISONER 888.

TWELVE - OUT OF THE KOMOROWSKA.

THIRTEEN - BEHIND THE HIDDEN WALL.

FOURTEEN   -   AMSTERDAM.

FIFTEEN   -   NUMBER 10 DOWNING STREET.

SIXTEEN   -   NEWSFLASH.

(EXTRACT FROM THE NEXT
'TIME-TRAVEL' ADVENTURE):

'SADDAM'S MISSING BILLIONS'

TASTER:

CHAPTER ONE   -   WAY TO GO!

'SPYSKI'

There are three key elements that interweave throughout this story, (a story that is a mixture of fact and fiction) – 'Faction.'

<u>Element 1:</u> Time-Travel.

<u>Element 2:</u> Colonel Oleg Penkovsky, Russian Master Spy.

<u>Element 3:</u> The Hidden Library of Tsar 'Ivan the Terrible' of Russia.

Ж

Element 1

'Time-Travel'

Once again, the leading protagonists in this 'Time-Travel' story are: Graham St Anier, a retired Police Inspector who resides in the delightful East Yorkshire market town of Beverley, and his friend, Hull based Scotsman Mike Fraser, the owner of the long-established and exclusive 'Time-Travellers Incorporated' 'T2-Inc' organisation whose main offices are based in the 'Time Travel Holiday Store' at Kingswood Retail Park on the outskirts of Kingston-Upon-Hull.

Although a proud 'Jock' - Mike is an 'Honorary' Yorkshireman. Both Mike and Graham thrive on a spot of 'Mystery, Mischief and Mayhem.' They are joined on this new adventure by their old friend, Dutchman Mike De Jong.

The main offices of *'T2-Inc'* is where all of the *'Time-Travel'* key planning and preparation takes place. Currently the only two Time-Machines – (the latest *'T3-Travellators'*) in the world are owned and operated under strict governmental license by *'T2-Inc'* and regularly *'bend time'* by *'teleporting'* from Humberside Travelport where *'T2-Inc'* has its own closely guarded secure hangar facility.

Ж

Element 2

'Oleg Penkovsky – the Master Spy'

Oleg Vladimirovich Penkovsky was born on the 23rd of April 1919 at Vladikavkaz, North Ossetia, Russia. He graduated from the Kiev Artillery Academy in the rank of Lieutenant in 1939.

After taking part in the Winter War against Finland and participating in World War 2, he had reached the rank of Lieutenant Colonel.

'Colonel Oleg Vladimirovitch Penkovsky'

A Soviet Military Intelligence Officer with the GRU (the Main Intelligence Directorate), Penkovsky was appointed Military Attaché in Ankara, Turkey, in 1955. He later worked at the Soviet Committee for Scientific Research. Penkovsky was a personal friend of the powerful Head of the GRU, General Ivan Serov and was also close to Soviet Marshal Sergei Varentsov.

Penkovsky, who had grown disillusioned with the Soviet regime, felt that Premier Nikita Kruschev was forever busy fomenting trouble and by doing so was leading the Soviet Union down the path to nuclear destruction with his relentless commitment to spreading Communism throughout the world. As a result he was constantly at loggerheads with the United Kingdom and the United States of America.

Wishing to prevent a nuclear war between the super-powers, Colonel Penkovsky delivered copious amounts of sensitive and highly classified documentary material to the 'opposition's' security forces, hoping that by doing so he was helping to level the 'playing field.'

As a representative of a Soviet Scientific Research Delegation, Colonel Penkovsky travelled frequently to Britain and France where he met both his CIA (Central Intelligence Agency) and Britain's MI6 (Military Intelligence 6) handlers for several intensive debriefing sessions. Whilst in Moscow he also passed over invaluable classified and sensitive documentary material at meetings with the wife of an officer from the British Embassy.

During the period that Penkovsky passed similar information to the USA and UK, he also:

- *Spoke to de-briefers for around 140 hours, passing on technical details of Soviet weaponry and their combat units.*
- *Delivered numerous rolls of microfilm and passed 5000+ photos of a significant number of secret papers to the CIA and MI6.*

- *Gave details of Soviet military preparedness.*
- *Informed MI6 and the CIA of the political intentions of the Kremlin hierarchy.*

Penkovsky's de-briefing sessions produced approximately 1,200 pages of transcripts, which the CIA and MI6 had around 30 translators and analysts working on. His information was immensely invaluable in helping to dispel concerns about Soviet strategic superiority and showed that in fact the US had the upper hand, at that time, in missile development and systems.

During the Cuban Missile Crisis, the information that Penkovsky had provided gave both the Kennedy and MacMillan Administration technical insights regarding the Soviet nuclear missiles deployed to Cuba, information that would eventually lead to a diplomatic solution.

Because of the information supplied by Penkovsky, President Kennedy knew that he only had three days before the Soviet missiles were made fully functional in Cuba, so was able to negotiate a diplomatic solution before they could be activated. It was a close run thing.

Penkovsky was responsible for informing the United Kingdom and the United States about the Soviet emplacement of missiles in Cuba, thus providing them both with the knowledge necessary to resolve the problem which was causing an increase in military tensions with the Soviet Union.

Colonel Penkovsky was the highest ranking Soviet official to provide intelligence for the UK at that time and as such is credited as being one of those who helped alter the course of what was termed the 'Cold War.'

In Moscow in the early hours of the morning of the 22nd of October 1962, Penkovsky was arrested by the feared KGB and taken to the Lubyanka Prison for interrogation by Alexander Zagvozdin, Chief KGB Interrogator. Zagvozdin stated that Penkovsky had been apprehended by the Soviet authorities for treasonable activities, he had then been tried, found guilty and, allegedly, executed. It was never revealed who or what had implicated Penkovsky.

There is a school of thought, however, that the long-time naturalised British subject, double-agent George Blake, (originally from the Netherlands) informed the KGB about Penkovsky's work for the US and UK, so from then on the KGB began to keep a very close eye on him. Blake also informed his KGB contacts of the details of British and American operations. It is claimed that Blake betrayed details of some 40 MI6 agents to the KGB, and by doing so ruined the majority of MI6's operations in Eastern Europe.

Because of information received, KGB Officers were stationed in apartments above and across the river from Penkovsky's home, from where they closely monitored his activities. His days were numbered.

After an extensive period of surveillance he was arrested by the KGB and placed on trial for Treason and Espionage. After being found guilty, his execution was ordered. Thus Penkovsky's career as a spy for the United Kingdom and the United States of America was brought to an abrupt end.

Colonel Oleg Vladimirovitch Penkovsky is still considered by the UK and the USA to have been one of the most valuable agents in history.

Element 3

'Tsar Ivan's Hidden Library'

Tsar Ivan Vasilyevich, (more commonly known as 'Ivan the Terrible') was the Grand Prince of Moscow from 1533 to 1547 then was proclaimed the first Tsar of Russia in 1547, reigning until 1584 when he died from a stroke whilst playing chess. He was proclaimed Emperor of all Russia at the tender age of 17. Ivan's reign was characterised by Russia's transformation from being a medieval state into a thriving empire. He was an able diplomat, a patron of the arts and encouraged trade, making him very popular with Russia's commoners.

'Ivan the Terrible'
(Painted by Klavidy Levedev – 1916)

Ivan was known to have had a very complex personality, described as being intelligent and devout, but was prone to paranoia, rages and episodic outbreaks of mental instability that increased with age. During one ferocious outburst he was believed to have killed his own son and heir, leaving the politically ineffectual Feodor Ivanovich to inherit his throne - which turned out to be a particularly bad move because it eventually led to the end of the dynasty as Feodor died without issue.

The Hidden Library

The 'Golden Library' (also known as the 'Hidden Library' or the 'Secret Library') is reputed to have been created by Tsar Ivan way back in the 16th century. The library is *rumoured to have contained rare Greek, Latin and Egyptian works from the libraries of Alexandria and Constantinople, as well as ancient 2nd century Chinese texts and many other such valuable artifacts, including precious metals such as silver, gold and a great deal of jewellery, including some of the Russian Crown Jewels.*

Tsar Ivan is believed to have instructed scholars of the time to translate ancient texts in the library so that he could gain knowledge of black magic, thus giving him the ability to cast evil spells. This terrible man is supposed to have placed a curse on the library prior to his death, so as to cause blindness to those that came into close contact with it.

Over the years many have tried to locate the 'Hidden Library' – but none have succeeded, despite massive efforts by Archaeologists, Treasure Hunters and even historical figures such as Peter the Great and the French Emperor Napoleon Bonaparte. It has long been considered that the library is situated somewhere beneath the Kremlin in Moscow and there it still sits, waiting to be rediscovered and reveal its priceless contents.

CHAPTER ONE

'SUMMONED TO NUMBER 10'

As Mike Fraser was chatting to Graham St Anier, Graham's eyes were slowly glazing over. *"So anyway,"* said Mike, *"straight after the caber tossing competition, the very sharp and dangerous crossed Claymore swords were laid on the ground in the approved manner, the drums and bagpipes were cranked up and then the Scottish Highland Dancing commenced."*

"Everything went swimmingly well until, that is, the young laddie, who'd had more than a dram or two, got a tad over-enthusiastic, his ankles clashed and he tripped over the swords, falling 'base over apex' right in front of the Royal Family. The Royals were ensconced in their marquee, partaking of a comforting wee dram themselves as they viewed the festivities - just to ward off the chill, you ken.

Anyway, as the young Jock was scrabbling around on the floor like a grounded salmon, trying vainly to regain both his footing and his dignity, there was a strong gust of icy wind straight frae the Trussocks, causing his kilt tae billow about his waist and in so doing revealing his family jewels and, alas, the 'crack of dawn.' The laddie was, in true Scottish tradition, wearing absolutely nothing underneath the kilt, apart frae that which mother nature had so generously provided."

'Hoots Mon!'

"Apparently the Duke of Edinburgh leant across to Her Majesty the Queen and was heard to mutter, "Well, there's somewhere to park your penny-farthing, cabbage!""

Mike slapped his thigh and roared with laughter at his own joke. Graham looked at him and smiled, "'*Ey up - there's another rib gone! You've told me that story about ten times. I keep hoping for a different ending!*" he said. "*Aye, well,*" said Mike, "*it improves with the telling. Always start the day off with either a wee dram or a wee titter, that's what I always suggest to myself.*"

"*So, why have you 'summoned' me here today then?*" asked Graham. "*Well,*" said Mike, "*if truth be known, old sport, I'm bored right oot of ma Scottish skull. We havenae got any 'Time-Travel' bookings for the next couple of weeks so I might just as well close the office down and send the girls home - on full pay I hasten to add,*" he said gloomily. "*Seeing as how there's not much going on here and I know that you're sat at home twiddling your thumbs, Graham, I just wondered if you fancied participating in a wee bit of 'Time-Travel?'*"

Just as Graham started to reply, Mike's telephone rang, "*Excuse me for a second whilst I take this call,*" he said. The call lasted a good ten minutes. There was a great deal of serious and intense nodding from Mike and several pithy comments such as, "*Aye, right, you dinnae say, God save us, well really, och you couldnae write it!*" Graham was intrigued.

Eventually Mike placed the handset of the 'phone back into its cradle and said, "*Wrong number!*"

"*Just joking, Graham! Would you believe it, here's me telling you that I'm bored stiff with nothing tae do and then Downing Street gets on the blower. That was a Mr Gregory - call me 'Greg' - Waterhouse, the Prime Minister's Chief of Staff no less,*" said Mike.

"*Downing Street?*" asked Graham. Mike nodded, "*Aye, it appears that the Prime Minster has instructed Greg to invite the pair of us to pop down to his gaff, Number 10*

Downing Street, to be precise, for a wee chatette with him. Some sort of problem has cropped up and he would like us to lend him a wee hand in resolving it, in our capacity as 'Time-travellers.'"

Graham looked puzzled, *"What do you mean, lend him a hand?"* Mike shook his head, *"No details other than that, I'm afraid. Just that you and I are required to report to Humberside Travelport at 1400 hours today." "Today!"* exclaimed Graham. Mike nodded, *"Aye, that's correct - today. There'll be an RAF HS-125 Executive Jet waiting at the Travelport, cranked up ready and waiting to whizz us both doon tae London, where the streets are paved with gold. All I know at the moment is that the use of a 'T3-Travellator' will be required for some 'Time-Travel' task or other. We'll have to wait until we get down there for further details."*

"Are you sure that they want us down there today?" asked Graham. Mike nodded, *"Aye, that's what the 'Man from the Ministry' said - and we both ken what 'invited' means."* Graham stood up and stretched, *"Mmmm, sounds rather intriguing. Right, well I'd better nip back to Beverley and let Mrs St Anier know that I won't be joining her for Tiffin today. I'll need to get changed out of these scruffy track-suit bottoms, can't be going to meet the PM looking like a scrap metal dealer,"* said Graham.

"Och, I think those paint splatters and cigarette burns look rather fetching, myself!" said a grinning Mike, elbowing Graham in the ribs.

Mike continued, *"OK pal, why don't you and I meet up back here at about half twelve and I'll get one of the office girls to run us across the Humber Bridge and drop us off at Humberside Travelport."* Graham glanced at his watch and said, *"I'd better get a move on then. See you shortly, Mike. I'll be as quick as I can."*

After Graham had departed, Mike was sat at his desk, thinking about the Prime Minister's invitation and doodling on a notepad, when his 'phone rang again. The small window on the handset flashed to indicate that the caller's details were being withheld. *"Now what?"* thought Mike.

It was the Prime Minister's Chicf of Staff, Gregory Waterhouse, calling back to confirm their flight details. Mike said, *"Thanks for that Mr Waterhouse, er Greg. Myself and Graham will be arriving at Humberside Travelport just before 2 o'clock. Who do we report to when we get there?"*

He paused to listen to the instructions, *"OK, and we're to drive straight onto the pan and up to the aircraft. Incidentally, Greg, are you able to give me any indication as to what this is all about?"*

After listening to the Chief of Staff's short explanation he then said, *"No, neither of us speaks Russian, apart from the odd word like "Da" and "Nyet," but I do have access to LI's here, that's Language Implants, so that wouldnae pose us a problem. Myself and Graham can insert them into our arms before we leave here."*

Mike paused, listening to the Chief of Staff, then replied, *"No, I haven't been to Moscow and as far as I can recall I don't think that Graham has either."* He laughed, *"I know that Graham appreciates a drop of quality vodka, if that helps! Och, you take a wee drop yourself now and again do you, Greg? Good man! Oh, hang on a moment, I speak with forked tongue. We have set foot on Russian soil now that I think about it."*

"Myself, Graham and our wives went to St Petersburg on a cruise ship a couple of years ago. It was just one of those one day touristy type things, off the ship, then a quick escorted trot in a bus around the centre of the breathtakingly beautiful St Petersburg to view the sights and then straight back to the ship clutching our goods from the duty free shop. All closely monitored by the KGB throughout no doubt. Not much use to you I suppose?"

Mike sat there listening and then nodding occasionally. He heard a familiar and cultured voice hollering in the background, followed by the P.M's Chief of Staff terminating the call rather abruptly, with a terse *"Must go, old chap. It's the PM. See you later on."*

"Och," thought Mike, *"that was a short, sharp farewell, no 'Bye - love you darling' or anything. He certainly didnae want to part with too much info on an open line, so I'm still not much wiser. Suppose the wee laddie's under a lot of pressure working for the head rancho. Wonder why we're needed though?"* as he replaced the telephone handset back in its cradle, then reached inside

his desk for the bottle of Glenfiddich that was kept there for medical emergencies and suchlike.

This, Mike decided, was a 'suchlike' occasion, so he proceeded to pour himself a generous stiffener.

Ж

CHAPTER TWO

'PRISONER 887'

Not that any of those who had the gross misfortune to have been detained by the KGB and imprisoned in the damp, freezing cellars of the Lubyanka Prison, Moscow, would have given a jot, but various things of note had happened earlier that particular year, 1963, amongst which were:

- *Double-Agent Kim Philby disappeared from Beirut having defected to the Soviet Union.*
- *The Beatles released their first album, 'Please Please Me.'*
- *The Polaris Sales Agreement was made with the United States of America, leading to the construction of nuclear submarine facilities at Faslane Naval Base in Scotland.*
- *The last British Servicemen were released from conscription as National Service drew to a close.*

- Kim Philby was named as the 'Third Man' in the Burgess & Maclean spy ring.

Meanwhile, back in the USSR, deep down in the dank, gloomy and fear-ridden cellars at:

'The Palace of Evil'
Headquarters Glaznoje Rasvedyvatel'noje Upravlenijie (GRU),
Soviet Military Intelligence Directorate & Lubyanka Prison,
No 1 Dzerzhinsky Street, Lubyanka Square, Meschansky District,
Moscow, Union of Soviet Socialist Republics

life went on as what could be mockingly termed as 'normal.'

A badly stained, olive green, badly chipped cell door was noisily unlocked then flung open. A man's voice, one that was obviously used to being obeyed instantly, bellowed, " 'Prisoner 887' - up on your feet and assume the position. Now!"

'Prisoner 887' an emaciated and frightened looking man, clad in filthy, smelly prison garb, jumped up from his chair and turned to face the blood spattered wall of his cell, legs spread apart, his hands placed on the wall where they could easily be seen.

The cold voice continued, *"Do not turn around until I tell you to do so, 'Prisoner 887!"* The voice belonged to the immaculately uniformed Major (KGB) Igor Chelpinski.

Amongst his other responsibilities within the KGB, Major Chelpinski had happily volunteered his services to act as an Executioner on behalf of the Soviet Government. He was a brute of a man who exhibited an unnatural enthusiasm for his work, particularly as State Executioner. Chelpinsky had moved up the KGB promotion ladder with indecent haste, particularly once his superiors realised that amongst his other talents he happily obeyed orders unquestioningly and was not afraid of employing particularly cruel methods of torture as a means of extracting confessions.

There had been several occasions when prisoners being interrogated by Chelpinsky had confessed to virtually anything just to put an end to the painful torture.

A humourless psychopath, Chelpinsky was totally without a conscience and always carried out his tasks with unquestioning obedience and obvious enjoyment. His KGB colleagues referred to him as 'Chiller the Killer' Chelpinski, (although never to his face). His ever present and loyal henchman, Lieutenant Ivanski Gregorovitch, who always stuck to him like glue, was known to all and sundry as 'Gormless' Gregorovitch.

'Gormless' wasn't the sharpest tool in the box but coupling blind-obedience with a great degree of animal cunning, made him very useful to Chelpinsky. In KGB terms, they were a dynamic-duo, although one senior KGB officer was heard to say of Gregorovitch, *"If he fell in a mincer as offal, he'd come out of the other end as a prime sausage!"*

Ivanski Gregorovitch was a tall, muscular man who unquestioningly and with unbounded enthusiasm undertook the 'heavy' elements of the small team's responsibilities, things like dishing out the slapping's, kicking's and beatings, which he greatly enjoyed on a personal level. His boss, Chelpinsky, was happy to stand aside and just let him get on with it, simply because he didn't like getting blood on his pristine uniform.

In the USSR, as a matter of principle, when confirming a death sentence (as had been the case with the unfortunate 'Prisoner 887' who had been found guilty of spying) the Russian State Judiciary never revealed the specific date or time of when an execution would be carried out. That information, like prisoners, would be left hanging in the air.

Each day, whenever the condemned prisoner's cell door was noisily unlocked and opened, it could either be the prisoner's meagre rations arriving, usually consisting of a bowl of watery, greasy, lukewarm liquid with perhaps a postage stamp sized piece of unrecognisable gristle floating in the middle of the whole unappetising mess, or it could be the 'Angel of Death' in the form of someone like Major Chelpinski, come to carry out the sentence of the court.

It was all part of the war of nerves and a punishment that had been purposely devised in order to stretch the twanging nerves of the unfortunate prisoner to their very limit. The condemned man or woman wouldn't have a clue if they were being given a bowl of food or were about to receive a bullet in the back of the neck. That little test of their sanity occurred at least three times a day.

Stood facing the cell wall, a trembling 'Prisoner 887' was so afraid that he wet himself. It happened to him quite a lot now; despite his efforts not to lose control of his bladder, he just couldn't help it.

Major Chelpinski, looked with disgust at the wet patch slowly spreading across the back of '887's' trousers, snickered then said, silkily, *"Don't worry, Comrade, there is absolutely no requirement for you to evacuate your bladder. We are not going to waste a good bullet today on a traitor like you. No, my colleague Lieutenant Gregorovitch and I have something rather special lined up for you today, is that not so, Ivanski?"* Gregorovitch nodded and smiled, *"Something very special, Comrade Colonel."*

Major Chelpinsky turned to his assistant, the ever-reliable plodder and said, *"The hood, if you please, Ivanski!"*

Ivanski stepped forward and from under his arm pulled a smelly hessian sack which he unfolded and placed roughly over 'Prisoner 887's' head, then tied the helpless prisoner's hands and ankles tightly together.

Once that was done, '887' was frog-marched across the cell to an old, well-used metal trolley that had been wheeled up to the door. 'Prisoner 887' was then lifted up roughly by Gregorovitch and tossed carelessly onto the trolley like a sack of potatoes.

As he laid there on the trolley, 'Prisoner 887' murmured, "*With respect, might I ask where you are taking me, Comrade?*" The Major replied, "*You will soon find out, my ex-Comrade. A little more patience and all will be revealed!*" then instructed his eager assistant to, "*Wheel this non-person along the passageway, Ivan!*" Chelpinski looked at his watch, "*And we need to get a move on, the trolley is booked for several other 'commuters' today!*"

Both officers grinned. They were well suited and in any normal society would have been shut away for life in a secure asylum somewhere, probably in some deepest corner of Siberia.

A clumsy and over-enthusiastic Gregorovitch swung the trolley around, eased it out of the cell then started whistling cheerfully as he wheeled it leisurely along the poorly lit passage. The ceramic yellow facings of the tiles on the passage walls reflected the flickering ceiling lights that cast an eerie, sickly pallor everywhere.

One of the wheels on the metal trolley gave a continuous and monotonous squeak as it rolled along, whilst the other three wheels rumbled noisily whenever they rolled over the cracks and gaps in the old and well-worn stone floor. It was a noise that all of the prisoners had come to fear.

The sound of the wheels echoed around the prison passages until suddenly stopping as the trolley arrived at its destination, then an ominous silence descended. 'Prisoner 887' lay there, rigid with fear. He knew in his heart of hearts that something very bad was about to happen to him and that it would more than likely be terminal. His trousers were wet again and his mouth was dry.

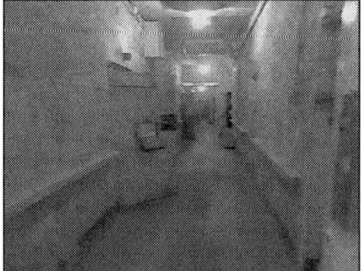

'Cellars of the GRU Interrogation & Holding Centre'
(Photograph – Brian (Harry) Clacy)

Underneath the thick, filthy and stained hessian sack that covered his head, 'Prisoner 887' was unbearably hot and finding it difficult to suck any air through the coarse material. His mind was racing as he tried to fathom out what was happening to him. *"What will they do to me this time?"* he thought. He knew that it wouldn't be pleasant; perhaps, if he was lucky, it would only be another long, cruel and painful interrogation?

His tormentors couldn't pull his finger-nails or toe-nails out because they'd already done that. Maybe it would be the turn of his teeth, those few that had not already been extracted with pliers, without the benefit of anaesthetic, by a cheerful Gregorovitch. Nevertheless, every second of his life was precious and so hope always sprang eternal.

As 'Prisoner 887' laid trembling on the trolley, he heard a key being inserted into a lock then being turned, followed by the sound of a metal door being pushed open, it's hinges squeaking in protest. The trolley wheels started squeaking again as it moved on past the door entrance and into the room.

Speaking to his enthusiastic assistant, Major Chelpinski glanced around the room and said, *"Everything is in readiness I see, Ivanski."* Lieutenant Gregorovitch nodded and replied, *"Yes, Comrade Major, everything has been prepared."* *"Excellent,"* said the KGB Major, *"then you may begin the process by removing the traitor's hood!"*

The hessian hood was jerked off 'Prisoner 887's' head and he immediately drew in a big breath of air. Once his watery eyes had adjusted to the light, 'Prisoner 887' gazed around at his gloomy surroundings and realised that he had been brought into some sort of furnace room. *"What is going on here?"* he thought.

"You didn't really need to be hooded, 'Prisoner 887,'" said a smiling Chelpinski, *"but it adds a touch of theatre to the proceedings, don't you think!"*

Chelpinski continued, *"Now, today, Lieutenant Gregorovitch and I have lined up something very special for you,"* he said, leaning over 'Prisoner 887,' *"a little something that is reserved just for those traitors who sell out their country to Western Intelligence Services as did you."* 'Prisoner 887' knew that something very nasty was about to come his way.

Chelpinsky sighed, *"Ah, Prisoner 887, you had it all, didn't you, but it was never enough - you were greedy and always wanted more!"* Chelpinski's assistant, Gregorovitch, said *"Excuse me, Comrade Major, sorry to interrupt but the KGB film crew has arrived. They are waiting outside."* The Major nodded, *"Excellent, bring them in here, Comrade, and tell them to set up their equipment quickly. The clock is ticking and we have much to do today!"*

After a few moments, two very nervous soldiers came into the room, one the camera-man, the other a young sound-man. They saluted Chelpinsky then began setting up a tripod and a relatively modern cine-camera. They'd also brought a large old-fashioned reel-to-reel tape recorder with them that the young sound-man had slung over his shoulder, attached by a heavy leather strap. He was also clutching a microphone in his trembling hand.

After a few moments fiddling about, the eldest of the two, the camera-man, coughed politely and said, *"Excuse me, we are ready, Comrade Major."*

"What is happening here? I have a right to know!" demanded a now very frightened 'Prisoner 887.' *"You have no rights and can demand nothing! For you, that boat has sailed! You are a filthy traitor who has been condemned to death for spying!"*

"It was decided that ending your life with a bullet would be a waste of good ammunition and that hanging would be too quick and easy for you, so it was directed that you would burn in hell - and that's precisely why we're here in this furnace room today. Now, no more clues!" said Chelpinski, winking at 'Prisoner 887.'

Major Chelpinsky turned to his assistant, *"Let's have the furnace door opened up then, Ivanski!"* As it finally sank in what was about to happen to him, a horrified 'Prisoner 887' shouted, *"Oh my God!"*

"He isn't going to help you, I'm afraid!" said a smiling Chelpinsky, who was obviously enjoying himself, *"Crack on, Ivanski!"* Gregorovitch nodded and did as his master instructed, walking across to a large, old, rusty steel furnace door. He pulled on a pair of heavy industrial gloves and unscrewed the substantial retaining bolts surrounding the door before heaving it open to reveal the cavernous, soot blackened innards of the well-lagged furnace.

The young sound-man was so overcome with nerves that he farted noisily. Chelpinski turned to look at him, tutted and said, *"Show a little respect for the about to be dearly departed, Comrade!"*

'The KGB Furnace'

He continued, "*Now, 'Prisoner 887' you will undoubtedly have noticed that the furnace has not yet been fired up, but don't concern yourself, that will soon be rectified!*"

He looked across at Penkovsky and said, "*After all, we don't want you catching your death of cold, do we, 887?*" Gregorovitch guffawed.

The Prisoner panicked, knowing that there would be no escape, "*You cannot do this to me - I am innocent!*" he screamed. Chelpinsky smiled, "*Yes, of course you are, 'Prisoner 887.' It's funny you know, everyone that has been in your unfortunate situation, and there have been many, say precisely that.*"

"*Anyway, I digress; you will be pleased to know that you will be making one final welcome contribution to the well-being of the KGB, 'Prisoner 887.' You will be helping to heat the upstairs KGB offices!*" said Chelpinsky who then burst out laughing. Ivanski sniggered. They were both definitely suitable cases for treatment.

As they too realised what was about to happen to 'Prisoner 887', the white-faced members of the film crew began trembling with fear. They'd been told that they would be filming an execution that morning, but never in their wildest dreams could they have imagined this horror. They'd assumed that it would be a straightforward shooting.

Major Chelpinski, who was enjoying himself immensely, turned to them and ordered, *"You may commence filming once this traitor is being wheeled inside the furnace, Comrades. Oh, and please make sure that neither my face nor that of my assistant appears anywhere in this film. Understand?"* The cameraman nodded.

Chelpinski waved his hand airily, *"Ivanski, let us begin, if you will!"* he said. *"Nooooo, please - I beg you!"* screamed 'Prisoner 887.'

"Come along now '887,' don't be such an old fuss-pot!" said Ivanski as he wheeled the trolley across the room and manoeuvred it expertly inside the belly of the furnace. 'Prisoner 887' was paralysed by fear - and even if he hadn't been, he was unable to resist in any way as his hands and feet were still tightly bound.

Once the trolley was in place, Gregorovitch rolled the helpless prisoner off it, letting him bounce down onto the concrete floor of the furnace, landing on his face and breaking his nose. Gregorovitch rolled him over onto his back, smiled and said, *"Whoops, sorry about that!"* then turned around and pushed the trolley out of the furnace, humming quietly to himself. The prisoner lay on the floor, gazing with horror at the surroundings.

Standing at the entrance to the furnace, Chelpinsky called out, *"This is precisely what happens to traitors like you, 'Prisoner 887.' Oh, and incidentally, if you're wondering why the film crew is here, we now recording these auspicious event for posterity and they are shown to all Trainee KGB Operatives in order to act as a salutary warning as to what will happen to them if they do what you did and go over to the other side - which, I suppose, in a manner of speaking, is where you will be very shortly!"*

He threw his heads back and laughed cruelly, *"However, all is not lost, 'Prisoner 887,' your death will not be in vain. You will be delighted to know that at the very least, your memory will live on, albeit on film. It is such a pity that it will only be in black and white."*

'Prisoner 887' started to scream and wriggle, the blood bubbling from the nostrils of his smashed nose as he fought for breath, *"Noooooo! I am innocent I tell you!"*
The Major, who was obviously enjoying himself, yawned, looked at his watch and said to Gregorovitch, *"This is getting boring, Ivanski. Let's get on with it."* He called out, *"Er, sweet dreams, 887!"*

Major Chelpinski stepped smartly aside as Ivanski heaved the heavy furnace door shut and then began tightening the retaining bolts, to ensure that there was a completely airtight seal. Very faintly from inside the sealed furnace, 'Prisoner 887' could be heard screaming and begging for mercy. His pleas, of course, fell on deaf ears.

Turning to the two members of the now horror-stricken film-crew, Major Chelpinski ordered the shaking cameraman to, "*Come, Comrade, get your camera lens against the glass viewing portal and make sure that it is in focus. Your predecessors filmed a couple of executions here the other week and, would you believe it, the camera was out of focus. As a consequence they will probably be filming the wild-life in Siberia by now in order to help them get their hands back in. You two don't want to miss anything, do you! There'll be no re-takes - not for 'Prisoner 887' anyway!*" His malodorous assistant, Gregorovitch, sniggered dutifully.

Both of members of the film crew quickly double-checked their equipment. The mortified camera-man gulped noisily and with shaking hands moved his camera lens into place, directly in front of the glass viewing portal. The young sound-man, who was equally horrified, stood beside him, his microphone pressed against the furnace door, the tapes on his reel-to-reel recorder spinning.

"*You'd better switch the furnace on now, Ivanski, it's starting to get a bit chilly in here, don't you think! Look, it's even making our poor film-crew tremble!*" commented Chelpinski.

His assistant nodded and with theatrical fervour threw the appropriate gas lever then began clicking the furnace's ignition switch. *"Oh and Ivanski, do try to keep the temperature fairly low initially, we don't want to let Prisoner 887 off too lightly, eh!"* Chelpinski's Lieutenant smirked and nodded dutifully.

Inside the darkened furnace, a terrified 'Prisoner 887' froze as he heard the ominous hissing of gas, followed by a loud clicking, then to his horror saw thin blue flames flickering out from the tiny holes in the line of pipes that were wound around the inside of the furnace. 887 couldn't believe that this was happening to him, but knew with absolute certainty that there was absolutely nothing he could do to stop it.

Gregorovitch slowly turned the gas dial, causing the flames inside the furnace to increase steadily in length and strength. 'Prisoner 887' could feel the skin on his face and hands starting to blister and burn. He thought, *"Please, dear God, please let me waken up from this nightmare!"* Sadly for '887' - God wasn't listening that day.

Struggling manically with his bindings, 'Prisoner 887' thrashed around on the floor as his hair and clothing slowly caught alight. The heat became unbearable and he was in indescribable agony. As the flickering blue flames slowly grew longer and reached out towards him, the heat inside the furnace gradually increased and his horrific screams grew louder. As he desperately sucked in what little oxygen remained, that too began to burn his lungs.

Chelpinski turned to the film-crew, "*You are capturing all of this, Comrades?*" Both men nodded, unable to speak.

The screaming from inside the furnace grew even louder, then suddenly it stopped. There was a loud crash behind Major Chelpinski as the film crew's sound-man fainted and fell to the floor, dropping his tape-recorder, the spools detaching themselves and rolling noisily across the room.

"*Pathetic creature!*" said Chelpinski.

Stood at the side of the now roaring furnace, after fifteen minutes or so had passed, the Major looked at his wristwatch, yawned and said, "*I am bored now, Ivanski. Turn the gas up to maximum for the last few minutes will you. Let us get this over and done with.*" Ivanski nodded and turned the control dial on the front of the furnace up as far as it would go, increasing the inflow of gas to the furnace to maximum.

Chelpinski tutted, gave the still unconscious sound-man a dismissive glance, then instructed, "*Keep the gas flow on maximum for a few minutes longer, Ivanski. There is to be nothing left of the late 'Prisoner 887' but a pile of ash.*"

"*Once everything has cooled down, collect 887's ashes then flush them down the nearest lavatory, will you. Don't bother depositing them at the Donskoi Monastery, there isn't time today.*" His assistant smiled and nodded. "*Oh, and Ivanski, I'll go and enter the details of his execution in the 'Book of Death' myself, we must keep an up to date *official record of these 'departures' for our masters!*" Ivanski nodded.

Chelpinski turned and walked towards the door of the furnace room, "*Right, I shall now go and inform my superior officer that the death sentence has been duly carried out and that 'Prisoner 887' is no more. Good morning gentlemen!*" then, stepping over the body of the still unconscious sound-man, he strode out of the furnace room, humming happily to himself. "*You can stop filming just for the moment,*" Ivanski said to the camera-man, "*you'd better to see to your friend.*"

As Ivanski was speaking, the sound-man, slowly sat up and then bent his head between his legs. Pointing at the door, he gasped, "*Who is that icy bastard?*" Ivanski smiled and replied, "*I should keep your voice down and your impertinent opinions to yourself if I were you, Comrade. That man is Comrade Major Igor Chelpinski - and let me assure you that he is not someone you would want to tangle with!*"

The camera-man helped his colleague up onto his feet. He turned to Ivanski and said, "*My apologies, Comrade Lieutenant, please excuse the young man. He is very new to this game and is clearly in shock. He doesn't realise what he is saying.*" "*Very well,* " said Gregorovitch, "*I will pretend that I didn't hear him, but only on this one occasion.*" The camera-man nodded, "*Thank you, Comrade Lieutenant, we are both of us much obliged.*" He nudged his sound-man, "*Say thank you to the Comrade

Lieutenant!" he ordered. The young man mumbled, *"Thank you, Comrade Lieutenant."*

Ivanski continued, *"Now, I suggest that once I have raked up the ashes of 'Prisoner 887' from the floor of the furnace, which you are also required to film for posterity, you should get your equipment out of here and go and develop the film. The Comrade Major will undoubtedly be required to show it to Comrade General Ivan Alexandrovich Serov, at the earliest opportunity."*

Rudely brushing the camera-man to one side, Ivanski had a quick peek through the viewing portal of the furnace and nodded with satisfaction at what he saw inside. *"Suppose I'd better give it another ten minutes or so before I open the door, just to be on the safe side. It might still be a little hot in there,"* he said, *"even though the extractor fans are now on,"* and thought to himself, *"anyway, I don't want to be blocking the bogs with clinker again."*

Some ten minutes or so later, the two members of the shaken film crew watched apprehensively as Ivanski undid the securing bolts of the furnace door, heaved it open and then after a moment or two to let the air clear, carelessly and cold-heartedly scooped up the ashes of what was 'Prisoner 887' using of all things a manky old dustpan and hand-brush, to sweep up and drop the ashes into an old metal fire bucket. For someone of 'Prisoner 887's' size, there was very little left of him, hardly enough grey ash to quarter fill the bucket in fact.

After switching their filming equipment off, the crew packed it all away with indecent haste and hurriedly exited the furnace room, greatly relieved to be away from the lunatic presence of Lieutenant Gregorovitch and such a mortifying place - one that positively oozed evil. It was a room that they hoped they'd never to have to see again, but they probably would. The horrific memory of what they'd witnessed in there that day would remain with them both forever.

After Gregorovitch had tipped 'Prisoner 887's' ashes down into the lavatory bowl, he began unbuttoning his trousers. *"Might as well take a leak whilst I'm here,"* he thought. Lieutenant Gregorovitch was secretly pleased that he didn't have to make yet another boring journey to the Donskoi Monastery Cemetery in Moscow to dispose of Prisoner 887's ashes, which was the usual procedure.

There had been so many executions already that year that the Monastery was running out of places to stash the ashes. The KGB had been very busy. *"There's so many naughty boys and girls to be dealt with just lately,"* thought Gregorovitch.

He often wondered just how many more containers of ashes would fit into the Donskoi Cemetery and what the alternative location would be once the place was declared to be full. The cemetery was such a miserable spot and one that he never seemed to be away from these days.

It always seemed to be raining cats and dogs whenever Gregorovitch and Chelpinsky went to the Donskoi

Cemetery to deposit the ashes of their victims. Once, when Ivanski had complained about the weather, Chelpinsky had replied, "*When it's raining, Ivanski, always remember that the graveyards are full of people that would love this weather!*"

Ivanski finished urinating, fastened the buttons on his trousers then heaved on the ancient lavatory chain to flush the contents of the pan noisily down to the ancient sewers underneath the Lubyanka Prison. "*Bon Voyage 'Prisoner 887!' That's another job well done*," he thought.

Ж

CHAPTER THREE

'GAME ON!'

"*My most sincere apologies for disturbing you, Comrade Chairman, but I thought you'd like to know that Comrade General Serov, 1st Chairman of the Committee for State Security and Leader of Soviet Security & Intelligence Services has arrived to see you.*" Khruschev nodded, "*Good, good, send him in immediately, Comrade,*" said Khruschev.

'NIKITA SERGEYAVITCH KHRUSCHEV'
1st Secretary Communist Party of the Soviet Union
(1953 to 1964)
Chairman of the Committee of Ministers (Premier)
(1958 to 1964)

General Serov strode confidently into the Chairman's office, gave a snappy salute and called out a business-like, *"Good morning, Comrade Chairman!"* The rotund Khruschev stood up, smiled and shook hands with Serov, then waving his hand at a chair said, *"Comrade General Serov, good to see you, please take a seat. How are you my dear friend?"*

General Serov grinned, *"I am in the rudest of rude health, Comrade Chairman. And your good self?"* Khruschev replied, *"I am doing 'OK' as our vulgar American 'friends' would say - and please Ivan Alexandrovitch, drop the 'Comrade Chairman' nonsense."*

"We go back a long time, you and I, to you I am and always will be Nikita Sergeyavitch. We are both life-long comrades-in-arms and brother Generals, are we not?" General Serov smiled and nodded, *"You are a little higher up the scale now than a mere General now though, Nikita Sergeyavitch."* Khruschev grinned, *"A rose by any other name is still a rose!"*

The two men had a long and colourful history stretching right back to before World War 2. Although after the war, circumstance had directed them along different career paths, they had both experienced great success in their chosen fields in the upper echelons of the relatively new Russian hierarchy.

Khruschev had clambered up to the top of the greasy political pole, whilst Serov had worked hard to become the 'Eminence Grise' in the shadowy world of security and espionage. Nevertheless, throughout their respective journeys they had remained close allies and were good friends who trusted each other implicitly.

Khruschev was known to be a very fiery, rumbustious and unpredictable individual who often jumped into tricky situations with both feet without, seemingly, bothering to consider the eventual repercussions or consequences; a dangerous trait when considering his elevated position as head of a nuclear power. He was of the, 'It's easier to ask for forgiveness than permission' school, (although it would have been a brave man who applied that particular work ethic whilst working for Josef Stalin, as both men had).

Conversely, General Serov greatly favoured the 'softly, softly, catchee-monkey' approach and his proven successes had helped him to rise rapidly to the top of the dung heap.

Khruschev poured himself and General Serov a generous glass of Vodka each then sat down. *"You'd better have a slug of that, Ivan Alexandrovitch, you'll need a stiffener once I tell you what has been uncovered,"* said Khruschev, tapping the classified file on his desk, headed *'CHAIRMAN'S EYES ONLY.'*

General Serov raised an eyebrow then his glass and said *'za ná-shoo dróo-zhboo!'* ('to our friendship!'), then tossed the vodka to the back of his throat. It made his eyes water as it burned its way down his throat, but it felt so good.

Khruschev gave a hearty belch, wiped his wet lips with the back of a pudgy hand then refilled their glasses. Serov noticed that Comrade Chairman Khruschev had dirty fingernails. *"Huh, you can take the man out of the trenches, but you can't take the trenches out of the man,"* he thought.

Once they had sat down and made themselves comfortable, Kruschev began, *"As we both know, my friend, the Americans have built the most powerful military machine that has ever been known - and quite naturally we would be failing in our duty to Mother Russia if we allowed ourselves to fall too far behind the damned Yankees!"* Serov nodded in agreement, wondering where all this was leading.

Khruschev continued, *"If we fail to do something positive to rectify this situation then not only will we have let our people down, but we would be finished as a world power. That cannot be allowed to happen and that is why, along with everything else, I instigated our current activities in Cuba, of which I know you are fully aware!"* Serov nodded.

There was a few moments silence whilst they sipped their vodka, then Khruschev continued, *"You are aware that we have a long-established, deeply embedded agent in the higher echelons of the British MI6 Security Services, are you not?"* Serov nodded, *"Yes, one of several, Comrade, but I think that in this instance you are referring to the man George Blake who has been in situ for the longest?"*

Khruschev nodded as he once again topped their glasses up with another generous measure of vodka, then continued, "*That is correct. Now, Comrade Blake has recently revealed to us that there is yet another undiscovered high-level spy in our own ranks who has been passing massive amounts of highly sensitive information from here in this very building to both the British and the Americans and has been doing so with apparent ease for quite some time. Undiscovered until now that is!*"

Serov shook his head, "*It was rumoured that there was someone and we have been keeping a close eye on matters and setting traps, but so far the name has eluded us and no-one has fallen into any of the traps that we set.*" Serov continued, "*I am at a loss to see how such a man could have slipped through the net, Nikita Sergeyavitch. There are so many checks and balances.*" "*By their very nature, spies are very clever and devious people,*" replied Khruschev.

Khrushchev tapped the file cover, "*Regrettably, this wretched person falls into that category. Fortunately, Comrade Blake has not failed us, indeed on this occasion he has exceeded himself. He has provided us with the traitor's name, and I have to say that when I read who it was I was shocked beyond belief. It rocked me back on my heels, I can tell you!*" "*Who the hell is it?*" thought Serov, glancing at the file on Khrushchev's desk.

"I thought that things couldn't possibly get any worse after the defection of the KGB's Yuri Nosenko, but I was obviously mistaken!" said Khruschev.

Serov had the good grace to blush at the mention of the name Yuri Nosenko. He had known and served alongside Nosenko and had taken it as a personal slight that Nosenko had escaped detection for so long. *"That is not an oblique criticism of you, my dear friend,"* said Khruschev, *"as we both know, such people are notoriously difficult to detect."* Serov sighed inwardly and wondered what was coming next.

Khruschev poured them yet another glass of vodka. It seemed to be having no effect on either of them. *"I take it that you are familiar with the name of Oleg Penkovsky?"* asked Khrushchev. Serov's jaw dropped.

Serov then nodded and replied, *"Of course, Oleg Penkovsky is a dear friend of mine."* *"Well, I am sorry to have to be the one to tell you this, Ivan Alexandrovitch, but it is Comrade Lieutenant Colonel Oleg Penkovsky who has been revealed as being a traitor!"*

Serov's vodka glass very nearly slipped through his now nerveless fingers, *"Oleg Vladimirovitch Penkovsky! I can't believe it!"* he said.

"Well, unfortunately it is true - and Comrade Blake has provided us with concrete evidence to that effect," said Khruschev, tapping the file in front of him. Sighing and shaking his head, he continued, *"These things happen I'm*

afraid. Like you, Ivan Alexandrovitch, I knew Penkovsky well and liked him. However, that aside, it would appear that along with other very sensitive information, he has been passing high level classified documents to Western Intelligence regarding our plans for establishing a static nuclear base in Cuba - along with the details of our nuclear weapon stocks there on the island and - would you believe it, our ORBAT (Order of Battle) - and the complete schedule of our nuclear weaponry stocks. He has caused us irreparable damage "

"As a consequence the English and Americans are now running circles around that segment of our foreign policy and plans. It is an unmitigated disaster. Years of planning and preparation have been ruined by the actions of Penkovsky. He has sold us down the river and what is worse, he has done it not because of some displaced ideology, he has done it for money!"

Serov slowly shook his head, "It greatly saddens me to hear this, Comrade Chairman. I cannot believe that my Comrade," he hastily corrected himself, "or should I say my 'ex-Comrade' Oleg Penkovsky could have been foolish enough to let himself be ensnared by either the British or the American Security Services. It is absolutely outrageous and unforgivable. I can hardly believe it."

"Well let me assure you that it is true, Ivan Alexandrovitch, and what makes it worse is that he's being doing it for filthy lucre. We have it on very good authority from our London contact that Penkovsky has been selling our secrets for a relatively few paltry English *pounds and American dollars. The damage he has caused because of his actions will take us years to recover from. It is unforgiveable!"* said Khruschev.

General Serov, slamming his glass on the desk, was furious, *"I can hardly wait to get my hands on the treacherous swine!"* he said, *"I will have him arrested and brought in immediately, Comrade Chairman!"*

"My sources tell me that Penkovsky is currently at his Moscow flat on leave," said Chairman Khrushchev, *"He has been given no reason whatsoever to suspect that we are aware of his spying activities. We must handle this situation very carefully. We don't want him dropping off the radar, so he is not to be taken into custody until first thing tomorrow morning and then brought in with the minimum of fuss, to be handed over to the interrogators"*

"Under no circumstances are the Americans or the British to know that he has been taken into custody. Once Penkovsky is safely inside the Lubyanka you have carte blanche to squeeze him like a lemon until there is no more juice or pips left in him."

"We need to know everything that he knows, everything that he has done and the names of all of his contacts, everything - and that is your job, Ivan Alexandrovitch. You are to ensure that Penkovsky is bled dry, then as punishment he is to be 'disposed' of in the usual manner that we employ for filth such as him!" Khruschev sighed and shook his head, *"Such a waste, I really did like him you know!"*

Serov nodded, *"I will get the Chief Interrogator, Alexander Zagvosdin, to take a personal interest in the matter. He can squeeze blood out of a stone - and has done so on many occasions! Oh how I despise traitors to the cause,"* he said, sorrowfully, *"and you know, he will be virtually impossible to replace. He is very knowledgeable."*

Khruschev smiled, *"Both you and I know full well, Comrade, that the graveyards are full of indispensable people. There should be no problem replacing him!"*

Sighing, Khruschev said, with an air of finality, *"As that unprincipled old rogue Sir Winston Churchill used to say – 'Action this Day!' - my friend."* General Serov nodded. *"I will get straight onto it!"*

"And after his trial, at which Penkovsky will be found Guilty, he is to make the same exit from this world as did 'Prisoner 887.' Do I make myself clear?" said Khruschev. The General nodded, *"Perfectly, Comrade Chairman. And let me tell you that it will be a pleasure. Now, if you will excuse me, I will go and make the necessary arrangements."*

"I do not wish to teach you to suck eggs, but make sure, Comrade, that Penkovsky is not 'despatched' until we are absolutely certain that we have obtained every single detail of all of his contacts and his traitorous activities. We must know precisely which information he has passed to the enemy so tha we can make amends!" ordered Khruschev.

Serov nodded and from the grim look on his friend's face, Khruschev knew that Penkovsky's fate was well and truly sealed. He wondered what other sordid details would be revealed by Penkovsky whilst under interrogation. Stir the murky pond with a stick and who knew what horrors would rise to the surface.

Once General Serov had left his office, Khruschev sat back and poured himself another generous measure of vodka then lit up one of his favourite traditional Russian cigarettes, the foul smelling 'Papyross.' Khruschev had been spitting feathers when he'd been informed of Penkovsky's treachery, which surprisingly had been revealed to him not by his own security people, the KGB, but via his ambassadorial contacts, who had received the information from George Blake.

On receiving the information, such was Khrushchev's incandescent rage that he would have had Penkovsky arrested and shot there and then until it had been delicately pointed out to him that Penkovsky needed to be 'persuaded' to provide details of all of the information that he had passed over to the enemy and reveal all of his contacts and co-conspirators before being 'topped.' God forbid that there were any more such serious leaks. Khrushchev was determined that Penkovsky would be made an example of.

"No wonder those sly, underhand dogs the Americans and British have been running rings around us of late," thought Khruschev, *"well, all that stops as of now! With*

the assistance of Comrade President Castro, it will be our turn to run rings around the Capitalist swine. I, Nikita Sergeyavitch Kruschev, will teach them a lesson that they won't forget!"

He poured himself another vodka.

Ж

CHAPTER FOUR

'A NEW TASK'

The year - 1962. Later that morning, Number 1 Dzerzhinsky Street, Moscow, USSR was a scene of manic activity, but conversely the inner office of the 1st Chairman of the Committee for State Security was in fact a relative haven of peace.

The current occupant of the office, General Ivan Alexandrovitch Serov, much preferred his day to build gently and was never at his best first thing in the morning. Up until mid-morning his staff trod on egg-shells when around him. T

That particular morning had started off very badly, with Serov having been summoned by Khruschev to inform him about the traitorous activities of Oleg Penkovsky.

'General Ivan Alexandrovich Serov'
1ˢᵗ Chairman of the Committee for State Security
Leader of Soviet Security & Intelligence Services
(Head of the KGB – 1954 to 1958)
(Head of the GRU 1950 to 1963)

(Motto: "I can break every bone in a man's body without killing him).

One of General Serov's staff officers, Major Chelpinski, had sought and been granted a rare late-morning interview with General Serov. Serov was rather fond of Chelpinski, who always reminded him of himself when he was a younger man trying to get a foot up the ladder.

There was a knock on his office door and Serov called out grumpily, *"Enter!"* The door swung open and Major Chelpinsky marched into the office, halted in front of Serov's desk and slung up a snappy salute.

"Ah, Comrade Major Chelpinsky, take a seat," instructed General Serov, giving Chelpinsky an insincere and not too reassuring smile. The robotic Major Chelpinsky immediately did as he was ordered. *"Now,"* continued the

General, "*let me have your report, Comrade!*" Chelpinsky to a deep breath and began making his report.

"*I am pleased to report, Comrade General, that the death sentence has been carried out on 'Prisoner 887,' precisely as per your instructions. I have film available of the event if you wish to view it?*" The General nodded, "*Mmm, perhaps later, after lunch. Mmm, I look forward to that little treat. Now, I have a new task for you, Comrade, which is somewhat sensitive, complex and demanding. Here, read this file that was handed to me today.*" General Serov slid a classified file across the desk that was marked, '**CHAIRMAN'S EYES ONLY**.' "*You can see for yourself just how sensitive the subject matter is.*"

When Major Chelpinsky opened the file and saw the name that was printed in red at the top of the first page he only just managed to stop himself from gasping out loud. The General nodded, "*Continue Major, plough through it and take your time, I can wait,*" he said as he sat back and lit a cigarette.

After a few minutes reading, a clearly shocked Major Chelpinsky closed the folder. "*You seem surprised, Comrade?*" said the General. "*If you will forgive me, that is something of an understatement, Comrade General,*" said Chelpinski, tapping the file cover, "*his is one of the last names I would have expected to see on one of our 'Spy' files. I have admired and respected Comrade Colonel Penkovsky and his work for many years.*"

The General sighed, *"Alas, it seems that very few people can ever be trusted, apart from a chosen few that is - such as me, our Premier, Comrade Chairman Nikita Sergeyavitch Khruschev, and hopefully you, Chelpinski!"* said Serov, with the merest hint of graveside humour.

Chelpinski kept his face straight, not wanting to risk an ingratiating smile just in case the General's comment was some sort of loyalty test. You never really knew where you stood with Comrade General Ivan Alexandrovich Serov.' It didn't pay to get it wrong. Careers and lives had foundered on much less.

Tapping the file, the General continued, *"That foolish officer was considered to be one of the chosen few, right up until now, that is. The world was his oyster. Fortunately for us, the covert activities of this this traitorous dog have been revealed by one of our deep-cover agents in the United Kingdom, otherwise the odds are that we would never have found out about him."*

"As you can see, he has been turned by both the British and the Americans, who now consider him to be a top access agent. It appears that Penkovsky, I can hardly bring myself to say his name, has been working for them for quite some time."

Serov sucked on his cigarette then blew several smoke rings towards the yellowed ceiling above his head. *"So where do we go from here, Comrade?"* he said.

Chelpinski began to answer but stopped when the General held his hand up, *"That was a rhetorical question, Chelpinski and does not require an answer from you! It has been decided that Penkovsky is to be arrested then taken to the Lubyanka Prison where he will be interrogated by Chief Interrogator, Alexander Zagvosdin, and bled dry. Then, after a trial at which Penkovsky will, naturally, be found guilty - he is to be disposed of in the usual fashion and that is where you come into the equation."*

"I am appointing you main case officer with immediate effect and require you to take full responsibility for and deal with this matter accordingly. You are to arrange for this traitor to be taken into custody, with the minimum of fuss, and then organise his eventual execution, which has already been authorized. He is not to be executed until I give you the nod personally. Do I make myself clear?"

"Perfectly clear, Comrade General." replied an attentive Chelpinski.

The General smiled again, *"You will be personally responsible for arresting him and bringing him in for interrogation. I do not want some typically clumsy, cack-handed KGB oaf ballsing things up, so take extreme care with this matter. The arrest is to be low-profile. It may not be as easy as it sounds because, between you and I, I have been led to believe that there is someone else here in this very building, yet to be discovered, drip feeding Penkovsky information and I suspect that the same person could well warn Penkovsky that he is about to be lifted, if the information becomes general knowledge."*

"Someone else?" asked a surprised Chelpinsky. The General nodded, *"But don't concern yourself with this 'someone else,' Comrade, he will be found and dealt with in due course. I have an idea who that person is and have plans for him too, but at the moment I want you to concentrate on Penkovsky. Tread on egg-shells, Chelpinski - 'softly softly catchee monkey!"*

Major Chelpinski said confidently, *"There will not be a problem, Comrade General. My small team and I will deal with this traitor quickly and efficiently now that we have been given the nod by you to do so." "Excellent. You must let me know what you will need in the way of assistance,"* said the General.

"I might need the services of a few trusted 'foot soldiers' for the surveillance and arrest segment, that is all, Comrade General," said Chelpinski. Serov nodded, *"Arrange it with my Chief of Staff when you leave here, but be ultra-sensitive about the name of this traitor, Chelpinski, from now on Penkovsky is to be referred to as 'Prisoner 888!'"*

Sliding his desk drawer open, the General reached in and pulled out two new rank slides, tossing them across the desk towards Major Chelpinski. He smiled and said, *"Incidentally, you have done well of late, Comrade Colonel. Here, put on your new badges of rank, you are improperly dressed!"*

Chelpinski flushed bright pink with pleasure at his totally unexpected promotion, *"Comrade General, I am deeply honoured."* he gasped. *"You have earned it, my friend. Continue along the path that you are treading, Comrade Colonel, and who knows what heights you could achieve. The world is your oyster, eh!"* said Serov.

Serov pressed a button on his desk and very shortly afterwards an attractive uniformed female orderly, his personal assistant, entered the office carrying a highly polished silver tray and on which sat a bottle of vodka and two glasses. Placing the tray on the General's desk, she smiled shyly at him then made a ghost-like exit. *"Lucky bastard!"* thought Serov.

The General removed the top off the bottle then poured a very generous measures of vodka into each glass, handing one of them to Chelpinski, *"Let us raise a glass or two to your promotion, Comrade Colonel, and to the success of your next mission - 'Prisoner 888.'"*

They both stood and the General bellowed, *"Davajte vupjem za to, chtobu mu isputali stolko gorya; skolko kapel vodka ostanetsya v nashikh bokalakh!"* *("Let us drink to the fact that we may have as much sorrow as drops of vodka that will be left in our glasses!")*

The newly promoted Lieutenant Colonel Chelpinski returned the toast, *"Za vashe zdarovje, Comrade General!"* *("To your health, Comrade General!").*

The General smiled and smacked his lips, "*A delightful tasting vodka is it not. It was originally produced in great quantities for the personal use of the dissolute Nikolai II Alexandrovitch Romanov and is considered to be the most perfect vodka ever made. 'The Tsar's Vodka!' as it is known, was distilled using diamonds no less. Well, the Tsar won't be needing it now, so we might as well drink it on his behalf, eh!*" said the General.

"*Now, let us get down to brass tacks and discuss precisely how you intend snaring the filthy traitor - ex-Lieutenant Colonel Oleg Vladimirovitch Penkovsky, 'Prisoner 888.'*"

The General turned and threw his vodka glass into the marble fireplace, shattering it into a thousand pieces. Chelpinski quickly followed suit. Serov pressed the bell on his desk and the female orderly returned carrying two replacement glasses. The procedure of drinking then smashing the glasses would, she knew, continue until the vodka bottle had been completely emptied.

Ж

CHAPTER FIVE

'PENKOVSKY CAPTURED'

It was a cold, wet and typically miserable 'Moscow' morning on the 22nd of October 1962. In the fairly select Sokol District of Moscow, sat shivering in his car, alongside his snoring assistant, Lieutenant (KGB) Ivanski Gregorovitch, was a thoroughly bored Lieutenant Colonel (KGB) Igor Chelpinsky. Chelpinski who elbowed Gregorovitch none too gently in the ribs. *"Waken up you idle oaf - here he is at long last!"* he hissed.

The 'he' that Chelpinsky was referring to was a weary and dishevelled looking Lieutenant Colonel Oleg Vladimirovich Penkovsky, who had been out on the tiles for most of the night. A dozy Gregorovitch stretched then wiped the sleep from his eyes, *"My apologies, Comrade Colonel, I must have drifted off, it's been a very long night,"* he said.

A sour-faced Chelpinsky replied, *"You don't know you're born, Ivanski; at least we are sat here in the comfort of this splendid Volga. I have lost count of the number of times I spent in East Germany crammed inside a tiny, freezing cardboard Trabant. You should think yourself lucky - and if you don't mind, I would appreciate it if you could stop blowing sailor's kisses!"*

"Sailor's kisses?" asked a puzzled Gregorovitch. *"Farting!"* replied Chelpinski, *"the inside of this vehicle smells like a pig farm. What little warmth there was in here escaped when I had to open a window to let some fresh air in!"* *"My apologies, Colonel,"* said a sheepish looking Gregorovitch, thinking to himself, *"from now on I'd better keep them silent but deadly."* Inside the car there was an unpleasant whiff of cheap air spray, fart and body odour.

'The Trabant - People's Car'

They were both sat in the fairly spacious, well sprung and well-padded faux-leather front seats of their government issue GAZ-23 'Volga.' Although comfortable, they were only able to run the Volga's engine intermittently in order to generate a little heat, as the belching clouds of smoke from its exhaust pipe and the rumbling engine might have revealed that the vehicle was occupied.

'The GAZ-23 'Volga'
(Neither the ordinary people nor Communist Party officials could use the Volga which was reserved purely for GRU and Secret Service use)

"How do you wish to play this, Comrade Colonel?" asked Ivan.

"We'll give Penkovsky ten minutes or so to get into his flat and hit the sack, then he'll think that he's safe and sound - that is when we will pounce." *"Usual procedure when we do, Colonel?"* Chelpinsky nodded, *"Yes, you kick the door in and I'll do the rest. Make sure that you keep him covered, Ivanski, he will undoubtedly be armed."* *"And if he resists arrest?"* asked Ivanski, *"Then I will knock some sense into him, but I mustn't overdo it!"* said Chelpinski. *'Shock and Awe' - it never fails, eh, Comrade Colonel!"* said a smiling Gregorovitch, relishing the opportunity for a spot of violence.

As a result of his pre-planning and preparation for the arrest, Chelpinski had discovered that some members of the Headquarters KGB staff had indeed been made aware that Penkovsky was known for spending large amounts foreign currency and living the life of Riley, but they had done nothing about it.

Chelpinski had ordered the arrest of those particular KGB staff members, who were now themselves languishing in the cells of the Lubyanka prison, awaiting disciplinary action. They had been issued 'prisoner' numbers and would more than likely not see the light of day again. Such gross inefficiency could not and would not be tolerated.

Chelpinsky and Gregorovitch both watched closely as Penkovsky heaved open the heavy wrought iron security gate leading to the apartments of the 'Comrade Stalin' block, where he had been allocated a nice flat, and trudged across to the main entrance of the grey, sombre-looking concrete five-storey tenement building, which was reserved purely for the use of the middle-ranking privileged families of Russia's elite KGB.

*'The unmarked gate leading to the 'Comrade Stalin'
Apartment Block, Moscow'*
(Photo courtesy Sara Langthorne)

Penkovsky, was dragging his feet, and looked as if he'd had a long hard night, which indeed he had. He'd been boozing and carousing in his usual hang-out, the 'Za Nashikh Milikh' night club, and was now going home to sleep the excesses off.

Penkovsky was relieved that on this particular occasion he wouldn't be getting his ear bent by his fearsome wife, Olga, as she had taken his daughter away from Moscow for a few weeks in order to visit Olga's aged parents who lived in Minsk. Much to his relief, Penkovsky had the apartment all to himself.

"As his wife is away, I'm rather surprised he hasn't dragged some vodka-soaked, raddled tart home with him; the man has the morals of a guttersnipe!" sneered Chelpinsky, *"That's the third time this week the dissolute swine has been out nightclubbing. I wonder he finds the time and energy to do any work!"*

"Don't know how he can afford it," said Gregorovitch. *"Oh, I do!"* said Chelpinsky, *"and that's precisely why we're here, my friend. Remember, I told you that the Comrade Colonel has had illegal access to a seemingly endless supply of foreign currency?"* Gregorovitch nodded.

"You and I, Ivanski, be inviting Penkovsky to explain the no doubt illegal source of supply and precisely what he has done to 'earn' it. Between you me and the gatepost, Ivanski, I have been informed that our man has been involved in a great deal of mischief with the Americans

and the British." Ivanski looked surprised. *"Yes, he has been a very naughty boy and as a result, I'm certain, will eventually be paying a visit to the furnace room in the cellars of the Lubyanka. But for the moment, let us not jump the gun, eh."*

An unsuspecting Penkovsky trudged up the stairs to his fourth-floor flat, wheezing and cursing; the damned lift was broken again. He would ensure that someone would be getting their arse kicked for that.

Once he'd reached the door of his apartment, he paused to regain his breath then smiled as he recalled yet another very pleasant night that he'd spent in the company of the delightful but expensive Ludmilla. She always made him feel young, strong, vibrant and wanted again. He'd been sneaking out to see her for a couple of months now and just couldn't get enough of her.

He smiled to himself as he thought of what a wonderful, amusing and attentive young lady Ludmilla was and how very experienced she was at pleasuring a man, particularly for someone of such relatively tender years. That she was only a little older than his teenage daughter made not the slightest bit of difference to him.

Ludmilla had perfected the precious gift of making him laugh until his sides hurt, whilst his wife, the overbearing Olga, seemed to have long-forgotten what fun and laughter was. Olga had cultivated a lip curling sneer that she now used more and more frequently. Penkovsky still loved Olga, but that love was wearing decidedly thin.

Strangely, Penkovsky was totally unaware that Ludmilla had been well trained in the 'dark arts' of seduction by the GRU and then planted, with others of her ilk, in the very popular nightclub that Russian senior officers and politicians were known to frequent, the 'Za Nashikh Milikh' ('To Our Lovely Ladies').

The nightclub was out of bounds to the 'ordinaries' and Penkovsky, who should have known better, felt as safe as houses there. Because of that, not for one moment had he suspected Ludmilla as being anything else other than a young woman earning a living as a hostess. She was completely off Penkovsky's security radar

As far as Ludmilla herself was concerned, the Colonel was an ideal 'customer' because he never knew when he'd had enough to drink and was easily susceptible to flattery. Ludmilla's job - which was to wheedle information out of unsuspecting victims, was made so much easier when their tongues had been loosened by drink.

Unlike Penkovsky, whatever was in her drinks glass was either fruit juice or Moscow's finest tap water. No alcohol for Ludmilla, she needed to keep her wits about her.

Penkovsky always seemed to have an endless supply of money, so the drink flowed unendingly. Ludmilla was very good at what she did and Penkovsky hadn't been the first man to fall victim to her charms. She enjoyed her work, was fully committed to it and regarded her employment as being patriotic. Ludmilla knew that when her looks and charms eventually began to fail she would be promoted and moved on. Currently though, as nothing was drooping, she knew that she was safe for a few more years.

Ludmilla was inordinately proud of what she did, after all wasn't it the Russian General Oleg Kalugin who'd said, *"There are many brave men we ask to lay down their lives for their country. But for brave women we simply ask them to lay down!"* That was good enough for Ludmilla.

Notwithstanding the ethics of it all, the lovely Ludmilla's activities almost certainly paid dividends for both her and the KGB. As a welcome bonus, she was allowed to keep the gifts that were handed to her by her 'customers' and the KGB was often handed valuable information on a plate.

It wasn't just Penkovsky that enjoyed the facilities of the night-club, there were many others, often those in the higher echelons of the military and government, who frequented the nightclub to enjoy what was on offer. The loose-tongued and louche Penkovsky was just one of many to fall into the state-funded honey trap.

Ludmilla had recognised that she was on to something good, right from the word go, when Penkovsky had been a little 'too flash with the cash.' He loved a drink or three and quickly became 'loose-lipped' - forgetting the old adage that 'whore's have ears.'

Even when had had a few too many vodkas though, Penkovsky had the good sense not to allude to any of his spying activities, which would have been a step too far even for him, (after all, even his unsuspecting wife Olga was completely unaware of that aspect of his life).

Penkovsky's mistake, however, was that he had been rather over-generous when spending his American dollars and that's what had made Ludmilla suspicious in the first instance, so she'd done her job and reported him to her KGB superiors. They had advised her to continue leading him along, submit regular reports and that they would monitor proceedings.

Ludmilla's reports had started the alarm bells ringing inside the Headquarters of State Security and Counter-Intelligence. The KGB section officer managing her activities, (now himself languishing in the Lubyanka Prison), had instructed her to gain Penkovsky's complete confidence, then continue to try and ease more information out of him, but not to make him suspicious Once a complete picture of his activities had emerged, the KGB 'experts' would then do the rest.

In the meantime, everyone had to tread very carefully because they were aware that Penkovsky was a senior and well-respected KGB officer with a lot of service under his belt and who had some very powerful friends and colleagues. Somehow, though, the Penkovsky case had slipped beneath the KGB's normally very efficient radar and nothing had been done about Ludmilla's revelations other than to keep a watching brief.

Initially there had been a flurry of activity in the KGB's Intelligence Headquarters as they set up an immediate and very covert 'Investigation and Observation' operation. A number of comments had been written in Penkovsky's bulky personal file regarding his high-level governmental contacts and clearance for access to very sensitive information. It had been noted that he had done a great deal of travelling outside of the USSR, had enjoyed the good life, enabling him to establish several important contacts with the Americans and the British.

He was considered to be an extremely safe bet and as such was trusted implicitly. Now, though, Penkovsky's excessive spending of foreign currency had given the hint that something may have been amiss, but for some unknown reason, nothing had been done about it. He'd just slipped through the cracks. However, his luck couldn't last forever and for Penkovsky, the game was now well and truly up.

The decision had finally been taken to haul him in and have him thoroughly interrogated. He now stood accused of selling state secrets, based upon the information provided by the traitorous MI6 collaborator George Blake.

Initially Penkovsky's interrogation would be relatively gentle, depending upon the level of his co-operation, then, if and when his guilt was established, things would go much harder for him.

What the lower level KGB operatives didn't know at that early stage of the investigation was that information regarding Penkovsky's alleged covert spying activities had already filtered through to Chairman Khruschev via another source in addition to that provided by Ludmilla, and that the information had then been passed on to General Serov by Khruschev himself. From that moment on, Penkovsky's days were well and truly numbered.

Once Penkovsky had 'coughed' to his spying activities - (and they always coughed, eventually, even if they were not guilty), then his interrogation would take a definite turn for the worse until every last detail of his activities was wrung out of him using a variety of well tried and tested torture and interrogation methods.

All hell had broken loose when it was discovered that it was known that Penkovsky had been involved in suspicious activity and that nothing substantial had been done about it. On hearing the news that Penkovsky was about to be arrested, the Headquarters KGB staff had mistakenly thought that the newly promoted Lieutenant Colonel Chelpinski had stumbled across the Penkovsky file and read the information provided by Ludmilla, then got things kick-started on his own initiative.

The lesser KGB mortals were aghast when they eventually discovered that it was in fact General Serov himself who had ordered the arrest and interrogation of Penkovsky and not Lieutenant Colonel Chelpinski. The General had gone ballistic when he'd been made aware that his staff had known all along of Penkovsky's profligacy, courtesy of Ludmilla, but had done very little about it other than instigating a bit of ongoing monitoring. All hell broke loose as everyone interrogated everyone else.

The sound of KGB umbrella's crashing open could be heard all around the building and it wasn't too long before three minor KGB operatives and their Senior Head of Department were immediately suspended from duty, arrested and taken away to be charged with gross negligence and inefficiency for failing to investigate the matter properly and progress their findings regarding the Penkovsky case up the chain of command.

In dealing with the matter initially and in their defence, the KGB operatives had trodden very carefully as they knew that the greatly feared General Serov himself was friendly with Penkovsky, so the investigation been handled with kid gloves. Somehow, and no-one knew quite why, the results of their investigation had not been passed up the chain of command by the Senior Head of Department and consequently the whole thing had gone 'tits up.'

The one thing that the surviving senior operatives in the KGB Headquarters didn't like was that the newly promoted Lieutenant Colonel Chelpinsky had been handed responsibility for the case. Chelpinski had always worked on the periphery of the KGB's more seedier activities and didn't really fit in with the rest of his Comrades. His rapid promotion to Lieutenant Colonel had put more than a few careerist noses out of joint.

The Headquarters staff of the close-knit KGB team were well aware that Chelpinski was a dark, unapproachable and ambitious character who bore close watching. He obviously had friends in high places and was on the way up. A smiling assassin. No-one, regardless of rank or position, was safe from him. The saying, "*Never trust a man with a small moustache*," certainly applied to Chelpinsky.

They also knew that there were unsavoury rumours flitting about regarding the personal relationship between Chelpinski and his Lieutenant, Ivanski Gregorovitch, so Gregorovitch would also have to be handled very carefully. It was a mine-field.

As Chelpinsky had been handed the task of arresting Penkovsky by General Ivan Alexandrovitch Serov personally, he was delighted beyond measure and thought the task a great honour. Serov held the post of 1st Chairman of the Committee for State Security and Leader of Soviet Security and Intelligence Services and as such his power was virtually limitless.

The Penkovsky case was undoubtedly extremely sensitive because Penkovsky was known to have been a close, personal friend of Serov's. Even so, that would not help him if it was confirmed that he was indeed a spy and a filthy traitor. If anything, his friendship with Serov would go against him. Serov was not known for his geniality.

General Serov had ordered Chelpinsky to make Penkovsky's arrest swiftly and with the minimum of fuss.

He was not to draw any attention to it. The fact that Penkovsky was probably still actively spying meant that he would more than likely have contacts in and around Moscow who needed to be brought out into the open.

Those contacts were to remain unaware of Penkovsky's arrest for as long as possible. Chelpinsky's excitement knew no bounds; he knew full well that if the arrest and interrogation of Penkovsky went well it would do his own career prospects no harm whatsoever.

Dawn was breaking as a totally unsuspecting Penkovsky let himself into his flat. He was relieved that he wouldn't have to make any explanations about his midnight meanderings to his wife, the ogre Olga. She'd been getting suspicious of his late night activities and only last week, during one tongue-lashing, had asked him dismissively if they'd taken to wearing perfume at the KGB Headquarters.

He'd managed to body-swerve his way out of that one by presenting her with a bottle of Chanel and explained that he'd given himself a quick spray of it just to see what the smell was like. Olga had then sprayed herself liberally with the perfume and just about ruined the intended effect, finishing up smelling like a tart's handbag.

Fortunately for Penkovsky she'd accepted his explanation and, much to his horror, his plan backfired as Olga had turned coquettish and for the first time in many months insisted upon a night of unbridled passion.

There was only so much marital sex a man could take, especially with Olga, who had the most annoying giggle which, when they'd first met, Penkovsky had found to be quite disarming, but now it just put his teeth on edge. He'd heard one of his brother officers commenting on a girl he'd met in a nightclub (not Ludmilla) that made him smile sardonically, *"You can put lipstick on a pig, but it's still a pig."* That, he'd thought unkindly, was Olga, although with her it wasn't lipstick, but perfume.

Penkovsky wandered into the thankfully empty bedroom, where he threw his uniform off, put his silk pyjamas on and then collapsed onto bed. He'd decided to clean his teeth and take a shower later on that day when he resurfaced, if there was any hot water available, which could never be guaranteed. He wasn't due to go into the 'office' for a few days so therefore he could take things easy and make time to recharge his batteries.

Penkovsky had made plans to meet up with Ludmilla again at the 'Za Nashikh Milikh' nightclub that very evening. He was going to make hay whilst the sun shone and especially whilst Olga was out of station.

Oleg had needed to return home for a bit of sleep, a change of clothes and also to replenish his rapidly diminishing funds. The cost of drinks in the 'Za Nashikh Milikh' nightclub was excessively high, but he considered that it was a price worth paying just to be able to have the delightful Ludmilla all to himself in a private curtained off booth at the night club.

He was going to have to get in touch with his American and British contacts before too long in order to drum up some more funds. Penkovsky wasn't too worried about his supply of money, there was plenty of it available to him - as long as he kept coming up with the goods.

Just as he was drifting off to sleep, Penkovsky heard a huge crash as the front door of his flat was battered open. Before he had time to jump out of bed and grab his pistol, Chelpinsky appeared at the bedroom door, waving his own pistol. *"Ah, good morning, Comrade Colonel Penkovsky. Stay where you are!"* he said, smiling.

"Who the hell are you, and what are you doing here in my apartment? Do you know who I am!?" demanded a shocked and outraged Penkovsky.

Chelpinsky smiled and nodded, *"We have crossed paths before. I am Lieutenant Colonel Igor Chelpinsky and I have orders from my superiors to take you into immediate custody, so as of this moment you are under close arrest, Comrade. You'd better get yourself dressed; we don't want you being seen out on the streets in your silk pyjamas. It would be bad for the KGB's reputation!"*

An astounded Penkovsky replied, *"Close arrest! How dare you! I don't think you know who you are dealing with!"* Chelpinski smiled, *"Of course I know who you are, and I know full well who I am dealing with. We were brother KGB officers, once! Now, you'd better get up and get dressed!"*

He turned to Lieutenant Gregorovitch, "*You'd better confiscate his personal weapon, Ivanski!*" Gregorovitch nodded and, spotting Penkovsky's pistol hanging from his leather belt on a chair at the side of the bed, quickly unholstered the weapon and unloaded it. "*You won't be needing that where you are going!*" Chelpinsky said to Penkovsky, who was hopping around pulling his trousers on.

A white faced Penkovsky said, "*There must be some mistake, a misunderstanding, surely? I have done nothing to merit this treatment, Comrade! I would advise you to contact General Serov, immediately!*" Chelpinski smirked, "*My dear fellow, that would be a complete waste of time.*" "*Why is that?*" asked Penkovsky. "*Because we are here under the direct orders of General Serov!*" replied a triumphal Chelpinsky.

It was at that precise moment that Penkovsky realised he was in the mire up to his neck and that the game was well and truly up. He'd often imagined that something like this would happen to him, but hadn't thought that it would be quite so soon.

A plan had been prepared for him to be extracted from Russia via East Berlin by his friends at MI6 in the event of his spying activities being revealed, but now there wouldn't be time to put it into operation. He doubted very much if he'd even be able to let them know what had happened to him.

"Before we leave here, I should give your face a quick swill if I were you, Comrade, and comb your hair. You look dissolute and you smell quite disgusting. Most unofficer-like!" said a triumphal Chelpinski, who was relishing Penkovsky's discomfort, *"After all, you will need to look your best when you meet the Chief Interrogator, no less!"* Penkovsky's legs nearly gave way under him. He knew precisely what the Chief Interrogator was capable of.

After Penkovsky had splashed some water across his face and wiped it dry on a fluffy towel, Chelpinsky ordered Lieutenant Gregorovitch to handcuff him. As the handcuffs clicked closed, Penkovsky asked, *"Is that really necessary?"* in what was for him an unusually querulous voice. Chelpinsky nodded, *"I'm afraid so, Comrade. I have no choice in the matter, we cannot afford to take any risks with you!"*

"What is all this about, I demand to know!" said Penkovsky. *"You can demand nothing - you are now a prisoner of the State. Everything will be explained to you once we get you to the Lubyanka Prison!"* replied Chelpinski, *"I suppose that it wouldn't do any harm, though, just to give you a little clue as to why we are here. You see, information was received that you have been rather over-generous, splashing out illegal foreign currency to your little tart, Ludmilla, at the 'Za Nashikh Milikh' nightclub. Someone wants to know where all that that money came from."*

"*I have no idea what you're talking about!*" huffed Penkovsky. "*Come, come, Colonel, the little 'shalava' (dirty slut) Ludmilla has told us all about your excessive spending and a few other of your other disgusting habits.*"

"*Incidentally, before we leave here, I have been instructed to find and confiscate any of the illegal money that you have undoubtedly stashed away.*" "*I have nothing 'stashed' away,*" said Penkovsky defiantly.

"*Let's not play games! Show me where it is hidden or we will take this place apart piece by piece until we find it. If you wish to avoid that, you can simply tell me where your stash of ill-gotten gains is tucked away!*" Penkovsky's top lip was beginning to tremble. "*Well, I'm waiting?*" said an impatient Chelpinsky.

"*Potsalot' moyu zadnitsu!*" *(You can kiss my arse!)* replied a defiant Penkovsky.

Chelpinski sighed, then slid his pistol out of its holster and unexpectedly struck Penkovsky a fearsome blow on the side of his face, causing the foresight at the end of the barrel to rip the skin on Penkovsky's cheek, making it bleed. Falling backwards onto the bed, Penkovsky gasped and spat two bloodied teeth onto the bedspread, "*You will pay dearly for that!*" he spluttered.

"*Would you prefer to make the payment in American dollars or English pounds?*" asked a laughing Chelpinsky. "*Oh, what a wag I am, eh! Now! Where do you keep the money? You'd better tell me now or you will be receiving* some more free dental treatment. *The arrest order said nothing about me not 'encouraging' you to co-operate!*"

Unfortunately for Penkovsky, one of the two teeth that had been hammered out of his mouth contained a glass suicide capsule for use in the event of his capture. He surreptitiously edged the two bloodied teeth off the duvet and onto the floor, then slid them out of sight under the bed with his foot. That particular avenue of escape had gone down the tubes.

"*I will not ask you again! The money - where is it hidden?*" demanded Chelpinsky.

Penkovsky nodded towards a dressing table in the corner of his bedroom, "*There is a hidden compartment in the bottom drawer of the dressing table. The money is there, inside my brief-case.*" Chelpinsky waved his pistol at Gregorovitch, "*Go find it, Ivanski!*" he ordered.

Gregorovitch went across to the dressing table, slid the bottom drawer open and ferreted around inside. "*I cannot see anything in here, Comrade!*" he said to Chelpinski. "*You will find the head of a small nail sticking up in the right hand corner of the drawer, underneath the clothing. Grip the nail and pull it up. There is a hidden compartment,*" said Penkovsky.

Gregorovitch nodded and threw some socks, underpants and several pairs of Olga's large flesh coloured knickers that were lurking inside there, onto the bedroom floor. "*I see that your wife has a healthy appetite, Comrade. Little pickers - big knickers, eh!" Penkovsky ignored the jibe.

Ivanski spotted a small screw sticking out in the corner of the drawer and pulled on it, lifting the false bottom of the drawer up, revealing a smart leather briefcase and a bundle of classified files neatly tucked away in the substantial concealed space there. Gregorovitch pulled everything out and chucked the items onto the bed, next to Penkovsky.

Waving his pistol at Penkovsky, Chelpinsky ordered, *"Off the bed! Go and sit on that chair over there - and do not move a muscle. Keep a close eye on him, Ivanski!"*

Chelpinsky strode across to the bed and attempted to click open the brief-case locks. *"The combination?"* he demanded impatiently, snapping his fingers. Penkovsky mumbled some numbers and Chelpinsky rolled the two barrel locks on the front of the briefcase which he then clicked open.

He eased the lid of the brief-case up and noted, to his delight, that stashed inside there were two large bundles of high denomination American and English currency, secured with elastic bands, an unopened bottle of Johnny Walker 'Black Label' whisky, several pairs of expensive French silk nylons, two bottles of very expensive perfume, some strips of South African gold sovereigns and four quality ladies gold watches.

"*A veritable treasure trove, Comrade,*" he said to Penkovsky, "*one wonders how you could have afforded to pay for these luxury goods on your salary as a Lieutenant Colonel. I know that I certainly couldn't!*"

Chelpinsky closed the brief-case, locked it and then reached over and picked up one of the files. "*I see that these are all classified files, Comrade. What are they doing here in your flat, tucked away in a dressing table drawer with that illegal contraband?*" he asked.

Penkovsky replied, "*It's no big deal. I bring them home to study them.*" "*You know full well that it is strictly forbidden and a serious offence for you to do that?*" said Chelpinsky. Penkovsky nodded, "*Yes, of course, but everyone else does it, not just me!*" "*Mmmm, well it looks to me like you've got rather a lot of explaining to do, wouldn't you agree Ivanski?*" The Lieutenant nodded dutifully, "*Yes indeed, Comrade Colonel. A lot of explaining!*"

Turning to Gregorovitch he said, "*We'd better make tracks, Ivanski. Take 'Prisoner 888' down to the car,*" he ordered. "*Prisoner 888!*" exclaimed Penkovsky. Chelpinski nodded and smiled, "*Yes, that is correct, 'Prisoner 888.' That is your new nomenclature and you must learn to answer to it!*"

Chelpinsky then leaned across and brutally ripped the Lieutenant Colonel badges of rank off Penkovski's uniform jacket, saying, "*I might as well keep these for myself. You won't be needing them anymore.*"

The three of them left the apartment and headed downstairs to the car. Penkovsky could hardly walk, his legs were trembling so badly and there was blood dribbling down his cheek and chin from where he'd been hit by the pistol. His mouth, where the teeth had been brutally knocked out, was throbbing fiercely. He wiped some of the blood away with the back of his handcuffed hand.

Penkovsky had been around long enough to know that a lot more of that sort of treatment would be waiting for him at the Lubyanka Prison. He'd seen it all before, many times and that was what was making his legs tremble.

"I will sit in the back of the car with 'Prisoner 888,' Ivanski," said Chelpinsky, *"we don't want him attempting to escape or doing anything stupid." "Prisoner 888?"* stuttered Penkovsky. Chelpinsky nodded, *"Yes, Comrade, that is who you now are - as I said before, you'd better get used to it."*

As he placed the briefcase and files onto the passenger seat of the car, a high-spirited Chelpinsky tapped Lieutenant Gregorovitch on the shoulder and said, *"As 'Prisoner 888's' American friends would say, Ivanski, hit the gas, baby, - then get on the car radio and tell the surveillance team to stand down!"*

Nodding, Gregorovitch replied, *"As you command, Comrade Colonel."* Gregorovitch glanced across at Penkovsky's expensive leather briefcase laid on the passenger seat and wondered if Chelpinski might consider removing some of the foreign currency from it for their own use. "*You never know, he might slip a decent chunk of it my way!*" he thought, but didn't hold out much hope.

As they drove off through the empty Moscow streets, a cheerful Chelpinsky said, *"Ah, look, it's stopped raining, Ivanski. You know what, things are looking up!"* Gregorovitch nodded and replied, *"Yes, it's turned out nice again, Comrade Colonel!"*

Ж

CHAPTER SIX

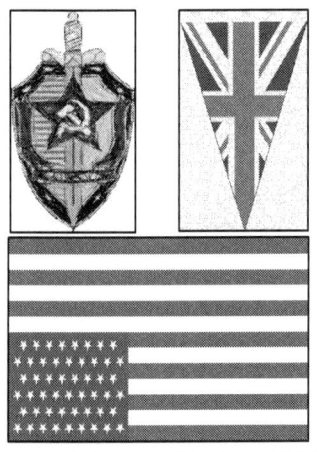

'FLASH TO BANG'

Background.

The 'Cuban Missile Crisis' took place during October 1962, when three major powers, the USSR, USA and the UK were balancing apprehensively on the very precipice of a full-scale nuclear war.

The angry confrontation, mainly between the Soviet Union and the United States of America took place over a 13 day period, from the 16th to the 28th of October 1962.

The reason for the confrontation - the Americans had discovered that the Soviets had covertly deployed some of their Luna Class ballistic missiles to Cuba and were keeping them there in pre-prepared locations, pointed threateningly at nearby America. The discovery of this

Russian skull-duggery caused fear and outrage in the USA and led directly to the nightmare threat of nuclear conflagration.

The Soviet Premier, the rumbustious and bellicose Nikita Khruschev, had concluded a secret agreement with President Fidel Castro, who had an intense dislike of the Americans. Castro had not only permitted the Russians to construct military bases and missile silos in Cuba but also granted permission for numerous Russian nuclear missiles to be stored on Cuban territory.

The missile bases would only be some 140 kilometres (90 miles) from Florida. A US manned U-2 spy plane had provided definitive high-resolution photographic evidence of the missile sites; further aerial photographs confirmed that work was ongoing preparing the sites for the arrival of Russian SS-4 (Medium Range) and R-14 (Intermediate Range) missiles.

The latest supply of Russian missiles were on their way to Cuba by sea, onboard the Russian merchantman 'The Kislovodsk.' Thus began what the Russians had designated 'OP ANADYR.'

On the 22nd of October 1962 the United States established a rapid-response naval blockade off Cuba in order to stop deliveries of the additional Russian missiles from reaching there. President Kennedy also demanded that the Russian weapons already sited in Cuba had to be dismantled immediately and returned to Russia, along with the Russian Ilyushin 11-28 light bombers, also on the island.

The hotline between Washington and Moscow was in constant use as negotiations between Kennedy and Khruschev teetered on a knife edge until finally, and to everyone's great relief, Soviet Premier Khruschev realising that his bluff had been called, climbed down at the eleventh hour.

Khruschev agreed to American demands to have the ship turned around, the nuclear weapons dismantled and all Ilyushin aircraft returned to Russia.

Nuclear 'Armageddon' had been avoided by a mere whisker.

As their part of the deal, the Americans had to agree not to invade Cuba. What wasn't known at the time, however, was that President John F Kennedy had agreed with Premier Nikita Khruschev that the Americans would dismantle all of the US-built Jupiter Missiles that were deployed in Turkey.

There was a gradual ramping down of tensions and there were palpable sighs of relief around the world; it had been a close run thing and could so easily have gone the other way. The world had definitely teetered on the brink of nuclear war and ultimately possible total annihilation.

'Hotline' - Key Players

Harold MacMillan
*Prime Minister of the
United Kingdom*

John 'Jack' Fitzgerald Kennedy
*President of the
United States of America*

Robert Francis Kennedy
*Attorney General of the
United States of America*

Nikita Sergeyavitch Khruschev
*Chairman of the
Union of Soviet Socialist
Republics*

In London, at Number 10 Downing Street, the telephone hot-line on the Prime Minister's desk began buzzing. The PM picked it up and immediately heard a clipped

American voice stating, "*Prime Minister, I have the President of the United States of America on the line for you, sir.*" There was a slight delay, then a few clicks before the PM heard the charming young President's very distinctive voice.

"*Hi, you there, Harry?*" asked a weary sounding John F Kennedy. "*Yes, yes, I'm here old boy,*" replied MacMillan, "*We never close!*" Jack Kennedy was one of the very few people that could get away with calling the erudite and polished Harold MacMillain 'Harry.' There was great affection and admiration between the two men.

Kennedy continued, "*Great. Well, I'd better get straight to the point, sir. It's those damned Russkies. Despite all of the evidence to the contrary, they have refused point blank to confirm that they have established a nuclear base on Cuban soil and deny absolutely that they are shipping additional missiles to Cuba by sea. That is also an outright lie, as we know full well that the missiles are on the high-seas as we speak.*"

Mr MacMillan snorted, "*Huh, those bloody Russkies! Could never trust them, not even during the last war. I never liked that awful man Stalin, his eyes were too close together. As usual, they're lying through their teeth! You and I both know that we have concrete evidence to the contrary, Jack!*"

"*That we do, Harry, but as you know, our key informant, Lieutenant Colonel Oleg Penkovsky, has been taken out of the loop, unfortunately having been arrested by the*

KGB. *So we're now having to rely on photographic evidence provided by the USAF's U-2's and the odd few scraps of intelligence that are coming our way from contacts inside Cuba,"* replied the young President.

"Yes, bit of a bugger that; don't fancy Penkovsky's chances, what!" said Mr MacMillan. *"Have we had any news regarding his whereabouts?"* asked the PM *"My CIA operatives tell me that the KGB were seen arresting him, not that they'll admit to it. We've been led to believe that the unfortunate man is being held somewhere in Moscow, more than likely in the cellars of the Lubyanka Prison."* said the President.

"Such a pity that, he was a bally good source of information," said MacMillan, tutting and shaking his head in sympathy, *"Don't give much for his chances now."*

"There's not a lot we can do for him at the moment thought, Harry, other than later on with the offer of a bit of damage limitation perhaps," said President Kennedy, *"we might be able to organise a spy exchange at some stage, but I don't believe that the Russians would even consider that at the moment."*

MacMillan sighed, *"So, Jack, dear boy, what's the state of play regarding the Russian merchant ship, the er, the 'Kislovodsk,' the one that's bringing the other nuclear weapons over to your neck of the woods?"* he asked.

"If you don't mind, sir, I'll just put my brother Bobby on the line for a moment, he's in a much better position than I to provide you with an update," replied the President, *"Just handing you over now."*

There was a slight pause then Robert F Kennedy, (the US Attorney General and brother to John F) came on the hotline, *"Good morning, Prime Minister." "Morning Bobby, I believe that you have an update for me regarding that bloody Russian scow?" "Indeed I do, sir,"* replied Bobby. *"the Whitehouse Situation Room has just flashed your security guys a detailed Sitrep, copied to the War Office, but in essence, despite several warnings, the Russian ship, the 'Kislovodsk' has failed to slow down or change course."*

"Oh dear," said MacMillan, *"so what do you intend doing about it?"* The PM knew full well that the Americans wouldn't hesitate to sink the 'Kislovodsk' if they deemed it necessary to do so.

Bobby continued, *"The USS Joseph P Kennedy is on station and has been ordered to clear for action, as have the USS Essex and USS Gearing. In the event that the Russian ship fails to turn around and head for home pretty darned soon there will be no alternative for us but to send it to the bottom of th ocean!"*

MacMillan tutted, *"Those damned Russian fellows always take things down to the wire. To make matters worse, my intelligence chaps tell me that apparently the missile sites in Cuba are still being actively worked on!"*

"*That's correct, sir,*" said Bobby.

"*Thunderation, the Doomsday Clock's ticking merrily away and, metaphorically speaking, were only five minutes from midnight, what!*" "*Indeed we are. O.K. well that's all I can tell you at the moment, so if I may, I'll pass you back to the President, sir.*" "*Thanks for that, Bobby,*" said MacMillan.

"*Hi Harry, me again,*" said the President. "*So, where do we go from here then, Jack?*" asked a now very concerned MacMillan. "*Well, as Bobby said, the worst case scenario is, Harry, that we'll probably just go ahead and sink the damned Russian ship. As for Cuba itself, I believe that only an invasion of the island would remove the threat to the USA once and for all,*" said President Kennedy, "*We cannot and will not allow that sort of regime to exist on our doorstep. It's as simple as that.*"

MacMillan replied, "*If you don't mind me saying so, old boy, I would urge you to exercise a great deal of caution here. The course of action that you are considering would only give Khruschev and his cohorts the excuse they seem to be looking for to press the nuclear button and start a war where, of course, we will all be the losers. Might I respectfully suggest that for the short term we both continue to apply both heavy diplomatic and military pressure and see how things develop. We mustn't lose sight of the grave likelihood of a nuclear conflagration.*"

After a slight pause, the President sighed, "*OK, I'll take your sage advice on that one, Harry, and step back from the brink. I will, though, order the low-level flights over Cuba to be increased from two a day to once every two hours, to see if that elicits a positive response from the Kremlin. They've gotta understand that we're serious about this."

"And if it doesn't elicit a response?" asked the Prime Minister.

After a brief pause, the President continued, "*If it doesn't, then I'll order the invasion preparations to be speeded up and, regrettably, I will also order a massive retaliatory nuclear strike on the Soviet Union - if they see fit to launch.*"

Kennedy's comment caused MacMillan to sit up straight in his chair and his jaw dropped.

"*And whatever else happens, I'm determined that one way or the other, the Russian ship will not pass through our blockade unscathed,*" said the President.

"Bit of a stale-mate then, what?" said MacMillan, "*The trouble is, Jack, that Khruschev is so bloody unpredictable. One can only hope and pray that his Generals and members of the Politburo persuade him see sense and caution him to step back from the brink, otherwise we're undoubtedly heading for a nuclear catastrophy. Nobody will win this one, old boy.*"

"I totally agree with you, Harry, but we're hog-tied with this. The President paused for a moment, then sighed,

"*OK, let's just see how things develop over the next few hours then. I'll give you a call on the hot-line should anything change.*" said the President, "*Speak to you soon, Harry, hopefully with better news.*" "*Grateful for that, Jack. Give my love to Jacquie and the family. Cheerio.*" said MacMillan, breaking the hot-line connection.

"*That bloody man Khruschev wants flogging!*" said MacMillan.

Ж

CHAPTER SEVEN

'NUMBER 10 DOWNING STREET'

The Prime Minister, The Right Honourable Sir Roger Peace MP, smiled wolfishly at Mike and Graham, *"Well, gentlemen, thank you for popping down here at such short notice; it's a pleasure to see you both again. I think the last time we got together under similar circumstances was when we asked you to travel forward in time to, er, 2119 wasn't it?"*

Graham nodded, *"That's correct, sir. We travelled forward in time for the first time ever, to Kingston-Upon-Hull, if you recall?"* (*See 'Tinkering with Time'). *"Ah yes, of course, that's it. And a veritable treasury of invaluable sensitive information you brought back from there too, as I recall. I'm told that it's being put to good use even as we speak,"* said the PM *"and because we've got a much better idea of the Chinese government's thought processes and pre-planned mischief activities we've managed to get* *them running around in circles, which makes a refreshing change! I doubt very much that it will prevent World War 3 but at least we can be prepared for when it happens. However,"* he continued. *"I've asked you chaps to come here today because we need your help once again."*

Mike nodded and replied, *"Aye, well we're always happy to do our bit for Queen and Country, Prime Minister, and I know that my oppo here is of the same mind, isn't that so, Graham." "Absolutely,"* said Graham. *"Jolly good show, chaps*," said the PM *"a volunteer is worth ten pressed men, eh!"*

Graham nodded enthusiastically in agreement, but in reality was thinking, *"Oh, hell fire, now what are we letting ourselves in for?"*

The Prime Minister continued, *"Very well, then I'll cut straight to the chase. Have either of you heard the name Penkovsky, Colonel Oleg Penkovsky, to be precise?"*

They both nodded. Graham said, *"To be perfectly honest with you, Prime Minister, Mike and I had a quick briefing from your Chief of Staff on that very subject just before we came in here, so we know who Penkovsky was and something of the historical background."* The Prime Minister nodded, *"Good, well if nothing else, that saves us some valuable time then."*

He continued, *"Now, gentlemen, what I am about to tell you must not under any circumstances go any further than this room. I am given to understand that you have both signed the Official Secrets Act, is that correct?"* Both men nodded. *"Bloody hell,"* thought Graham, *"this is getting a bit serious."*

Sir Roger continued, *"Excellent, then I will proceed. Incidentally, I must warn you that if it is subsequently discovered that anything I'm about to tell you has leaked out, then you will both be heading for HM Prison Belmarsh faster than you can say 'Tony Blair!'"*

Mike's jaw dropped and Graham visibly paled.

After a heartstopping moment the Prime Minister guffawed heartily, *"Just joking chaps, but I'm sure you get my drift."* Both men nodded, knowing full well that the Prime Minister wasn't joking. Sir Roger wasn't known for his sense of humour.

"Now, I'm sure you're asking yourselves what all this is about?" said the Prime Minister. Without waiting for them to reply, he continued, *"Well, as you now know, Colonel Penkovsky was arrested by the KGB in Moscow, on the 22nd of October 1962 to be precise. It's not general knowledge but I's since come to light via our intelligence 'sources' that he was arrested as a direct result of a leak from our very own George Blake, who unbeknowns to us was a double-agent in the pay of the Kremlin."*

"Blake is a dreadful creature; he disclosed many of the names of our agents and informers who were operating inside the USSR on our behalf at the time to the KGB. As a direct result, they were taken prisoner, more than likely

tortured and then executed. We did eventually catch Blake and put him in prison, back in the early 60's, but he was smuggled out in 1966 and eventually resurfaced like the creature from the swamp, in Moscow. I'm told that he now lives a life of ease in a dacha given to him courtesy of the Russians. Huh, if anyone deserves a bullet in the head, that reptile Blake does."

The PM sighed, *"I digress. We don't know for definite what happened to Colonel Penkovsky. It's rumoured that he met a horrible end by being burned alive in an industrial furnace somewhere in the cellars of the Lubyanka Prison, either that or he was shot. Not really sure."*

"There is another option that's been mooted - which is even worse as far as we're concerned, and that is that he was in fact acting as a double-agent, feeding us false information for years and was still alive, tucked away out of sight somewhere in Mother Russia, possibly Minsk!"

"I've actually seen the mortifying KGB film of his execution – or should I say 'an' execution, but it is by no means certain that the unfortunate victim was Penkovsky."

"My God," exclaimed Graham, *"how dreadful! To think that the Russians would actually film something as horrendous as that. It's mind blowing. They're as bad as the Nazis!"* The Prime Minister nodded in agreement, *"Yes, it was rather hideous. I've been unable to touch pork crackling ever since!"*

"Er, so what precisely is it that you want us two to do, Prime Minister?" asked a grimacing Mike.

Sir Roger smiled, "Well, I'd like you both to travel through time in your 'T3-Travellator' Time-Machine back to 1962, locate Colonel Penkovsky, then rescue him and bring him back here. We believe that he was possibly being held in the Lubyanka Prison in central Moscow around about then but are not absolutely certain of that. The Russians were playing this very close to their chests. Probably thought that we might try to mount some sort of rescue mission, like they themselves did with the wretch George Blake."

"You see, for starters, we need to know if Penkovsky was definitely working for both us and the Americans, or if he was simply acting as a double-agent, charged by the Russians to feed us mountains of false information, deliberately designed to mislead us. The only way to do that is to go and get Penkovsky and bring him back here for an in-depth interrogation."

The Prime Minister paused, sighed, then continued, "Why bring him back here after all this time, you might ask? Well, and this is where things get really sensitive, we believe that back then there was someone else working alongside the notorious traitor George Blake here in London."

Mike and Graham both nodded, as the PM continued, "The mystery man that we are interested in was also working in the upper echelons of our Secret Service at the *time. Blake was relatively young back in 1963 and was deemed to be a high flyer, as was this other 'mystery man.'We believe that the 'mystery man' is now very senior and has reached the very higher echelons of our Secret Service. Indeed, there is a distinct possibility that he is in line to take over from 'M' as Departmental Head of MI6 at the end of this year when 'M' retires."*

"We need to know for definite if Blake's colleague was also spying for the Russians at the time and indeed has continued to do so, for obvious reasons" The PM shook his head, *" It would be an utter disaster if that were found to be the case. We can produce no physical evidence to that end so want to go right back to the very beginning to when all this kicked off - and that's why we need to speak to Penkovsky. You see, Penkovsky would undoubtedly have been in a position to know the name of our 'mystery man.'"*

"Ah, right,' said Mike, *"so we just 'Time-Travel' back to the Lubyanka Prison in 1962, blag our way in there, lift Colonel Penkovsky - if in fact he's there, and then transport him back here for questioning. Doddle actually!"* The Prime Minister had the good grace to laugh.

A smiling Sir Roger said, *"Now come on chaps, don't be backwards at coming forwards, you know full well that you can pull this one off. You two are a quality act. I mean if we thought that it wasn't a feasible proposition then we wouldn't be sat here right now discussing it would we?"*

Graham coughed, *"If I might interject, sir. It's all very complex is this 'Time-Travel' business, Prime Minister. You, more than anyone know that we're not allowed to 'tinker with time,'* "*Your point being?*" asked the PM *"If we do rescue this man Penkovsky and save him from execution then we'll have done precisely that, 'Tinkered with Time,'"* said Graham.

"Well, Graham" said Mike, *"I suppose that at a push we could always take Penkovsky back to the Lubyanka Prison after he's been interrogated here and then let Russian nature take its course." "That's not going to happen, is it! How could we knowingly take someone back to face that sort of cruel fate!"* said Graham. *"It's just a wee thought for consideration,"* said Mike.

The Prime Minister nodded, *"Under normal circumstances I would agree with you about tinkering with time, but on this occasion you have my prime ministerial authority to do just that. The 'National Interest' is a stake here. If there's the slightest chance of there being a bad hat at the very highest level of our Secret Service than he must be rooted out and dealt with before he can do any further damage - and that's why we must get Penkovsky safely back here!"*

"But, sir," said Graham, *"you said that there was a chance that Penkovsky might be a double-agent, in which case he won't want to come back with us, if indeed he's going to be there in the Lubyanka Prison. He may have been living the 'Life of Riley' tucked away in some luxurious dacha on the edge of the Black Sea for all we know!"*

"It's a calculated risk that we, or should I say you two, are going to have to take. We must have answers. If you locate him and he doesn't volunteer to come back with you then you must 'persuade' him to do so," said the PM *"It won't be easy,"* said Graham, shaking his head.

"I didn't think for one minute that it would be. Tell you what, I'll give you both twenty four hours to mull it over," said the PM *"then I would like you both to come back here and tell me that 'a' you're definitely going to do it and 'b' just how you intend going about doing it."*

"Sounds like it's 'Hobsons Choice' then, sir?" said Graham. *"Got it in one!"* replied the Prime Minister, nodding and smiling at them. *"I need not remind you both, but I'm going to, that this is a highly sensitive matter and must go no further. Not a squeak to anyone!"* Both men nodded.

"Now then chaps, my Chief of Staff, Greg, has booked accommodation for you both over at the Ritz Hotel. You can have a good think tonight about what we've discussed, then pop back here tomorrow and let me know of your decision." Said the PM.

Mike and Graham nodded, stood up, shook the Prime Minister's hand then left for the Ritz. They both knew full well that the decision for them to go and rescue Penkovsky had already been rubber stamped, despite what their concerns might be.

Once they'd departed, the PM picked up his 'phone and put a call through to the Head of MI6. *"Right 'M.' I've given them both the full Monty and they've gone off to the Ritz Hotel to talk things through. Make sure that you've got someone lurking to keep a close eye on them whilst they're there if you would"*

"I don't want them sliding off to Soho for the night like they did last time they were down here. I want them both back here bright eyed and bushy tailed at ten o'clock tomorrow morning - on the dot!"

The following morning, just as Big Ben could be heard striking ten o'clock o'clock, a fully refreshed but apprehensive Mike and Graham were once again sat in front of the Prime Minister.

"Well chaps, what've you decided to do?" he asked. Mike said, *"We will, of course, have a crack at it, sir. Not only for you, but for Queen and Country and all that."* The PM smiled, *"Jolly good show!"*

"There is just one little proviso though," said Mike. The PM raised an eyebrow, *"Oh really - and what might the, may I ask?"* he said.

"We'd like permission to take our Dutch friend, Edward De Jong, along with us," said Mike, *"like me, Ed was Special Forces, he's an intelligent hard-case and will come in very handy should we fall foul of the Russians and need a bit of muscle to get us out of a tight spot."*

The Prime Minister thought for a moment then nodded, *"Oh, very well. It's highly unusual, but then this whole thing is highly unusual, isn't it. I'll instruct my Chief of Staff to see that the necessary background checks and clearances are carried out on your Mr De Jong, as a matter of priority. If and when your friend is given the nod, then you'll be good to go. If he doesn't get clearance then you're on your own, I'm afraid."* "Fair enough," said Mike.

"How long have we got before we leave, sir?" asked Graham *"I would like you to be on your way to Moscow by no later than a week from now. Time is of the very essence. The MI6 Promotion Board sits in a fortnight and we want to have everything well and truly ironed out by then,"* replied the Prime Minister.

"Can we warn Ed De Jong off then?" asked Graham. *"Absolutely not!"* said the Prime Minister, *"I want him to be closely vetted and cleared before he hears even a whisper about any of this. Not a squeak, do I make myself clear?"* Both men nodded.

"Right, well you two had better cut along and make your plans and we'll have a further meeting at the end of this week. On your way out of here, please pass your colleague Mr De Jong's contact details to the Chief of Staff and he'll take it from there," said the Prime Minister,

"Now, if you'll excuse me, gentlemen, I have to prepare myself for the delight that is Prime Minister's Questions. Bloody nuisance, but it's got to be done!" Mike and

Graham stood up, shook hands with the Prime Minster and left.

The PM summoned his Chief of Staff, "*Greg, there's a little something I'd like you to do for me, if you wouldn't mind. There's a chap called Ed De Jong, a Dutchman, that'll be needing flash top level security clearance so that he can accompany Messrs St Anier and Fraser when they 'Time-Travel' back to Russia for the extraction. See to it will you - and let me know of there are any problems*"

The PM's Chief of Staff nodded, "*Consider it done, sir,*" he said as he bustled off, thinking, "*Bloody hell, as if I haven't got enough to do. I'm supposed to be taking my wife to Fortnum and Mason today.*"

Ж

CHAPTER EIGHT

'VILLEFRANCHE-SUR-MER'

"Hello, who's this?" asked Ed De Jong. *"Hi Ed, it's me Mike, Mike Fraser." "Morning Mike, how are you my dear friend?"* said Ed. *"Oh, stunningly average, thanks,"* replied Mike. *"Listen pal,"* said Mike, *"we, that's me, you and Graham, need tae have a wee chat about a particularly sensitive governmental project that we'd like your help w"*

"I was wondering if you'd care tae pop across to Hull for a wee chin-wag in the very near future?" "This all sounds very mysterious, Mike. Are you able to tell me anything about it now?" asked Ed. *"I dinnae really want tae say too much about it over an open line. I'd rather speak to you face to face,"* replied Mike.

"Well my friend, I'd be more than happy to come over and see you, but just at the moment I'm on the Côte d'Azur in a most picturesque place called Villefranche-sur-Mer." said Ed. *"Och, the life of the idle rich, eh! What mischief are you up to there then? I'll bet you're no there just for the sunshine; is there a wee French chick lurking on the periphery?"* Ed grinned, *"No chicks, Mike, although*

there is a Russian lady involved, but she's a bit of a 'coffin dodger' as you would say. "All sounds delightfully mysterious, something going on?" said Mike. "I have what you would call a 'wee' project in mind," replied Ed.

"How long are you going to be there for?" asked Mike. "Not for too long, in fact I'm hoping to be on my way later this evening," said Ed, "I've just got to have a chat with the little Russian lady and then I'll be heading straight back to Amsterdam. Tell you what, I'll give you a bell once I get back home and we can sort something out." "OK Ed, but don't hang about mate, the clock's ticking on this one," said Mike.

"I'm intrigued," said Ed, "I should be back in Amsterdam early tomorrow morning, so I'll ring you straight after breakfast, if that's OK?" "That'd be great," said Mike. "OK, speak to you later then. Oh, and give my regards to Graham." said Ed. "Wilco," said Mike and rang off.

"Sounds very interesting, wonder what that's all about," thought Ed as he headed along the picturesque Avenue Feodorovna at Villefranche-sur-Mer, towards what was referred to by the locals as the 'Russian House.'

The 'Russian House' was a large, beautiful old fashioned stone building, set slightly back from the road and facing directly out onto the glorious bay. On arrival at the house, Ed opened the front gate, strode up to the door then rang the doorbell. After a few moments, the door swung open and the elderly, soberly dressed manservant standing there bowed his head respectfully then in a quavering voice politely asked Ed what was it that he required.

Ed informed him that he was the one who had telephoned earlier requesting an appointment with Princess Anastasia. *"Ah, of course Monsieur, forgive me. Her Royal Highness is expecting you. Would you care to come in and I'll inform Her Royal Highness that you have arrived."*

On the large, marble floored external balcony outside the receiving room of the 'Russian House' the manservant, Vladimir, who had answered the door to Ed, tottered up to the distinguished looking old lady who was perched in a high-backed chair, gazing out at the ocean.

He bowed his head deferentially and raising his voice said, *"Excuse me, Your Royal Highness!"* *"Yes, what is it, Vladimir - and Vladimir, there is no need to shout, I am only slightly hard of hearing?"* replied a smiling Princess Anastasia. Vladimir was himself as deaf as a post and therefore assumed that everyone else was. *"Forgive me, Your Royal Highness, the Dutch gentleman who telephoned here earlier has arrived."*

Anastasia nodded, *"Good. You'd better bring him out here then - and Vladimir..."* *"Yes, Your Royal Highness?"* *"He is to remain here for no longer than thirty minutes, by which time our business will have been concluded - one way or the other. Is that clearly understood?"* *"Of course, Your Royal Highness. I'll show him in then,"* said Vladimir, who withdrew from the royal presence.

The Princess opened her small purse, took out a delicate crystal perfume bottle and sprayed herself liberally behind the royal ears, then called out, "*Oh and Vadimir, you might care to bring him a glass of iced tea, it's unbearably hot today?*" Vladimir, misunderstanding, smiled and replied, "*Half past three, Your Royal Highness.*"

'Princess Anastasia'

Perched on a slightly uncomfortable chair in the corner of the large balcony, immediately adjacent to the 'Russian house's receiving room, Ed was sat facing the very distinguished looking elderly lady, Princess Anastasia, wishing that he hadn't worn a suit because of the sticky heat.

After the initial social niceties, Princess Anastasia had invited him to take a seat. The Princess informed Ed that she was slightly hard of hearing and had politely asked him to enunciate distinctly, so he leant forward whenever he spoke to her. Notwithstanding that little problem, it was quite evident to Ed that she was still as sharp as a pin and didn't miss a trick or a nuance, as Ed had soon discovered whilst chatting with her.

When Ed had been introduced to the Princess, or 'presented' as Vladimir had put it, he'd caught a distinct whiff of the original fragrance '4711 Eu de Cologne' that she was wearing, which reminded him of his late grandmother who had also splashed herself liberally with the same scent, and it sort of set him at his ease.

The two had agreed to converse in English, a language common to them both. *"And so, Mr De Jong, I presume that you have brought the gold sovereigns with you in anticipation that I would agree to whatever it is you might wish to suggest?"* she asked.

"Indeed I did, Your Royal Highness, although I would not wish to be thought presumptuous," Ed replied, *"If you are unhappy with any of what we are about to discuss, I will instantly take my leave and you may retain the sovereigns."*

Anastasia gave a world-weary sigh, thinking, *"I hope that I am not selling my soul for a mess of pottage,"* She continued, *"Very well. Might I have a look at them?"* she asked, *"I'm sorry to appear so forward, Mr De Jong, but times are hard and I have little income other than a very small pension that I receive from the French Government, which just allows me to keep my head above water. It will bring me much joy to receive something of value for a change. Who knows, I might even be able to afford a decent sized bottle of Kölnish Wasser!"* she said, smiling at Ed. *"How delightful she looks when she smiles,"* thought Ed.

"Forgive me, Ma'am, but do you receive nothing from the Russian Government?" asked Ed. She shook her head, *"Not a damned kopek!" "That surprises me!"* said Ed.

"Not a bean, my dear man. Huh, and I am only allowed to reside here in this house under sufferance. 'They' the Russian authorities prefer me to be here so that they can keep a watchful eye on me and see that I don't get up to any mischief. I'm a bird in a gilded cage."

Anastasia gazed around and sighed, *"It's not quite the same as the Winter Palace in St Petersburg, but it keeps a roof over my head,"* she said, her piercing blue eyes twinkling.

Mike passed Princess Anastasia an expensive looking and highly polished wooden box which, after prising the lid open, she saw to her immense delight that it contained several strips of gleaming and chunky gold sovereigns. *"Perfectly delightful,"* she said, running them through her fingers, *"and strikingly beautiful. Now, perhaps you'd better tell me what it is that I am required to do to earn these trinkets?"* she said, closing the box lid and placing it by her side.

"I can kiss that box goodbye," thought Ed.

The little old lady, Princess Anastasia, daughter of the Russian Tsar Nicholas the 2nd, claimed to be the last surviving member of the Russian Imperial family.

Fortunately for her, (or so she would have it), she had, purely by chance, avoided the mass execution of her family that took place in the cellars of the house at Yekaterinburg on the night of the 16th/17th of July 1918. Purely by good fortune, she had left the house on the afternoon of the 16th of July 1918 and by doing so escaped a similar fate.

Anastasia's family, including her dear father Tsar Nicholas the 2nd, had been brutally massacred, firstly being shot and then bayonetted by representatives of the provisional government in the cellar of the house where they were being kept prisoner. After searching their bodies for hidden loot, the guards threw the Royal Family's remains unceremoniously into the back of a truck then carted them away to be dismissively tossed down a mine shaft and left there to rot for all eternity. A truly uneccessary, heinous and cowardly act.

Anastasia, the only Royal survivor, had wandered all around the world like a lost soul for many years until eventually settling down in Villefranche-sur-Mer under the protection of the French government, who had sought and surprisingly received permission from the Russian government for her to reside in the 'Russian House' for her remaining years.

The Princess had never forgiven the British Royal Family for not rescuing them as promised, in particular King George the 5th, whom Anastasia felt had let his cousin Tsar Nicholas and family down very badly.

Tsar Nicholas had implored King George, to whom he was personally very close, for help. King George had solemnly promised the Russian Royal Family asylum and a safe haven in England but had withdrawn the offer at the very last minute, cutting the Romanovs adrift.

Apparently one of King George's senior courtiers had whispered in his ear that the Russian's desire for Republicanism just might rub off on his British subjects - which the King didn't want to happen, for obvious reasons – his own position and that of his family might have been compromised. So the offer of asylum was withdrawn and the Romanovs, King George's close relatives, were dropped like hot cakes and abandoned to their cruel fate.

Anastasia said, *"I'm sure you know what then happened to my family, Mr De Jong, it is general knowledge, is it not?"* Mike nodded, *"Yes indeed it is, Ma'am, and if I might say so, it was unforgiveably cowardly, cruel and totally unnecessary."*

Gazing off into the distance, she sighed then continued, *"Truly terrible. On the 17th of July 1918, during the early hours, my family was awakened and ordered to get dressed. Once dressed they were led downstairs into the basement at the back of the Ipatiev House. My father, the Tsar, was informed that the family had been moved down there because the anti-Bolshevik forces were heading for Yekaterinburg and it was thought that a rescue attempt might be made."*

"They told my father that Ipatiev House might be fired upon and no-one wanted any of my family to be injured, in view of which they were being moved downstairs to the safety of the basement."

With a slight break in her voice, she continued, *"What my beloved family didn't know was that a firing squad had been assembled and was waiting for them down in the basement in an adjacent room. The firing squad was commanded by a Bolshevik fanatic, Yakov Yurovsky."*

She paused momentarily, *"Am I boring you yet, Mr De Jong?"* Ed shook his head and said, *"No, not at all, please continue, Your Royal Highness, this is all deeply touching quite fascinating."*

Anastasia continued, *"You know, those men didn't even have the common decency to provide chairs for my exhausted and frightened family to sit on. My mother, who was carrying my sickly brother in her arms, complained and so eventually a couple of chairs were brought in"*

"A few moments later the firing squad filed into the room and Comrade Yurovsky informed my darling father of the family's pending execution. Before my father or anyone else had time to react, the Bolsheviks opened fire and the slaughter began."

Anastasia paused and dabbed at her eyes with a small, frilly lace handkerchief. *"Not only were they shot out of hand by those unprincipled cowards, Mr De Jong, but they were also cruelly bayonetted. I can still hardly bear to think about it, even after all these years. The pain does not go away."*

A compassionate Ed wanted to reach across and give Anastasia a comforting and reassuring hug, but refrained from doing so. She looked far too regal and distant for that sort of thing. A very sincere, *"I'm so very sorry,"* was all he could manage.

Continuing, Anastasia said, *"Of course, I had the good fortune to escape by the skin of my teeth. That is another story. Since then, for whatever reason, no-one seems to believe that I survived and I have continually had to try and prove that I am who I say I am. Quite ridiculous."*

"From the very start the Bolsheviks attempted to discredit me, saying that I was an impostor. It would have been much more convenient for them had I been 'disposed' of with the rest of my family. So, I am now considered to be something of a threat to Mother Russia, presumably because whilst at least one Romanov survives, there is a chance, however slight, that the Imperial throne might be reclaimed."

"My journey has been a long and difficult one, Mr De Jong. I have been pushed from pillar to post, pilloried, mocked and villified. At the end of a very long road, I was eventually offered the sanctuary of this little villa in which

to spend the remainder of my days. It was, as we Russians say, like a mountain had fallen off my shoulders and I accepted the offer with alacrity. I was free, had a safe place to stay and had been promised that the Russians wouldn't lay a finger on me - just so long as I didn't make any fuss. "Da poshlee onee vse. Da mne gluboko naplevat!" (*'To hell with all of them – I don't give a spit!'*) she hissed!

After a few moments whilst she composed herself, she then gave a heartfelt sigh, "*So, my Dutch friend, very briefly, that's my story. Quite sad really, isn't it. You couldn't write it.*"

Lifting the lid of the box containing the coins, she let her long, slim fingers caress the gold sovereigns. Smiling at Ed and pointing to the sovereigns, Anastasia said, "*You have met your part of the bargain and ,as I'm long enough in the tooth to know that there is no such thing as a free dinner, I am intrigued to know precisely how you think I am able to reciprocate?*"

Ed smiled back at her, "*Well, your Royal Highness, I'm sure that by now you've gathered that I'm something of, er, how would you describe it, an 'adventurer.'*" The Princess smiled, "*In Russian we would say an 'Avantyurist.'*" Ed nodded and continued, "*I want to assure you, however, that I need nothing from you other then a little 'historical' information.*" She smiled and said, "*Please continue, I am intrigued.*"

Ed told her, "*I am on a quest to seek out the 'Lost Library' of Tsar Ivan the Terrible, if indeed such a place exists.*"

Anastasia laughed, then, looking at him shrewdly, after a moment or two she said, "*Ah, the 'Lost Library.' Well, let me assure you, Mr De Jong, that the so-called 'Lost Library' definitely does exist, or it once did. My father knew all about it, had seen it and told me of its existence.*" She gazed off into the distance again. "*Just give me a moment or two to gather my thoughts.*"

As she was thinking, the elderly manservant, Vladimir, tottered onto the patio, Anastasia waved him away, "*Another thirty minutes if you please, Vladimir, and Vladimir, perhaps a glass of iced tea for our visitor?*" Nodding, the deaf as a post Vladimir, said, "*I have an umbrella stood by just in case, Your Royal Highness,*" then bowed and left.

Anastasia sat, deep in thought for a couple of minutes, then said, "*As far as I can recall, the earliest reference to the secret library was made in 1518. There is a long and complicated history as to the supposedly invaluable contents of the library. The main proponent of the library was, as you say, Tsar 'Ivan the Terrible.'*"

She sighed, "*It is difficult. The passage of time, as you would expect, has dimmed my memory somewhat.*" Ed thought that Anastasia was holding out for more gold sovereigns, but she continued.

"What I do remember, though, is that despite many searches, the 'Hidden Library' lay undiscovered for many years until being found purely by chance by workmen who were doing some digging beneath what is now the Lubyanka Prison."

"After having ordering that a comprehensive list be made of the library's contents, my Father ordered that the library and all of its contents, not just the books - but many other treasures, was to be resealed and hidden away for safe-keeping."

"Once the entrance had been re-sealed, the poor unfortunate workmen - and their families were immediately despatched to Siberia and never heard from again. I'm afraid that you must draw your own conclusions there."

"Military Engineers were then instructed to disguise the entrance to the library - and they too were sent away, never to return. The Salt Mines - that is how things were done in those days, I'm afraid."

Mike nodded, then asked, *"And did your father, the Tsar, ever tell you of the precise whereabouts of the library?"* Anastasia nodded, *"Oh, much better than that, Mr De Jong, he actually took me and my brother there one day."* She smiled, *"It was such an adventure. We all went down to those gloomy cellars beneath the Lubyanka and he showed us the entrance to the 'Hidden Library' and described what was hidden behind the bricked off wall."*

She continued, *"It had been re-sealed and very cleverly concealed by then, some sort of alcove as I recall. You would never had guessed it was there in a million years. My brother and I were sworn to secrecy as to its precise location. Yes, it was quite an adventure."*

Sighing wearily, Anastasia said, *" I shouldn't get your hopes too high about finding it, though, because as I said, it is located in the cellars of what is now the Lubyanka Prison in the Meschansky District of Moscow. I would imagine that you would prefer not to pay a visit to that particular establishment which I believe remains full of political dissidents and other such unfortunates."*

"I can, however, draw you a diagram of the area if you so wish. My memory is still quite clear on that subject, although the layout of the cellars may well have changed somewhat by now. Knowing those swine the Bolsheviks, they've probably added many more cells. Let me send for a pencil and some paper."

She reached across to a side table and rang a tiny silver bell to summon Vladimir. A moment or two later, Vladimir tottered onto the patio carrying a tea tray which he laid down on the side table at the side of Anastasia.

"Thank you, Vladimir, now - a pencil and a sheet of paper, if you please," Vladimir nodded, *"Yes, your Royal Highness, it is freshly made."* Anastasia sighed and said, slightly louder, *"Vladimir, a pencil and a sheet of paper, if you please!"*

Vladimir smiled, nodded, bowed then exited. It was quite obvious that Vladimir adored his Princess.

Ed was thrilled to bits. So here was confirmation that there was indeed a 'Hidden Library' and it sounded is if there was a good chance that it could still be there, unseen and untouched by anyone for years. What an adventure it was going to be trying to rediscover it.

Being beneath the Lubyanka Prison, though, could make it very complicated unless, that was, one had the use of a 'T3-Travellator' and some trustworthy buddies. He was excited at the prospect and couldn't wait to get over to Hull where he could discuss it with Mike and Graham.

Vladimir re-entered, handed Anastasia a pencil and a sheet of paper, then withdrew. Princess Anastasia started to draw a diagram of the Lubyanka Prison cellars. *"Of course,* " she said, *"one can hardly imagine how you propose gaining access to the Prison. It will be knee-deep in armed guards, security systems and the like. The building always was an impregnable fortress."*

Ed smiled, *"I never could resist a challenge, Ma'am,"* he replied.

Ж

CHAPTER NINE

'THE TIME-TRAVEL HOLIDAY STORE - KINGSTON-UPON-HULL'

Mike leapt to his feet and threw his arms around recent arrival, Ed De Jong, *"Ed, my old Dutch mucker, great to see you. Your flight across here OK?"* Ed smiled and gazed around the newly refurbished office, *"Yeah, no prob. It's great to see you too, Mike and I see that you've had the office tarted up since I was last here. Looks very Gucci!"* Mike smiled, *"Yeah, it's had a lick of paint and we've replaced all of the carpets. Place was like me, looking a bit ragged at the edges! Cost me an arm and a leg, looks the dog's though!"*

Ed turned to Graham, *"And my thanks to you Graham, amigo, for meeting me at Humberside Travelport and giving me a lift over here; that saved me a lot of faffing about with taxis. Very kind of you."* Graham smiled and nodded, *"For you - the world, old cock!"*

"Now, come and take the weight off your feet and tell us all about your trip to, er, where was it you said?" said Mike. Ed replied, *"Villefranche-sur-Mer on the Côte d'Azur."* *"Sounds very exotic. Have a nice time there?"* asked Mike. *"Yes, I was only there for a couple of days, but I got what I went for,"* said Ed, *"and once you've revealed why I've been invited here today, Mike, I will then reciprocate the gesture by sharing some rather interesting information with the pair of you."*

"Before we crack on," said Mike, *"do you fancy a cup of tea or would you prefer something a wee bit more fortifying?"* Ed shook his head, *"Ah, my Scottish friend, even for me it is a little early in the day for that. A nice cup of your 'Yorkshire Tea' wouldn't go amiss. The coffee at Schipol Airport is well known for stripping the enamel from off your chompers!"*

A grinning Mike replied, *"Well, ease your clogs off, stick your briefcase at the side of the desk and make yourself comfy whilst I go and put the kettle on. Once we've got the tea and biccies organised then we can get down to brass tacks."* *"I must admit, you've got me intrigued!"* said Ed, sliding his shoes off and wriggling his toes. *"Back at you!"* said Mike as he toddled off towards the kitchen.

"So, how's it hanging, Graham?" asked Ed. *"Oh, fair to middling,"* replied Graham, *"to be perfectly honest, it's all been a bit too quiet around here for my liking."* Ed

nodded, *"Well, my friend, I suspect that that is all about to change."*

Ten minutes later the three of them were sat around Mike's desk slurping their hot tea. Mike held out a tin of biscuits and they snaffled a couple each. *"Mmmm, 'Hob Nobs' - delicious,"* said Graham, *"put hairs on your chest will these - and they're good dunkers too."* *"OK,"* said Ed, settling back in his seat, *"you to go first then, Mike."*

"Right," said Mike, *"well, just over a week ago, me and Graham were summoned to Number 10 Downing Street by no less than the Prime Minister's Chief of Staff, on behalf of the man himself, The Right Honourable Roger Peace MP."* Ed smiled, *"Ah, so your knighthoods have come through at long last?"* he said. *"Dream on,"* snorted Graham, *"we were lucky to get offered a cup of char at Number 10, never mind a bloody knighthood – and you've got to be a pop singer to get one of those!"* *"Tea?"* said Ed. *"No, a chuffing knighthood!"* said Graham.

Mike continued, *"Now, with respect Ed, like me, you're of an age to remember a chap called Colonel Oleg Penkovsky, are you not?"* Ed thought for a moment then nodded, *"Yes, I vaguely remember the name. I think you are referring to the, er, Russian spy?"* *"That's the very man,"* said Mike. *"So, what about him?"* asked Ed.

Mike continued, *"Well, to keep a long story short, the PM wants us to jump on board our 'T3-Travellator' and go back in time to Russia to the beginning of the 1960's and see if we can locate Colonel Penkovsky, snatch him and bring him back to London. Graham and I thought that you might like to be in on this one, particularly as you like a challenge!"*

Graham chipped in, *"And we also need some of your 'brains and brawn' as back-up!"* *"Snatch and extract him, you say?"* asked Ed. *"Yes,"* said Graham, *"apparently he was being detained in the cellars of the Lubyanka Prison at the time – and that's where we'll be going."*

Ed laughed out loud then said, *"When you said Russia, I was hoping that you were referring to Moscow and not some icy gulag in Siberia, where we'd be thrashing around freezing our collective nuts off?"* Mike shook his head, *"No Siberian gulags, although I would imagine that the Lubyanka Prison isn't too dissimilar."* *"So what precisely will we be doing in Moscow then?"* asked Ed.

"We'll be punching a hole through the time dimension and transporting ourselves back to 1962 to the cellars of the Lubyanka Prison in Moscow where, apparently, Penkovsky was supposed to be being held prisoner, prior to allegedly being executed in the most brutal way." Ed raised an eyebrow. *"What do you mean?"* *"Well,"* said Mike, *"apparently he was put in a furnace whilst he was still alive and kicking."* *"Bloody hell!"* said a visibly shocked Ed.

Mike said, *"Our task, which we have accepted,"* *"Not that we were given much choice!"* grumbled Graham. Mike continued, *"Our task is to locate Penkovsky and get* him out of there before the alleged execution happens then transport him back to England in the 'T3-Travellator!'".

"*You say 'alleged' execution? Does that mean that there's a possibility his execution wasn't carried out?*" asked a surprised Ed.

Mike nodded and turned to Graham, "*OK, G, give Ed the full monty, but before Graham begins Ed, I'm duty bound to warn you that if you do decide to come along with us, which we both sincerely hope that you will, you'll be required to sign the British Official Secrets Act, with all of its ramifications - and what we are about to tell you now must go no further than these four walls, on pain of immediate imprisonment!*"

Ed grinned and nodded, "*More than happy to do that - and don't worry, my lips are well and truly sealed. I'm up for the challenge, especially when you hear what I have to tell you,*" he said. "*Hello, he's got something else up his sleeve!*" said Graham. "*You go first, Graham,*" said Ed.

After Graham had filled Ed in on the general background and then outlined the Prime Minister's precise requirements, Ed turned to Mike and said, "*I'd better have that whisky now, Mike.*" Mike smiled, reached into his desk and pulled out a bottle of whisky and three glasses.

He poured a generous measure for each of them and said, "*Ah, the old team - back together again, 'The Three Musketeers.'*" "*Cheers team!*" said a delighted Graham, knocking his drink back and holding his glass out for more, "*Seconds?*" he asked hopefully.

"*Och man, you're like Oliver Twist, always asking for more!*" said a smiling Mike as he poured Graham another slug of whisky. "*You're no getting treats like this every day!*" said Mike. "*Bloody nipscrew. You could peel an orange in your pocket!*" replied Graham.

"*You know what, boys, I wouldn't miss this gig for all the tea in Yorkshire*," said Ed. Raising an eyebrow he asked, "*And it'll just be the three of us, you say?*" Mike nodded. "*So I can't bring my two boys, Diederick and Ludo along as additional back-up then?*" asked Ed. "*Not this time I'm afraid,*" said Graham shaking his head, "*the PM was quite insistent that it could only be the three of us. Something to do with 'damage limitation' if we get caught, he said.*"

"*Huh, as if we're going to get caught. That's never going to happen!*" said Ed. "*I'll put that in my book of famous last words,*" said Graham.

After taking a sip of his whisky, Ed smacked his lips and said, "*Yeah, I'm definitely up for it, guys. Life's too short to be sat in an armchair, drooling and dreaming about what might have been and where the next bowl of soft food's coming from.*" "*Och, I knew that you wouldn't be able to resist the opportunity. That's great news!*" said Mike. "*Yaay - the old team back together again. We're going to have some good fun!*'" said Graham.

132

"*Right,*" said Mike, "*before Graham gets down to the boring details of our task - what's your news then, Ed?*"

"*Well, I wanted to update you on what I've been up to in the past few weeks and why I was lurking in Villefranche-sur-Mer, chatting with an old Russian Princess.*"

Graham gazed quizically at Ed, "*An old Russian Princess you say. You don't mean that lass, er, Anastasia do you?*" Ed nodded, "*Yes, that's the one.*" "*Hey, well done, Graham,*" said an admiring Mike, "*I'm very impressed, you're not just a pretty face!*" Graham smiled, "*It's a gift I have - knowing a little bit about everything and a lot about nothing. I'm a mine of useless information!*"

"*What on earth did you want to go and see her about, Ed? I mean, she's a bit long in the tooth, even for you, pal!*" said Mike. "*There's many a good tune played on an old fiddle! Isn't that what you once told me, Mike?*" replied Ed. Mike smiled and nodded, "*Especially if it's a Stradivarius!*"

Ed continued, "*The reason I went to see her will become apparent when I explain. You see, after our last exciting little 'Time-Travel' adventure together, I was looking for some sort of project to commit to. As you both know, I soon get 'stir crazy' when I've got time on my hands.*"

"*I was bored stiff just sitting there in Amsterdam counting my money and 'twiddling my thumbs' as you fellows say.*"
"*There's nowt wrong with polishing your brass, my*

friend. It's a true Yorkshireman's favourite pastime!" said Graham.

Ed smiled and continued, *"One afternoon, whilst doing a bit of channel surfing on 'Google' I discovered purely by chance, and to my amazement, that supposedly there's something called a 'Hidden Library' tucked away somewhere beneath the Lubyanka Prison in Moscow."*

Mike and Graham looked at each other and both said, *"The Lubyanka - Moscow!" "Oh aye, and where's all this going?"* said Graham.

Ed nodded, *"Yes, what a coincidence, eh." "You couldn't write it!"* said Graham. Ed nodded in agreement, then continued, *" I read that 'Ivan the Terrible' had not only filled the 'Hidden Library' to the brim with priceless antique books but also treasures beyond our wildest dreams."*

"The place is supposed to be cram-packed with gold, silver, crates of jewellery, some of the Russian Crown Jewels, precious religious artefacts, those sorts of things - and it's been added to over the years with precious items like Fabergé eggs."

Graham rubbed his hands together and said, *"Fabergé eggs! I'm getting a very warm feeling in my off-shore bank account!"*

Ed continued, *"And now you're telling me that we'll be 'Time-Transporting' into the Lubyanka Prison to try and find this man Penkovsky!" "And your point is?"* asked Mike. *"Well, with a bit of careful planning we could 'kill two birds with one stone,' although it's a big ask."* He shook his head, *"Such a remarkable coincidence is it not? It's written in the stars!"*

"A 'Hidden Library' you say. Must say, I haven't heard of that one, have you Graham?" said Mike. Graham shook his head, *"No, nary a squeak."*

Ed continued, *"Apparently, many have tried to locate it over the years, but as far as I know, all have failed - and that's where we three come in. My suggestion to you both is that whilst we are there in Moscow, we have a look for this 'Hidden Library' and if we find it - remove some of the more choice items for ourselves. Simples!"*

"I'm well up for that," said Graham. *"Me too,"* said Mike, *"but how are we going to succeed when you say that so many others have failed?"* Ed continued, *"Well, what I did discover when I was doing some sniffing around was that one of the very few other persons believed to have seen the Library since the days of 'Ivan the Terrible' - and survived the experience - was Tsar Nicholas the 2nd, his daughter Princess Anastasia and her little brother, Prince Alexei Nikolaevitch - and I'm not saying that twice!."*

"Gold, silver and crown jewels you say. Well that's tickled my Scottish fancy - and I certainly prefer Fabergé eggs to Scotch eggs, although only just!" said Mike. *"Me too, cocker!"* added Graham.

Ed smiled, "*Just as a matter of academic interest, I also carried out a little research on Fabergé eggs. I know you're interested in that sort of thing, Graham*"

"*Do tell, we are intrigued,*" said Graham.

"*The first Fabergé egg was made for one of the Tsars who wanted it as a present for his wife,*" said Ed, "*That was way back in the year 1885. Apparently she liked it so much that she had another one made and so it snsowballed. Eventually the eggs became a fashionable gift for the idle rich. I can easily understand why. Such beautiful thing - that's the eggs, not the idle rich!*"

Ed reached into his briefcase and pulled out a sheet of paper, "*Take a look at this.*"

Handing a photocopied sheet of paper to Mike, Ed said, "*It's a photograph and an explanation to give you an idea of how lovely and intricate the Fabergé eggs are, and - according to Princess Anastasia - the 'Hidden Library' contains a display case with several of the eggs tucked away inside it, along with lots of other precious Fabergé goodies. There's plenty of them to go around, apparently.*"

"*Anastasia also mentioned shelving in the library that was stacked right up to the ceiling with gold bars. She was very forthcoming and a mine of information, although I had to cross her palm with quite a few gold sovereigns to get her to co-operate further!*"

"What put you onto Princess Anastasia then?" asked Mike. "Just a simple article I stumbled across on Google about Crown Jewels. It mentioned that Princess Anastasia was currently residing in Villefranche-sur-Mer and then it went on to list some of the things that she had been claiming were rightfully hers."

"In the article, the Princess stated that as she was the last surviving member of the Russian Royal Family, she still had a rightful claim to various land, properties and so forth in Russia and, more importantly, the Russian Crown Jewels. So I decided there and then that I would travel to Villefranch-sur-Mer and try to have a chat with her."

"Now, I managed to get to see her and when I was chatting to her, and this is the important bit, she told me that she knew where the Crown Jewels were hidden. As you can imagine, a light went on in my head! Show Graham the drawing of the egg, Mike."

Mike passed the piece of paper to Graham. After a few seconds gazing at the piece of paper Graham said, "*Wow, these are the sort of things I'd like to get my sticky paws on,*" as he passed the sheet back to Ed. Ed nodded, "*Yes, they're true works of art.*" "*Och aye, a couple of those eggs would look rather fetching sat on the mantleshelf at Fraser Towers!*" said Mike.

Ed continued, "*Anyway, back to Anastasia. You see, when she was a young girl, just for a bit of fun, Anastasia was taken beneath what is now the Lubyanka Prison by her father to see the 'Hidden Library' and she claims to remember where it was."*

"We chatted about it for a while and after I made her an offer she couldn't refuse i.e. some gold sovereigns and a share of whatever valuables we found, then she agreed to draw a diagram of where she thinks the 'Hidden Library' was. I have that very diagram here with me in my briefcase."

"Och, well we're more than halfway there then!" said Mike enthusiastically.

"I fully intended travelling over here to Hull, once I got the information," said Ed, *"to see if you two vagabonds fancied going on an exploratory expedition with me beneath the Lubyanka Prison to discover if Anastasia was telling me the truth; either that or her Royal Highness was just coming up with a clever ruse to con me out of some gold sovereigns."*

"I got the distinct feeling, though, that she was telling me the truth. She appeared to be a very nice, approachable old lady."

"So did Myra Hindley!" said Graham.

*'A young Princess Anastasia Nikolaevna Romanov,
the daughter of Tsar Nicholas
and Tsarina Alexandria'*

Ed continued, *"If I did go to the Lubyanka and find the 'Hidden Library' she made me solemnly promise to get her a Fabergê egg or two - said that her Father had told her that he'd seen plenty of them in the room! I promised her that if I found them, then I'd put a couple to one side for her, those and a few other jewels."*

"And now, to my utter astonishment, you tell me about this Penkovsky thing. The Lubyanka Prison. I can hardly believe it!"

"Oh, right, well I don't see it as being much of a problem then," said Graham, *"we just nip across to Moscow in the 'T3-Travellator' - blag our way into the Lubyanka Prison, top a few of the KGB guards, find Colonel Penkovsky and the 'Hidden Library' - stash him and as much loot as we can into the 'Travellator' and then bring the whole kit and caboodle back here, via Villefranche-sur-Mer to drop off a few Fabergé eggs for the old Russian bird. Sounds perfectly straightforward to me. Shouldn't take us more than a couple of hours."*

Ed smiled, *"Well, obviously it won't be quite as easy as all that, guys, or everyone would be doing it - but I know that we all relish a challenge - and the financial rewards will, of course, be tremendous."*

"I totally agree with, Ed," said Mike, *"it's all down to a bit of planning and preparation. If we get all that right, it'll be a doddle. And dinnae forget, we've got the benefit of having a 'T3-Travellator' at our disposal, which no-one else has!"*

"You say that, Mike, but it'll certainly be a challenge. That Lubyanka place will be a right nest of KGB vipers and if we're not careful they'll be using us lot for target practise!" said Graham.

"What's the time-frame for your 'rescue' segment?" asked Ed.

"The Prime Minister wants the Penkovsky thing done and dusted by the end of next week; so the clock is already ticking. There's other complications that we don't need to go into at the moment," said Mike, *"so we need to make a decision here and now if we think that this whole thing is feasible and if we're going to proceed - or just call the whole thing off."*

"I don't think that we should call it off," said Graham, *"but what are we going to do first, rescue Penkovsky or do the 'Hidden Library search?"* asked Graham. *"Why don't we do both at the same time?"* said Ed, *"It's all in the*

Lubyanka Prison!" "That's pushing it a bit time-wise isn't it?" said Graham.

"Well, we'd be over there doing one job or the other, so we might as well do both. As Ed said, it's all there in the Lubyanka, just waiting for us, Graham," said Mike.

"I imagine that you have some sort of date in mind for us to go back there and snatch Penkovsky?" said Ed. Graham nodded, "Yes, well we were looking at the 16th of May 1963." "What is the significance of that particular date?" asked Ed. "We're told that Penkovsky was in the cells in the Lubyanka Prison then, and also apparently that was the day scheduled for his alleged execution," said Graham.

"Well, there you are then. Simples.com! We can arrive there first thing in the morning, sort the little 'snatch of Penkovsky' task out and then go and look for Ivan's 'Hidden Library.'" said Ed.

Mike nodded, "It won't be a problem, especially as we've got the 'T3-Travellator.' We can just de-materilise in Penkovskys cell, stick him inside the 'T3-Travellator' then zoom off to where the 'Hidden Library' is supposed to be, using the diagram kindly provided by Princess Anastasia as a locator tool," he said. "It's all very broad brush, but it's entirely feasible" said Ed.

"What if there's an armed guard, or guards in the cell with Penkovsky?" asked Graham. "No problem. Mike and I are trained killers, so we'll just knock seven bells *out of them,"* said Ed, *"now come on, lighten up Graham, where's your sense of adventure!"* *"And if things do go tits-up, Graham, we'll just clamber back on board the 'T3-Travellator' and leg it back home. We can always 'Time-Travel' back to the Lubyanka Prison and try again later, or sooner,"* said Mike.

There was a few minutes silence whilst they gave the matter some thought. Breaking the silence, Mike said, *"Well, I don't know about you two, but I'm definitely up for it."* Ed nodded to signify that he was in too, then he and Mike looked across at Graham. *"Oh, bugger it - to be honest, I wouldn't miss it for all the tea in Yorkshire, speaking of which, it's time for a refill."* said Graham.

"What, no more whisky?" asked Ed. Mike shook his head, *"'Fraid not, we'd better keep clear heads from now on. We'll need to work out a concrete plan of action and, as time is of the essence, we'd better make a start asap. The Prime Minister's Chief of Staff will no doubt be ringing me for an update before too long."*

Shaking his head, Graham said, *"It's unbelievable, I mean what are the chances of these two projects arriving on your desk at the same time, eh Mike?"* *"Aye, strange that,"* said Mike. Ed smiled, *"In the Netherlands we call that sort of thing 'Happenstance.' In reality, it shouldn't be too difficult to 'dove-tail' the two tasks together, not with the technology and the know-how that we have to hand."*

Mike stood up, *"Well, that's it then, decision made. Let's get the show on the road. 'One Team - One Dream' eh!"*

"Whilst you two make a start on compiling an outline plan, I'll go and sort oot the cup that cheers. Then, once we've made some headway, we can all slide over the road to 'Ginos' Restaurant and tie on a nose-bag. My stomach's beginning to think that my throat's been cut!" Mike toddled off to the kitchen.

Graham picked up a pen and started scribbling on a large yellow legal notepad, *"Bit of a Gordian knot this, Ed. Which bit do we do first, do we find Penkovsky and then go looking for the 'Hidden Library' or vice verce?"*

"I think that it would be better to get Penkovsky first," said Ed, *"my reason being that as he's a KGB man - he'll more than likely know his way around the cellars of the Lubyanka Prison and can help us to avoid any hidden poo traps, eh!" "Good point, well presented,"* said Graham,

"The other alternative, Ed, is that we could go and get Penkovsky, bring him straight back here and hand him over to the Secret Service, then return to the Lubyanka and carry out a search for the 'Hidden Library.' Either that or we could go and find the 'Hidden Library' and bring some loot back home, then return for Penkovsky. It's 'six of one - half a dozen of the other." said Graham.

Ed smiled, *"Why not just keep it simple, let's get Penkovsky first, then find the 'Hidden Library' and see what's in there. After that, we can bring both him and whatever loot we choose to remove then transport everything back here. Better to kill two hares with one shot, as the Russians say!"

Mike returned carrying the steaming tea-pot, tea, milk and sugar etc on a tray. "*There's something else we need to take into consideration, chaps. Remember, Graham, the PM intimated that Penkovsky might have been a double-agent, in which case, if we do locate him, he might not be too keen to co-operate or accompany us.*"

Ed grinned evilly, "*If he's a spy under sentence of death then he'll bite our hands off at the opportunity we'll offer to get him out of there in one piece. If not, and it turns out that he is still working for the KGB, then we'll just have to get a little heavy with him.*" "*Or maybe we can make him an offer he can't refuse and persuade him to join our little team and take a share of the profits. They told us at the security briefing that Penkovsky wasn't averse to accepting bribes!*" said Mike. "*One way or the other, he'll be coming back with us. That's the deal!*" said Ed.

Graham looked puzzled, "*Call me old fashioned, but I keep thinking - why would he be down there in the cells if there's a chance that he's a double-agent?*" he asked. "*Och, we can sort all of that out once we get there, dinnae fuss yerself,*" said Mike, "*either way we've got to find him and bring him back with us!*" "*It all sounds a bit tenuous to me,*" said Graham.

"*Look, if he's not there and we can't get our hands on him, the worst case scenario is that we can use the opportunity to locate the 'Hidden Library.' We can always go back to Moscow later and search for Colonel Penkovsky. He's bound to be there somewhere,"* said Ed. Graham sighed, *"Come on, let's get the chuffing brainstorming session started then."*

Mike picked up the tea-pot, *"I'll be Mummy,"* he said. Graham reached for biscuit tin and Mike smacked his hand, *"Naughty! We're going for some scran when we've finished this. You'll ruin your appetite!"* *"Why did you bring the chuffing biscuits then?"* asked Garaham, rubbing his hand. *"It was a tactical error!"* said Mike.

A few hours later they'd come up with what they considered to be a basic but eminently suitable working plan. It would need padding out, but the bare bones were there.

Ed had come up with the brilliant suggestion that in the first instance it would be better for them to make a quick visit in the 'T3-Travellator' to the GRU Headquarters situated at Moscow's Khodinka Airfield, preferably during the silent hours. Ed had said that he was familiar with the layout of the place from a previous mission in the area but wouldn't go into any further detail.

He thought that there could well be some information held there in the building relating to the location of Penkovsky and that it would save hours of searching the Lubyanka Prison cellars if they could find it..

"*Hells Bells! I thought that getting inside the Lubyanka Prison would be bad enough and now you're on about blagging our way into the GRU Headquarters?*" said Mike. Ed explained that it was more than certain that there would be a file or some information in the Headquarters building regarding Colonel Penkovsky and his whereabouts.

Finding it would save some valuable time in the long run. The GUR Headquarters offices, Ed assured them, was where all of the KGB records were kept. He said that if someone so much as '*farted out of tune*' it was noted in their personal file.

If push came to shove, they could even have a little 'chat' with a member of staff there. Ed said that he always carried a 'persuader' with him, in the shape of a loaded pistol, when he was 'out and about.'

Graham thought that it the whole idea was a bit of a long shot but agreed to go along with it. "*In for a kopek, in for a ruble,*" he said, "*but I still think that it's all a bit iffy.*" "*Trust me,*" said Ed, "*I know just how these people work. In Russia there's a file on everyone - including Penkovsky. They never get rid of them!*"

They decided that once they'd discovered the whereabouts of Penkovsky, then after finding and briefing him, hopefully with his assistance, they'd go and seek out the 'Hidden Library,' offering him shares in whatever they might find in there, which, if Princess Anastasia was to be believed, could be worth many millions. *"That sort of offer would turn anyone's head,"* said Mike.

In addition to that, the UK Government would undoubtedly have a selection of other tempting 'goodies' to dangle before Penkovsky, things like a new identity and relocation to somewhere safe like Canada, depending upon what useful information he could impart that would be of value.

If he refused to co-operate, then he'd be swopping one cell for another, the only difference being that in his British cell he'd have a colour TV and three square meals a day - and also be without the constant fear of a KGB executioner arriving at any time.

Yes, if he thought about it, for Colonel Penkovsky it could be a 'win win' situation. The only downside for him would be, of course, that an enraged and vindictive KGB would definitely put out a 'wet-job' order on him which would remain extant for the rest of his life. Like the Mafia, the KGB neither forgot nor forgave.

Ж

CHAPTER TEN

'THE AQUARIUM'

Background

The Headquarters of the GRU - (Glaznoje Rasvedyvatel'noje Upravlenijie) the Soviet Military Intelligence Directorate, is located at Khodinka Airfield, on the site of the old Moscow Central Airport. Khodinka Airfield, which as you would expect, is an ultra-secure area that not only contains the GRU Headquarters, where the KGB Planning Department is located, but also the Headquarters of the Russian State Airline, 'Aeroflot,' the National Aviation and Space Museum, the Military Aviation Academy and the Moscow Aviation Institute. Added to this complex tapestry of organisations, on one side of the airfield is also the Institute for Cosmic Biology. A busy place.

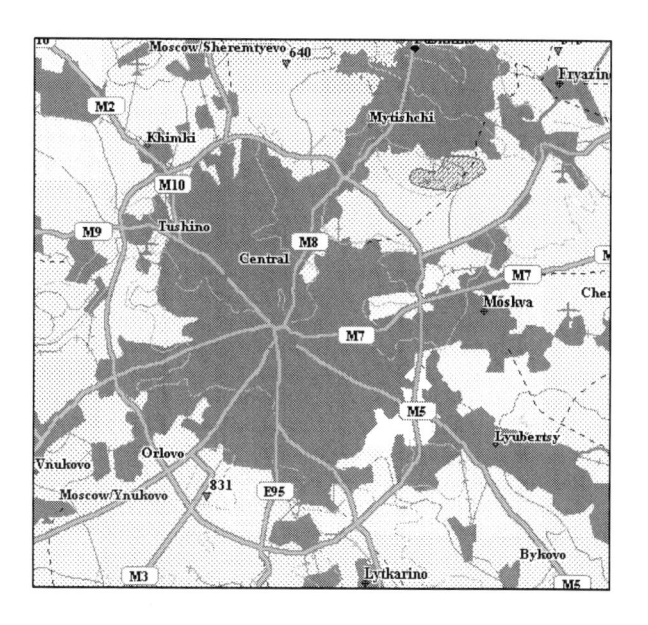

'The Aquarium' – *(as the GRU Headquarters is referred to) - is reached by accessing a narrow lane, passing through a ten-metre high wall, which then sits behind the Institute for Cosmic Biology. The main office of the GRU building is encased by glass in a nine-storey tower which itself is surrounded by a two storey structure. Adjacent is a 15 storey structure, just outside the secure area, which is also a GRU facility. It includes offices and residential accommodation for current GRU personnel and also their families, where security is also ultra-tight.*

The Head of MI6, 'M,' was reaching the conclusion of his classified briefing to an attentive Prime Minister, "*And in closing, Sir Roger, these documents were copied by one of our deep under-cover agents, Vladimir Rezun, from the original classified files held in the office of Major General Oleg Shalovski."*

He showed the PM the documents. "*These are quite genuine, 'M'?*" he asked. 'M' nodded, "*Absolutely, sir, cast iron guaranteed.*" "*Excellent,* " said the PM "*listen, old boy, I'm seeing the 'Time-Traveller' chaps this very afternoon and I'll brief them accordingly. Am I permitted to give them your copy of the 'Aquarium' and Lubyanka Prison's layout?*"

'M' shook his head, "*Prefer it if you didn't, Sir Roger, not those particular documents anyway. I've had 'doctored' copies drawn up by hand just in case something goes awry and the 'Time-Travellers' get captured by the bad guys. I wouldn't want the KGB finding a copy of the original documents in our team's possession. Just might give the Russkies a clue as to who our 'deep-throat' is, what!*" The PM nodded "*Quite, quite. That makes sound sense 'M'.*"

"Right, well I'll leave the copies of the drawings with you and be on my way, Sir Roger. *Viel Glück!*" said 'M.' 'M' slid the copies of the drawings across to the PM before tucking the remainder of the original highly classified documents away safely in his briefcase. Wouldn't do to risk leaving them in Downing Street - you never knew who might read them; either that or they'd finish up in a waste bin in the nearby St James's Park, tossed in there by some witless politician or be left on a park bench by a careless civil servant.

As he locked his briefcase, 'M' said, "*So, the game is well afoot then, Prime Minister!*" The PM nodded, "*Yes, the game is quite definitely afoot, 'M.'* The 'Time-Travel' chaps have agreed to have a crack at it. It's just a matter of them tying all of the loose ends together.*" "*With respect,*" said 'M' "*I hope that we can rely upon them to get the job done. There's a great deal at stake here - and when all's said and done, they are untrained volunteers.*"

The PM nodded, "*Well, you say that but I have absolute faith in them. As you're no doubt aware, two of them were Special Services, one Dutch, one British, and the remaining one was an experienced fire-arms trained police officer. We've used them before and they certainly didn't let us down then. Remember the Kingston-Upon-Hull visit when they travelled forwards in time to 2119, that was most successful - and I'm sure that you'll agree with me when I say that the information they obtained was most productive.*"

'M' nodded, "*Oh, yes, that op had slipped my mind. A hypothetical question, sir, but what happens in the event that they fall into the hands of the KGB?*" he asked. "*There's always a chance of that happening I suppose, but if they are captured then, regrettably, we will of course claim that we know absolutely nothing about them. Usual damage limitation procedure, total deniability etc until we can get some sort of 'swop' organised,*" replied the PM

"I can't quite get my head around it, Prime Minister," said 'M,' *"I mean, if they're captured, then they'll be captured back in the early 1960's won't they?"* *"Yes, well as there's nothing on the historical record to that effect, we can only assume that they are going to be successful, even though it hasn't happened yet. It's all very complex and you've got to approach this 'Time-Travel' business with an open mind,"* said the PM.

"I'll have to take your word for it, sir." replied a still puzzled 'M.' *"And what happens if the Russian's don't want to do 'swopsies?'"* asked 'M.' *"We'll have to cross that bridge when we come to it 'M.'"* replied the PM.

'M' nodded, *"OK, well I'd better be making tracks, Sir Roger. I've got that Turkish submarine business to get sorted."* The PM smiled, *"Oh, that. Still rumbling on is it?"* 'M' nodded. *"Yes, I mean who would have thought that they'd go limping into Scarborough of all places for engine repairs. I mean, really!"*

The PM smiled, *"Nothing wrong with Scarborough, old boy. Used to go their for my school holidays when I was a lad. First class beach, lots of crabs. Anyway, I digress, Will I be seeing you later at the COBRA meeting, 'M?'"* asked the PM. *"Oh, I wouldn't miss it for the world, Prime Minister. TTFN,"* said 'M' waving a cheery farewell.

Mike, Graham and Ed De Jong sat in front of the PM having listened very carefully to what he'd had to say. *"So there you have it, chaps. You now know as much as I do."*

A confident Mike said, *"Well sir, now by some miracle that we have a diagram of Major General Shalovski's office layout in the 'Aquarium' I suppose it's simply a matter of us de-materialising inside there back in 1962, courtesy of the 'T3 Travellator,' then having a good old root around to see if we can find any information relating to the precise whereabouts of Colonel Penkovsky at that time."*

"And then getting out of the 'Aquarium' in one piece," said a gloomy looking Graham, *"that building is probably more secure than your wallet, Mike!"* *"I doubt that very much,"* replied Mike. Unusually for Graham he looked very apprehensive.

"Och, cheer yourself up man and get yer face straightened!" Mike said to Graham, *"You love a good challenge - and if things do go wrong, we'll just leg it home in the 'T3-Travellator' and then go back to the 'Aquarium' the day before. That sort of thing."*

"Well you say that," replied Graham, *" but originally we thought that we were just going to have a sniff around the cellars underneath the Lubyanka Prison, but now we're off to the KGB's Headquarters as well. Double jeopardy there!"*

Ed smiled, *"We need to be 'Fluid and Flexible!' Have a bit of faith, Graham, my friend. We'll be in and out of both places before you can say Jack Robinson - and when all's said and done we're doing it for your 'Queen and Country!"*

Graham thought to himself, *"Aye, well that bloody 'Hidden Library' isn't for 'Queen and Country' Ed. Thank goodness the Prime Minister doesn't know anything about that!"* The Prime Minister, keeping his face straight, was thinking, *"Hah, the cheeky buggers. They don't know that I know about the 'Hidden Library!'"*

The PM nodded and said, *"And in the unlikely event that something does go amiss, chaps, and you do fall into 'enemy' hands, don't worry. You can rely upon H.M. Government to do absolutely everything in its power to have you brought home at the very earliest opportunity, unharmed. I give you my solemn promise on that."* The PM had his fingers crossed behind his back.

If Graham had seen a pig flying past the Prime Minister's office window at that precise moment, he wouldn't have been in the least surprised, he didn't trust politicians as far as he could throw them. He was convinced that the whole operation was doomed.

Sir Roger continued, *"Now, if you'd like to pop along the Chief of Staff's Office, gentlemen, he's prepared an in-depth briefing for you, after which you can fire any questions that you may have at him. He has also been tasked to provide you with anything else that you feel you might require, such as weapons, that sort of thing."*

"The combination to Major General Shalovski's office safe in the 'Aquarium' would be nice, sir!" said Mike.

"I think you'll find that the Chief of Staff will more than likely have that precise information available for you." said the PM - winking.

"Right chaps," said Sir Roger waving his hand towards the door, *"if you'll excuse me, I must crack on. I've got the Chancellor of the Exchequer coming in for his 'weekly whinge' very shortly. The value of the pound's dropped against the Euro again and he's blaming me for it."*

Smiling, the PM said, *" So, all that remains for me to do is wish you bon voyage. I'm sure that everything will go swimmingly. Almost wish that I was coming with you. The Chief of Staff will keep me in the loop as to the state of play throughout the Op!"*

Sir Roger stood up and shook hands with the three men, who then trooped out of his office, heading for the Chief of Staff's office and their promised in-depth briefing.

A few days later, early one morning and precisely as planned, the 'T3-Travellator' de-materialised inside General Shalovski's darkened office inside the 'Aquarium.'

"OK guys, we've arrived," said Ed. *"just let me have a wee peek through the porthole and check that there's no-one lurking or working out there,"* said Mike.

Mike scanned the office, and, as per the intelligence that they'd received, saw that it was empty, which was only to be expected at three o'clock in the morning - but you never knew. "*It's all clear, boys. We're good to go,*" said Mike.

Ed wasn't too concerned, he'd brought a taser with him, just in case anyone in the office needed 'calming down.'

"*Into the valley of death*," murmured a gloomy Graham

As the 'T3-Travellator's' door swished open, Ed, Mike and an apprehensive Graham stepped out into General Shalovski's huge office.

Looking around at the plush wall-to-wall carpeting, the expensive and highly polished carved oak wood panelling, the crystal chandeliers and chunky antique furniture, Graham whispered, "*To say that they're bloody Communists, they certainly know how to look after them pigging selves. Feast your mince-pies on this little lot!*" he said.

Pointing at the office wall, a smiling Mike said, "*Och, would you look at that, chaps, Major General Shalovski's got a picture of Comrade Stalin hanging on the wall. I can feel his eyes following us!*" Hung on the office wall was a very large portrait of a stern looking Stalin, staring down accusingly at them.

"*Bloody hell, I would have like to have bumped into him on a dark night*," said Graham. "*Och, he looks a sweet guy,*" said Mike.

**The greatly feared
'Josef Vissario Novich Stalin'**

"*And you know what, he looks just like Saddam Hussein's favourite uncle!*" said Mike. "*Right lads, come on, let's get the General's wall-safe open and see if we can find any info on Penkovsky, then we can hightail it out of here before anyone finds us,*" said Ed.

They walked across the plush carpet to the wall-safe. "*As we were informed, it's a standard Russian rotational blister lock,*" said Ed, "*which is absolutely no problem, especially as we've been given the combination. Rather surprisingly the numbers relate to the General's birthday. Basic error is that. They never learn!*"

Ed started to spin the combination lock on the front of the safe, factoring in the series of numbers that he'd been given, then stopped when he heard a sharp click. *"There we are,"* he said, *"easy peasy!"*

Twisting the dial to zero and turning the door handle on the front of the wall-safe, he swung the thick, heavy metal door open. The inside of the wall-safe was jam-packed with classified files. *"Looks like we've struck gold!"* said Mike.

"Bloody hell, it's like a small library in there, it'll take us all night to filter through that lot!" said Graham. Mike shook his head, *"Nah, we're not doing that. We'll just take all of the files back to London and then let the experts plough through them,"* *"Yes, but the Russians will know that they've gone missing when they look in the safe, won't they?"* said Graham.

"Graham St Anier, dear boy, might I remind you that we are thrashing around the universe in one of only two existing' Time-Machines.' We can nick these files and have them read and translated by the experts, then once they've told us where Penkovsky is, we'll bring them back here ten minutes before we arrived this morning!" said Mike.

Graham smiled, *"Yes of course, sorry, I forgot the strange 'tinkering with time' world that we occasionally inhabit."* *"Come on then troops, let's load these files into the 'T3-Travellator,'"* said Mike.

Just after they'd finished cross-loading the files from the office safe into the 'T3-Travellator,' they froze as they heard loud giggling outside the General's office door. The giggling was followed by a key being noisily inserted into the door-lock.

Mike, Ed and Graham dashed across to the 'T3-Travellator' and leapt inside. Mike pressed the button that operated the door, which slid shut quickly and noislessly. Mike then peered through the port-hole to see what was going on.

The door of the office opened and a portly, uniformed and bemedalled General Shalovski, belched loudly then tottered inside.

He was obviously the worse for wear, hat on the back of his head, tie askew and shirt tail hanging over the back of his trousers. Gesticulating with his podgy nictoine stained fingers he said, "*Step into my office, my gorgeous darling. Quickly now, we do not have a great deal of time. I am expected home within the hour.*" A very butch looking male soldier stepped inside the office and closed the door behind him.

"*Lord save us,*" whispered Mike.

"*Can I tempt you to a glass of vodka, my dear sweet boy?*" the General asked him. The soldier shook his head, "*I do not drink any form of alcohol, Comrade General, that is why I am your driver,*" replied the man.

"*Oh, let's hope that that is the only vice that you deny yourself!*" replied the General, laughing, "*And do call me*

Oleg when we are alone like this. Now, over here and help me to ease these damned boots off. Come along now, and be gentle with me."

The soldier hesitated and looked slightly embarrassed. The impatient General said, "*Now don't be shy. If you're a good boy, there could be a spot of promotion in this for you!*"

Inside the 'T3-Travellator' Mike said, "*Saints preserve us, the dirty wee dobber is about to give that squaddie the good message, methinks; it's time we made a swift exit. Because we're tucked away in the corner of the office they haven't spotted us yet.*" "*Hit the TSS switch, Mike and let's get out of this den of iniquity!*" said Graham.

Mike tapped the TSS (Time Sequence Starter) switch and the 'T3-Travellator' silently and immediately materialised. Having been pre-programmed, it flew back through the ether, heading towards London.

"*Hell fire!*" said Graham, "*I've just had a thought! Did you close the wall-safe door, Ed?*" Ed nodded, "*Yes, but unfortunately I didn't have time to twirl the blister lock to secure it.*" "*Let's hope that the General doesn't notice,*" said Graham.

"*Dinnae panic chaps, I think that he's probably got his mind on other things just now,*" said Mike, "*and anyway, we'll have everything done, dusted and returned before he touches the safe,*" "*I bloody well hope so,*" said a gloomy

Graham. "*Is it being so cheerful that keeps you going, my wee hen?*" said Mike.

"*So,*" said the PM "*the Russian files revealed that Colonel Penkovsky was indeed being held captive in the cellars of the Lubyanka Prison pending his execution! That resolves the double-agent theory then. So, where do we go from here then, chaps?*" he asked. "*It is our intention, Prime Minister,*" said Ed, "*to return the classified files to General Shalovski's safe at the 'Aquarium' and then we'll go and get Penkovsky out of the Lubyanka.*"

"*Easier said than done, I suspect!*" said the PM "*I'm sure that the damned prison is like a rabbit warren and unlike the 'Aquarium at three o'clock in the morning it's likely to be well guarded. Still, it's got to be done, eh! How will you know where to find Penkovsky once you reach the Lubyanka?*"

Ed smiled, "*We've extracted the information from the Russian's classified files and, along with the diagram provided by your Security Services, we have a map of the Lubyanka's cellar layout, kindly provided by a contact of mine.*" "*I'm not even going to ask you about that,*" said the bemused PM "*I'll leave you to it. You chaps seem to know what you're doing.*"

"*When are you heading back to Russia?*" "*Straight after this meeting, sir, we need to get those classified files back inside the wall-safe before the General notices that they've gone missing.*" said Mike. "*I'd better let you crack on then,*" said the PM.

After they'd returned to the 'Aquarium' to return the classified files back inside the wall-safe behind General Shalovski's desk and ensured that everything was ship-shape, they prepared to leave for the Lubyanaka Prison.

Just before getting back inside the 'T3-Travellator' Mike decided to relieve himself in the General's metal waste-paper bucket. When he'd finished peeing, he zipped the fly on his trousers up, smiled and said, *"I'll leave that with you, General!"* Mike looked up at Stalin's portrait, winked then flashed him a 'V.'

Turning to the others, Mike said, *"Right gentlemen, sorry about the pee - 'pre-flight' nerves."* *"Needs must when the devil drives!"* said Graham. *"Thank goodness you didn't need a Number 2!"* said Ed.

They jumped into the 'T3-Travellator' strapped themselves in and began preparations for next the flight through time, which was scheduled to take them across to the Lubyanka Prison cellars where Colonel Penkovsky was being held. Graham punched in the relevant co-ordinates, then paused.

"I don't know why, but I've got a very bad feeling about this," said Graham. *"Och, hod your whisht, you old Yorkshire tart!"* said Mike, *"When we're next sat in the 'Dog and Duck' in Beverley quaffing a foaming ale, you'll look back and laugh at all this. Now shut the door and let's get cracking!"*

As Graham was about to close the 'T3's' door, they fell silent as they heard loud giggling outside the General's office door, followed by the sound of a key being noisily inserted into the door lock.

"Ah, it's the action replay. Sounds like the salacious General Shalovski's back with his lover boy for a spot of naughties!" said Mike, *"We'd better head for the hills. Shut the door and get the pedal to the metal, Graham. The Lubyanka awaits!"* *"At least the wall-safe's locked this time!"* said Ed.

"Let's hope that the General doesn't kick the bucket!" said Mike.

Ж

CHAPTER ELEVEN

'PRISONER 888'

Ex-Lieutenant Colonel Penkovsky, or 'Prisoner 888' as he was now known, was sat rigidly to attention in the corner of the cell, perched on the edge of a battered three-legged hard wooden stool, hands clasped behind his head,. The cell was situated deep in the damp, gloomy cellars of the Lubyanka Prison.

He was utterly exhausted and would have sold his soul for just a few minute's sleep, but it was absolutely forbidden for him to sleep or indeed, close his eyes and drift off, even for a few precious seconds.

Sleep deprivation was just one of the many punishments currently being meted out to him. Disciplinary rules were strictly enforced by his KGB captors and harsh chastisement was swiftly meted out to anyone that transgressed. His oafish KGB guard loitered outside the cell in the constant hope that Penkovsky would fall asleep so that he could beat him .

On the one occasion that Penkovsky's eyelids had drooped and his head had fallen forward onto his chest, hands flopping onto his lap, he had received a vicious, stinging blow in the ribs, delivered courtesy of the metal-edged rifle butt of the ever watchful KGB prison guard - who took great delight in carrying out his duties to the letter, particularly as he'd been told that 'Prisoner 888' had once been a senior KGB officer. It was a heaven-sent opportunity for the guard to get a bit of his own back on a despised officer.

As he gazed around the cell with red-rimmed, tired eyes, an exhausted Penkovsky once again read the words that were scratched into the filthy plaster on the cell wall, directly opposite him, 'Gospodi, pomilny – Derzhee - karman sheereh!' (*God forgives – but don't hold your breath!*) written by a previous desperate occupant of the cell. It was just something for Penkovsky to focus on whilst fighting to remain conscious.

There were countless dried blood splatters on the walls of the cell, presumably left there from other vicious beatings or torture sessions, some of it relatively recent and now some of it Penkovskys.

He was at the very end of his tether and knew that he couldn't last for very much longer. Both mentally and physically he was utterly drained. Since his arrest, he'd been interrogated many, many times and his persecutors had tortured him until he'd confessed to absolutely everything.

He'd been stripped naked, left in the freezing cold for hours, badly beaten, starved, water-boarded, mocked and demeaned, electrodes attached to his private parts - just about the full tick list of tortures available to his experienced tormentors.

Now he would do anything and say anything just so that 'they' wouldn't hurt or abuse him any more. He just wanted the ever-present nagging pain and fear to stop – and oh what he would give for just a few minutes sleep..

As a consequence of his forced confession and admission of guilt, he'd been sentenced to death on the direct orders of his one time friend and mentor, General Ivan Alexandrovitch Serov, 1st Chairman of the Committee for State Security who'd made a personal appearance in the cell to give Penkovsky a severe slapping. The General had also informed Penkovsky that there would be no appeal. against the death sentenc, before smashing the toe-caps of his highly polished boots into Penkovk's shins.his .

Penkovsky's 'Days of Wine and Roses' were a distant memory.

Although Penkovsky was fully aware that he was going to be executed, he didn't know how or even when. It was the way those sort of things were done in the Russian penal system.

Every time Penkovsky's cell door swung open it could signal either the delivery of some disgusting, unpalatable food or the arrival of the State Executioner come to carry out the sentence of the court by firing a bullet into the back of his badly shaven skull.

When ever 'Prisoner 888' heard the sound of the key turning in the cell-door lock his bowels turned to ice and, despite not wanting to, his whole body would start to tremble uncontrollably.

The fear and horror of what might be about to happen to him was unimaginable. His guards thought that it was hilarious and noisily opened the cell door many times just for the fun of watching him quail.

Only a few days earlier Penkovsky had been paid a visit by the official State Executioner, Lieutenant Colonel Igor Chelpinski, accompanied by his lick-spittle assistant, Lieutenant Ivanski Gregorovitch. They were both there to metaphorically 'measured him up' and they'd made a point of making sure that he was aware of their creative and various cruel methods of despatching condemned prisoners. It seemed that a bullet to the head was not the only option being considered.

Both Chelpinski and Gregorovitch were studiously avoided by their 'brother' KGB officers, who considered them both to be odious creatures who themselves were suitable cases for psychiatric treatment. It didn't do to meet their eyes. Unfortunatley for him, Penkovsky knew of their reputation.

Chelpinski had taken great delight in explaining to Penkovsky that, "*We have something rather special lined up for you,, 'Prisoner 888,'* " but wouldn't tell him what that something 'special' was, which made the veiled threat even more nightmarish as it allowed Penkovsky's imagination to run riot.

What Chelpinsky did tell Penkovsky, however, was that his execution had been purposely designed not only to punish him but also to act as an example to other would-be traitors, showing precisely what fate would befall them if they were caught selling out, as Penkovsky himself had done.

Penkovsky was very, very frightened at the prospect of what he knew would be a cruel and undoubtedly painful execution. Much of his fear was in not knowing what to expect, but what he now knew was that it wouldn't be quick or easy. He was certain that it would more than likely be a long drawn out affair and would be as unpleasant as the 'Gruesome Twosome' could possibly make it.

Suddenly, and unusually, the fetid air in the corner of his windowless cell was disturbed. Penkovsky glanced across and saw what he thought looked like a mini-whirlwind, the unusual movement in the air swirling the dust particles around.

Penkovsky blinked several times and assumed that his exhausted brain was playing tricks on him. No, the air was definitely being disturbed by something. Then the weirdest thing happened as some sort of large, colourful box-like shape appeared in front of him.

His jaw dropped open and he stared at the apparition in shock as a door in front of the infernal machine slid open and a man wearing some sort of flight-suit stepped out. *"Am I going mad, or is this to be the means of my execution,"* thought Penkovsky.

Penkovsky noticed that the new arrival was clutching a pistol. He in turn was closely followed by two others who were similarly dressed. Penkovsky didn't know it, but it was Ed De Jong, accompanied by Graham St Anier and Mike Fraser.

Glancing around him, Ed said, *"Welcome to the Lubyanka Prison, my friends!"* *"Ah, the condemned suite! Very fetching, love the decor!"* whispered Mike, Looking across at Penkovsky, he said, *"Looks like we've found our man, Oleg, too!"* *"You are Colonel Oleg Penkovsky?"* asked Ed. A dazed and still slack-jawed Penkovsky nodded and replied croakily, *"Yes, that is correct."*

Penkovsky was astounded and was unable to speak momentarily. *"What is happening here?"* he thought, *"Is this some clever piece of KGB theatre, devised to torment and frighten condemned prisoners, or some new piece of equipment that I haven't heard about. Either that or perhaps it is some sort of drug induced lunacy."*

Penkovsky made an effort to speak - but Ed held a finger up to his lips, warning him to remain silent.

Ed then tip-toed across to Penkovsky and whispered quietly, "*Colonel, we are your friends. We have come to save you, but to do that we need your help. In a moment I want you to allow your head to droop forward as if you have fallen asleep.*"

"*Is this a KGB trick? Are you going to execute me?*" asked Penkovsky. "*Certainly not, my friend, we are here to rescue you! Just trust me and do as I have asked. Now, when I tip you the wink – let your head fall forward!*" said Ed,

A confused Penkovsky nodded, thinking, "*Lies, this is all lies. This is it – once my head droops they are going to put a bullet in it.*" Nevertheless, he decided that he'd better do as he'd been instructed. If they were going to 'top' him - let them get on with it - at least the pain would stop.

The three visitors slid quietly across the cell and tucked themselves away behind the door, away from the spy-hole and out of the field of vision of the KGB guard. Ed nodded at Penkovsky who, as instructed, closed his eyes and let his head droop down until his chin was resting on his chest.

After a few moments, there was a sound of the metal cover on the spy-hole being slid to one side, then a key being inserted in the clunky lock, before the heavy cell door was heaved open.

A cruel-faced, jack-booted KGB guard stormed into the cell and slapped Penkovsky hard across the face with the back of his hand, *"It is forbidden for you to sleep! Waken up, 'Prisoner 888'!"* he roared, slapping Penkovsky again. Inflicting pain on helpess victims who were uanble to retaliate was one of life's little joys for the KGB career guard. He regarded it as being one of the perks of the job.

A dazed Penkovsky sat there, head lolling and peering at the guard through red, bleary eys. *"I am going mad,"* he thought. The guard stamped on the helpless Penkovsky's bare feet, crushing his toes and making them bleed, *"Sit up straight, you swine!"* bellowed the guard.

The guard was so keen to punish Penkovsky for falling asleep that he'd failed to notice the 'T3-Travellator' parked in the corner of the cell. His focus of attention was elsewhere. He took great delight in swinging his rifle and striking Penkovsky a sharp blow in the ribs with his metal-edged rifle butt, *"You know full well that you are not permitted to sleep, 'Prisoner 888'!"* he shouted.

Mike stepped out from behind the door, tapped the guard on the shoulder and said, *"Excuse me!"* The guard, swung around to face him, his jaw dropping in surprise and started to say something. *"That poor man might not be allowed to sleep, but you certainly are, you arsewipe!"* said Mike as he punched the guard on the jaw with his large, bunched, meaty Scottish fist. Mike had hands as big as workhouse shovels and when used 'in battle' they were very effective. The guard's eyes rolled up into the back of his head and he sank to the floor unconscious. *"Take that, you wee clawbaw!"* said Mike.

Graham pushed the cell door closed. *"Nice one, Mike. Couldn't have done it better myself!"* Turning to Ed, Graham asked, *"So, what now, Ed?"* *"Just let me have a quick chat with Penkovsky and clear a few things up,"* replied Ed.

Colonel Penkovsky was white-faced and trembling, his crushed toes were bleeding were they'd been stomped on by the guard. He didn't have a clue what was going on and now his ribs felt as if they were on fire. Ed reached into his jacket pocket and pulled out a packet of cigarettes, *"Sorry about all that, Colonel. Would you care for a cigarette?"* he asked. Penkovsky nodded and gratefully accepted the cigarette.

His hands were trembling so badly that Ed had to light it for him. Ed noticed that Penkovsky's fingers had also been badly crushed and that where his finger-nails hade been, there were just torn stumps.

Ed turned to Graham and said, *"Graham, go and get this poor man a spare flight suit from the 'T3.' He's freezing."* Graham nodded, *"I'll bring the first-aid box and bandage his hands and feet as well,"* On his return, they helped a grateful Penkovsky to pull the flight-suit on over the filthy prison rags that he was wearing. *"We'll clean and bandage your hands and feet properly once we get on board the 'T3' - there's some good pain-killers in there as well,"* said Graham. Penkovsky nodded his thanks.

"Mike, can you get the guard's rifle and stick it in the 'T3' please, it might come in very useful later on," said

Ed. Mike nodded and picked up the rifle, *"I've a good mind to give this KGB git a swift crack in the ribs, but then I'd be as bad as him!"* he said, walking off towards the 'T3' with the guard's rifle.

Turning to Penkovsky, Ed said, *"Now, Colonel, let me try and explain precisely what's going on here. I know that you speak good English, so that is the language we will all use from now on, OK?"* *"You are English?"* asked a nodding Penkovsy, drawing the smoke from the cigarette into his lungs and coughing, making his ribs hurt even more. Ed shook his head, *"No, I am Dutch actually, but my two friends here are English,"* he said, nodding at Mike and Graham.

"I beg to differ, but I'm Scottish actually," said Mike.

"What are you all doing here - and what is that strange machine over there that you have arrived in?" asked a bemused Penkovsky, nodding towards the 'T3-Travellator.'

"Well, let's try and make things a little easier for you to understand. Have you ever read the book 'The Time Machine' by the author H G Wells?" Penkovsky nodded, *"Yes, I have. It is, of course, forbidden reading here in Russia, but I purchased a copy once when I was over in London on a cultural visit."*

Ed pointed at the 'T3-Travellator' - *"Well, in principle, the H G Wells 'Time-Machine' was something like that contraption over there. The Wells 'Time-Machine' was, of course, purely a figment of his colourful imagination, but as you can plainly see, ours isn't. We call our Time-Machine the 'T3-Travellator.'"*

Now, in case you were wondering what all this is about, we've been sent here, back through time, by the British Government in order to extract you from this miserable hell-hole and rescue you from a fate worse than death!" "Sent here? Sent by whom?" asked an astounded Penkovsky. "*The British Prime Minister*," said Ed. "*And back through time? From when?*" asked an astounded Penkovsky. "*From the year 2019,*" said Ed.

"*The year 2019!*" said an astounded Penkovsky. Then he smiled for the first time in many weeks, "*You have come to rescue me, you say?*" he asked, then his face fell, "*Wait a moment! How do I know that this isn't some sort of cunning KGB trick?*" "*It's no trick, let me assure you, Colonel,*" said Graham. All three men nodded.

"*Rescue me and take me to where, precisely?*" asked Penkovsky. "*We've been tasked to take you back to London to meet the Prime Minister, after which you'll be fully debriefed by the American and British Security Services. Don't worry though, you'll be well look after by them. Your treatment won't be anything remotely like that which you've obviously suffered here, I can assure you!*"

Penkovsky's head drooped and he started to sob, "*I can hardly believe it. Are you certain that this isn't some sort of obscene KGB trickery?*" he asked plaintively. "*Absolutely not, you have my bounden word as a bona-*

fide Jock on that!" said Mike, patting Penkovsky comfortingly on the shoulder, *"Just trust us."*

"Thank God!" whispered a weeping Penkovsky as he wiped his tear-stained cheeks with the back of his filthy bruised hand, the finger ends bloodied and torn. The tears had left grimy trails down his dirty, emaciated and bruised face. *"Cheer up, pal,"* said Mike, *"we'll take good care of you. You'll soon be back to your old self!" "I cannot really understand what is happening to me,"* said a confused Penkovsky, *"My mind cannot take all of this in."*

"Let me explain," said Ed, *"We'll be taking you forward in time to the year 2019 in our 'T3-Travellator' - the Time-Machine, where the British Prime Minister, the Head of the British MI6 and the CIA's Head of Station London want to have a nice long chat with you about certain matters!"* said Ed.

"Ah, the British Prime Minister," said Penkovsky, *"and how is Mr MacMillan?" "Oh, 'SuperMac' - he's long gone,"* said a smiling Graham, *"it's a very different bloke at the helm now. Don't forget that when you get back to London it won't be 1962 any more. Sir Roger Peace is the man in Downing Street now. Don't worry about all that, we'll get you up to speed with that sort of information later. Our main job is to get you out of here safely."*

Ed said, gently, *"Graham is quite correct, you can relax, we're taking out of here and on to the year 2019, where the KGB will not be able to harm you."* Ed noticed that Penkovsky had stopped shivering. The flying-suit was doing its job and helping him to warm up. Whilst they'd been speaking, Graham had very carefully bandaged Penkovsk'y hands and feet.

A grateful Penkovsky said, *"Thank you. I have been in this terrible place for so long that I have lost track of time. I don't care where you take me, or when, or even to whom I speak once I get there. Anything is better than this hell on earth."*

"There is just one tidgy little thing, though," said Mike, *"before we take our leave of the Lubyanka cellars, there is something a bit out of the ordinary that we want you to help us with." "Just ask, it's the least I can do,"* said Penkovsky.

"Now, this is going to sound a wee bit strange, but we have had it on good authority that Tsar Ivan the Terrible's 'Hidden Library' is tucked away down in these cellars. Have you ever heard of it?" asked Mike.

Penkovsky nodded, *"Ah, not that hoary old chestnut. Yes, I have heard of it, but I'm not sure if there is such a thing or even if there is, precisely where it is situated. These cellars are never ending; not even the KGB knows everything about them. Huh, even a rabbit would get lost down here. Anyway, everyone believes the story of the 'Hidden Library' to be nothing but a fairy-tale, like King Solomon's Mines."*

Penkovsky looked across at Mike and said, mischieviously, *"or even your famous Loch Ness*

Monster. *The true facts are shrouded in the mists of time. We often chatted about it though, upstairs in the KGB offices, although as far as I can recall, no-one ever did anything about it." "Let me assure you, my friend, that it's no fairy-tale,"* said Graham, *"show him the diagram, Ed."* Ed reached into the map pocket of his flying suit.

They froze as suddenly, the KGB guard groaned and started to sit up. Ed leaned across and smacked him on the temple with his pistol butt, promptly knocking him out again. *"Better that he stays out for the count whilst all this is going on. It's one less thing for us to worry about!"* said Ed.

Spitefully tapping hot cigarette ash on the guard's face, Penkovsky smiled, *"It's such a pleasure seeing this swine being dealt with in such a positive manner. He is a sadist. If I had the strength and my hands worked properly I would greatly enjoy hitting him myself!"*

Ed pulled a piece of paper out of his flying-suit pocket, carefully unfolded it and showed it to Penkovsky. After a few moments reading it, a squinting Penkovsky pointed at the diagram with a trembling finger and asked, *"Might I ask where you got this information from?"*

"It's a long story Colonel, but it was drawn for me by the fair hand of a certain Russian Princess, Anastasia Romanov," replied Ed, *"and we transposed the details provided by her onto the Architect's drawings of the original cellar layout, so now we have a good idea where to go to find the 'Hidden Cellar.'"*

Penkovsky smiled, *"Princess Anastasia you say. I didn't know that she was still alive."* He examined the drawing, *" I won't ask you where you got the Architect's drawings from!"* Mike tapped the side of his nose, *"That's need tae know, pal, and you dinnae need to know!"*

Penkovsky smiled, *"I have definitely gone stir crazy. Russian Princesses, Time-Machines, Hidden Libraries and purloined Architect's drawings. I must be dreaming all of this,"* he said, shaking his head.

"No, what we're telling you is all true, pal, every word of it. Now what do you think? Can you make any sense of what's on the diagram?" asked Mike. Penkovsky examined the drawing closely and then nodded, *"Possibly."*

"Incidentally, Ed," said Mike, tapping his wrist-watch, *"we need to be getting a move on, we're pushing our luck a bit here. Somebody's bound to notice that the KGB guard is missing from his post oputside the cell before too long."* said Mike. Ed nodded in agreement. Ed looked at Penkovsky and asked, *"Well, Colonel, the drawing, what do you think?"*

"This drawing looks vaguely familiar, and it's very precise," said Penkovsky, peering at the diagram. He tapped the drawing with his bandaged hand, *"Yes, I think I remember that depression in the wall there. It is right next door to the Furnace Room, if I remember rightly."*

Mike looked across at Graham and said, "*We want to stay out of the Furnace Room, don't we boys and girls!*" They all nodded their heads in agreement.

Penkovsky continued, "*Yes, that concave depression in the wall there, it looks familiar. It's the only one of its sort down here. They sometimes have a KGB guard sat on a chair in front of it. I believe that the alcove was built in such a way as to cleverly disguise a hidden doorway, but I never could discover what was behind it, none of us could. Whenever we asked about it we were told to mind our own business and that the information was above our pay grade.*"

Penkovsky shrugged his shoulders, "*We just assumed that it led to a bomb shelter, or perhaps to an emergency exit leading to the Moscow Metro for our glorious KGB leaders to scuttle out of in the event of war breaking out, something of that nature.*"

Ed nodded, "*Well, we're here today not just to haul your irons out of the fire, if you'll pardon the phrase, but to discover what lies behind that particular hidden door,*" he said, tapping the drawing, "*and perhaps you'd like to give us a hand.*"

Penkovsky nodded, "*Gladly, if I have the strength. Although, as you can see, I'm in a terrible physical condition.*" "*You won't be required to do anything physical,*" said Ed, "*if you can just point to where you think that the hidden door is then that would be of great assistance. We don't really have the time to carry out a lengthy search."

"And you think that the concave wall concealing the doorway might lead to the 'Hidden Library' of 'Ivan the Terrible?'" said Penkovsky. Mike nodded, "*Aye, that's a distinct possibility, based on the information provided by Princess Anastasia and now alluded to by your good self.*"

"And how do you intend gaining access there, if you do find it? It's bricked in," asked Penkovsky, "*Presumably you have neither the time nor the equipment with which to demolish the wall that conceals the doorway? Not only that, these passageways are continually patrolled by armed KGB guards, accompanied by fierce guard dogs. Even those oafs would become a little suspicious if they found us there trying to demolish a wall.*"

Graham pointed towards the 'T3-Travellator,' "*No problem there, cocker. As long as we've got a good idea where the entrance is we'll just jump on board our 'Time-Machine' then I'll adjust the travel co-ordinates and with a bit of luck and a fair wind we'll de-materialise at the far side of the door of the 'Hidden Library'- simple as that!*" "And the patrolling KGB guards will be none the wiser," said Mike.

A puzzled Penkovsky shook his head, "*This is all to much for me to take in at the moment, although I'd sell my soul to the devil if it meant getting out of this place in one piece.*"

A smiling Graham said, *"Bit excessive is that, lad! Anyway chaps, we'd better be making a move. We're pushing our luck - we've been here for far too long already! It's time to make good our escape ...."*

As Graham was speaking, there was a startingly loud 'crash' as the cell door was kicked open, startling them all and hitting Ed on the arm, knocking his pistol out of his hand and causing it to skitter across the floor.

In the doorway, brandishing his own Makarov semi-automatic pistol, stood a sneering Lieutenant Colonel Chelpinski. *"Place your hands in the air, Comrades, and no tricks!"* he ordered. No-one moved, *"I will not tell you again!"* said Chelpinski.

'The Makarov Semi-Automatic Pistol'

"Och, buggeration, the wee fellow looks a bit peeved - and the hammer's back on his pistol!" said Mike. *"Now we're in deep cack. I just knew that something like this'd happen!"* said Graham. *"Hands up!"* shouted Chelpinsky, waving his pistol at them. They all raised their hands as ordered.

Chelpinski turned to Lieutenant Gregorovitch, who was stood behind him, *"Quickly, Ivanski, pick up that man's pistol, hand it to me and then search them all carefully -*

make sure that they have no other weapons on them. If any of these dogs tries anything, step smartly to one side and I will shoot them down!"

Ivanski moved into the cell, picked up Ed's pistol then started patting the men down.

After a few moments Ivanski turned and said to Chelpinski, *"They are all unarmed, Comrade Colonel!"* *"Excellent,"* said Chelpinski, waving his pistol, *"now, you three 'guests' may sit on the prisoner's bed, hands behind your heads, whilst you, 'Prisoner 888' may now return to your seat. By the way, you look very fashionable in your new suit although the bandages spoil the effect - and put that cigarette out, you are not here to enjoy yourself!"*

With an air of desparation, Penkovsky dropped the cigarette from his nerveless fingers onto the floor and sat down.

"What about this poor fellow here, Comrade Colonel?" asked Ivanski pointing at the still unconscious KGB guard. *"Leave him there, he'll resurface in his own good time. When he does, I will arrange to have him re-allocated to another post. He is obviously an incompetent who has failed in his simple guard duties."*

Chelpinski back-heeled the cell door closed, *"Now that we are all cosy, let me try and discover precisely what is going on here,"* he said, glancing across at the 'T3-Travellator' his eyes narrowed slits, *"and perhaps someone could explain to me precisely what that box of tricks over there in the corner of the cell is. Do you have a spokesman?"*

Ed stood up and stepped forward, *"That will be me, Colonel,"* he said. *"And you are?"* said Chelpinsky.

Ж

CHAPTER TWELVE

'OUT OF THE SKOVORODKA'

(*) 'Skovorodka - Frying Pan.

"*Now then Gentlemen, before your leader speaks, permit me to introduce myself. I am Lieutenant Colonel Igor Chelpinski of the Komitet Gosudarstvennoy Bezopasnosti.*" Mike called out, "*Hey pal, why don't you just say 'KGB' and save us all a couple hours of crashing boredom!*"

Chelpinski barked, "*Be silent! You may all lower your hands and place them on your laps, but not you 'Prisoner 888.' I warn you all, no tricks - and as for you, you impertinent Englishman, I would advise you ...*" Interrupting him, a scowling Mike said, "*I'm a Scotsman actually.*"

Chelpinski smirked, "*Ah, obviously the 'wag' of the group - there's always someone with a big mouth, eh,*

Ivanski. We must think of something 'special' for him." Ivanski nodded and smiled.

"I'm rather partial to a nice bowl of porridge actually, if you can see your way to getting that organised, my good fellow," said Mike. Chelpinski replied, "*In here we call it Kasha - and if I have my way, you'll soon get used to the taste!*"

Chelpinski continued, "*So, gentlemen, let us agree that we will all speak in English, apart from my colleague Ivanski here who doesn't understand it.*" "*That doombrain doesnae even look as if can speak Russian properly!*" Mike said to Graham.

Glaring at Mike, Chelpinski continued, "*As you have no doubt noticed, my command of the lumpy English language is perfectly adequate for our needs,*" he glared at Mike, "*particularly when I'm speaking to a Scotchman.*"

Mike snarled, "*You cheeky wee bawbag, I've just told you, it's Scotsman!*" Graham chipped in "*Aye Chelps, your English isn't too bad at all, old cock. I'm very impressed.*" Chelpinski bowed his head, "*Why, thank you, my dear sir.*" Glaring at Mike he said, "*At least one of you possesses some semblance of manners. So, before we all die of boredom, I would like to get to the bottom of the how and why you are all here, but perhaps we could begin with the why!*"

Mike chipped in again, "*Well, Chelpers, my old son, we were just having a wee shufty around the place with a view to putting in an offer,*" he said, smiling sweetly.

Chelpinski's face hardened and he moved towards Mike, raising his pistol and was obviously about to strike him with it. He said, "*I'm warning you for the final time, Scotch, er, Scotsman!*"

A defiant Mike grinned and said, "*Och, I care not one jot! And let me warn you - I'm no a wee half-starved, defenceless prisoner, pal. Come any closer with that spud-gun of yours and I guarantee that you'll be sucking on soft food for your meals with what few gnashers you'll have left in your obnoxious Russian gobski, you wee zoomer!*"

Deciding that descretion was the better part of valour, an angry but nevertheless cautious Chelpinski took a pace backwards, "*I might need to have the majority of that translated! I warn you though, make a move towards me and I will have no hesitation in shooting you down like the dog you are!*"

Chelpinski glanced at his watch, "*Now, there is time enough for me to get to the bottom of this little mystery, but first I have a small but enjoyable task to carry out. You three 'visitors' can remain here in this cell whilst I complete a little task!*"

He turned to 'Prisoner 888' - "*On your feet, Penkovsky! I will deal with you first,*" then waving his pistol towards

Mike, Ed and Graham, said, *"after which I will return here and enjoy cracking you three little nuts."*

Mike chipped in again, *"Don't you mean 'six' little nuts?"* Chelpinski ignored his jibe.

Ed asked, *"Might I ask where you are taking the Colonel?"* *"He is no longer a Colonel, he is 'Prisoner 888' - and you do not need to know where he is going,"* snarled Chelpinski, *"what I will tell you, however, is that he has a prior appointment and will not be returning here in the forseeable future. Stand up, 'Prisoner 888' - the moment has arrived, your time has come!"*

As a trembling Penkovsky heaved himself to his feet, Mike said, *"Just a moment, Colonel Penkovski,"* then turned to Chelpinski, *"When you were ear wigging at the cell door,"* Chelpinski interrupted him, *"Ear-wigging? What does that phrase mean?"* *"It means that you were listening to summat that was none of your chuffing business!"* said Graham.

Mike smiled, then continued, *"When you were ear-wigging at the door, you may well have heard us discussing the 'Hidden Library?'* Chelpinski sneered, *"Yes, I did, but that is all frothy nonsense. Let me assure you that no such place exists!"*

Mike continued, *"You are quite wrong, my amigo. It certainly does exist and, might I just remind you that it is alleged to contain great treasures."* *"It's a lot of* nonsense. You are just playing for time. Come along, Penkovsky!" said Chelpinsky waving his pistol.

Ed said, *"He is speaking the truth, Colonel, the 'Hidden Library' does exist and we have rock-solid evidence to that effect."*

"What, you mean evidence provided by the ridiculous female impostor who claims to be the Russian Princess Anastasia! When I heard you talking about that, it was all I could do not burst out laughing!"

"Hah, it's not possible, the Bolsheviks dealt most appropriately with the Romanovs in the cellar at Yekaterinberg!" said Chelpinski, *"They were all slaughtered like the pigs they were and are now 'resting' at the bottom of a mine for all eternity, including your Princess. The woman you met with is nothing but a glib trickster. Had she lived in Russia and made those ridiculous claims she would have been placed inside a mental institution long before now!"*

Shaking his head, Ed said, *"Well, you're completely wrong there, my friend. That particular Romanov escaped from Ipatiev House on the afternoon prior to the executions taking place and managed to get out of Russia in one piece. Princess Anastasia now resides in a lovely little house in Villefranche-sur-Mer on the Côte d'Azur with, I might add, the approval of your government."*

"I spent some time with her at Villefranche recently and she described to me in great detail the location of the

Tsar's 'Hidden Library. She even knows where the entrance is." "And how could she possibly know that?" sneered Chelpinsky.

"Well," said Ed, "one day, her Father, the Tsar, took both Anastasia and her brother the Tsarevitch, Alexei Nikolaevitch Romanov, on a little family adventure down to these very cellars, just for a bit of fun and to have a look around. A sort of magical mystery tour."

"Her father explained to Anastasia precisely what was in the 'Hidden Library' and swore her to secrecy. He would have had no reason to lie to her about the presence and contents of the 'Hidden Library.' So, in view of that, I am confident that not too far from this cell there are great riches to be had. You just need to believe what I am telling you!"

Shaking his head, Chelpinski replied, "This is all nonsense. Do you not think that if this so-called 'Princess,' Anastasia had really survived that we Russians would be aware of it?

"Be honest, you people are not known for your openess, are you!" replied Ed, "Let me assure you that she did survive and as I told you, she lives in a house in Villefranche-sur-Mer, which surprisingly is owned by the Russian Government. I would have thought that as a senior officer in the KGB you'd be aware of that sort of thing!"

"It's probably beneath his pay grade!" said Mike.

Graham chipped in, "*And ask yourself, Colonel, just why would the Russian Government be providing her with funds and letting her live in their villa at the sea-side then, eh, clever clogs?*"

"*What absolute nonsense!*" said Chelpinski, haughtily, "*You'll be telling me next that the moon is made of green cheese!*" "*It is,*" said Mike, "*the Americans have been up there a couple of times to take a look!*"

Chelpinski said, "*And this nonsense about the so-called 'Hidden Library' being down here in the Lubyanka cellars? Why should anyone want to hide a Library down here of all places , eh?*"

Graham said, "*You obviously weren't paying attention when you were ear-wigging! Listen, old pal, although it's referred to as being a Library, it doesn't just contain precious books! According to Princess Anastasia it's supposed to be full of Imperial treasure - jewels the size of pigeons eggs, tons of gold, mountains of precious royal artefacts, Fabergé Eggs, all those sort of things.*"

Mike interrupted, "*And not only Fabergé Eggs - dinna forget the Scotch Eggs!*" Apart from the Russians, everyone else laughed.

"*Now I don't know what your annual KGB salary is, Colonel,*" said Ed to Chelpinsky, "*but this could be a 'golden' opportunity for you to become extremely wealthy and upgrade your whole lifestyle for very little effort on your part."* "*How so?*" asked Chelpinsky, suddenly showing a spark of interest.

"*Here's the deal. We're offering you and your friend, the Lieutenant, the opportunity to join our team. We have the ability to programme our 'Time-Machine,' the 'T3-Travellator,' to take us to the 'Hidden Library.' You must also have heard us describing its capabilities to Colonel Penkovsky. Our 'pilot' Graham just has to revise the T3's on-board co-ordinates so that we'll leave here and dematerialise behind the wall where the 'Hidden Library' is supposed to be.*" said Ed.

Chelpinski laughed, "*A 'Time-Machine! You mean that clapped out old shed in the corner of the cell. Whatever next!*" "*Aye well the proof will be in the pudding, old chap – and don't be so rude about our 'T3-Travellator!'*" said Mike.

"*That's right,*" said Graham, "*and we can use the 'Travellator' to go and find out if what Princess Anastasia told us is true and if there actually is a shedful of loot hidden away in the Library. If there is, then we can then load some of the chocer pieces onto our 'T3-Travellator' and take it away from here.*"

"*And if there isn't anything there?*" asked Chelpinsky. "*Well, we won't know until we go and have a look, will we, Mr Pessimist!*" said Graham. "*You've got nothing to lose and everything to gain!*" said Ed.

"And if we do find something, which I very much doubt, how are we to get it out of here without being seen? This is a high security prison in case you hadn't noticed" said Chelpinsky.

Graham sighed, *"How do imagine we got in here, genious?"*

Mike said, *"Easy peasy lemon squeezy! We just load the treasure into the 'T3' and then make several journeys backward and forward to off-load it. We have the ability to go anywhere and enter any time-zone."*

"We can easily drop you off to stash your portion of the ill-gotten gains wherever and whenever you want and then bring you back here at a time of your choosing, after which we'll just leg it back to our time with our portion of the loot."

"Not only that," said Ed, *"we can make sure that you're back here in Moscow at the right moment in time so that no-one can question what you've been up to or know where you've been. That's one of the benefits of 'Time-Travel.'"*

Ed could tell by the glint of animal cunning that appeared in Chelpinskis eyes that he was interested in the unsual proposal. It was quite obvious that Chelpinski was a ruthless opportunist. *"Come on man, you've got everything to gain, and nothing to lose,"* said Ed.

Chelpinski turned to Ed and said, *"Assuming that I believe you, which I'm not sure that I do, what about 'Prisoner 888' - what happens to him. I can't have him running around on the loose?" "Oh, he can come to 2019 with us,"* said Ed. *"And precisely how am I going to explain his absence to my superiors?"* asked Chelpinski. *"You won't need to,"* said Ed, *"we're well aware of your 'disposal' methods!"*

Arching an eyebrow, Chelpinski said, *"My disposal methods?" "The furnace!"* said Mike. Ed continued, *"We know that there would have been very little, if anything, left of Penkovsky - so you could claim to have done the dirty deed and then disposed of his ashes in your usual efficient manner. Therefore no-one would be any the wiser."*

Penkovsky had turned as white as a sheet when he'd heard the furnace comment. *"And what will happen to him?"* asked Chelpinsky, pointing at Penkovsky. *"As Ed said, he can come back to 2019 with us and we'll tuck him away somewhere where he'll never be found. No-one will be any the wiser,"* said Graham.

"And my Lieutenant and the KGB prison guard?" asked Chelpinski, indicating the still unconscious guard. *"Och, we'll take both of them along with us when we leave here and deposit them in the 'Hidden Library.' I doubt if they'll be able to escape from there. They can stop in there for all eternity and guard what's left of the loot once we've all gone,"* said Mike, turning and winking at Graham.

"*This is all quite fanciful. How do I know that the pile of junk over there really is a 'Time- Machine, eh? The whole concept is ridiculous!*" said Chelpinski, pointing at the Travellator. "*Well, we didnae smuggle it in here piece by piece, did we, you numpty! This a high security hoosegow, in case you hadnae noticed!*" said Mike.

"*Tell you what,*" said Ed, "*a picture is worth a thousand words, so why don't we all jump on board the 'T3-Travellator' and let's take you to the 'Hidden Library' – that way you'll be able to see for yourself. You've got the gun so there's nothing untoward that we can do. What do you say, eh? You've got everything to gain and nothing to lose!*"

Chelpinsky thought it over for a moment then decided. "*Very well, but if you are planning to try and pull a fast one, as you people say, then let me assure you that I will take great pleasure in shooting you all. 'Da mne gluboko napelvat!' Sorry, in English - 'I don't give a spit!'*"

He looked across at his Lieutenant, then gave him a quick explanation, ommitting to mention that Ivanski might well be left to rot in the 'Hidden Library' with the KGB prison guard, "*Ivanski, there may be something in what they say. I'm willing to go along with them. We have little to lose. Are you with me?*" Ivanski nodded, "*To the bitter end, Comrade Colonel.*"

Turning to Ed, Chelpinski said, "*Very well, let us clamber on board this 'T3-Travellator' contraption of yours, and see if it does what you say it will. Let me warn you though, if I suspect that you are lying to me and this is some sort of trick, I will not hesitate to put a bullet in the back of all your necks!"*

Mike nudged Chelpinski with his elbow and said, "*You ken what, Chelps, I'll bet a pound tae a pinch of faeces that your Dad's really proud of you and what you've achieved, particularly the sunny personality side, eh!*"

Chelpinski looked puzzled. "*What has my Papa got to do with any of this?*" he asked. "*Leave it, Mike!*" said Graham as Mike was about to hurtle a further insult at Chelpinski.

Chelpinski waved his pistol at Penkovsky, "*Very well, the decision is made. 'Prisoner 888,' get inside their 'T3-Travellator' - you go with him Ivanski and cover me when I follow the others in.*" Ivanski nodded and pushed Penkovsky across the cell and into the 'T3-Travellator.'

Turning to the others, Chelpinsky said, "*After you, gentlemen, oh - and better bring the guard along with you We must leave no witnesses behind.*" Dragging the unconscious guard across the floor, they entered the 'T3-Travellator' with Chelpinski bringing up the rear.

"*Mmm, this is deceptively large once you get inside,*" said Chelpinsky. "*As you can see, Colonel,*" Ed said to Chelpinski, "*there are only the six seats, so might I suggest that my 'team' take their normal seats and you, Colonel Penkovsky and the Lieutenant plonk yourselves downwhere you can.*"

The still unconscious guard was propped up in a corner of the 'T3-Travellator.' Chelpinski nodded and they all took their seats. *"Very well, let the 'adventure' begin - and remember what I said - no tricks, or else!"* he said, gazing ominously at his pistol.

"Right, fasten your seatbelts, lads, here we go." said Graham as he flicked a switch on the console to close the door of the 'T3-Travellator.' *"Graham,"* said Ed, *"if you could kindly work your magic on the console and input the co-ordinates to transport us to the inside of the the 'Hidden Library' that'd be great."*

"I can certainly give it a good try," said Graham, *"as you know, I can land this thing on a sixpence when I put my mind to it." "Aye, you're not just a pretty face!"* said Mike.

Graham had a quick look at the Anastasia drawing and the Architecht's original diagram then started tapping the new co-ordinates onto the console's keyboard. He threw a switch and the computer on the console whirred into action.

The lights inside the 'T3-Travellator' dimmed and the standard materialisation process began. *"If you like we can return to 'Ivan the Terrible's' time and see what he was up to with the 'Hidden Library' back then?"* said Graham.

Mike shook his head, *"I dinnae think we want to be tangling with the likes of him, Graham. Anyway, we've got enough trouble on our hands with 'Chelpinski the Churlish' here and his mates,"* he said, looking at Chelpinski, Gregorovich and the guard.

"Let's just crack on and see if we can find the 'Hidden Library' in the here and now, shall we, eh!" replied Ed. Graham laughed, *"OK, it was just a thought."*

Graham double-checked the co-ordinates into the master board of the 'T3-Travellator, *"Now bear with me chaps; if those drawings are correct then we should de-materialise somewhere inside the 'Hidden Library' or thereabouts,"* he said.

"I bloody well hope so," said Mike *"we dinnae want to be dematerialising somewhere dangerous like the KGB Headquarters!"*

Chelpinski sat back in his seat, his pistol laid on his lap, thinking, *"What on earth have you got yourself into here, Igor. Still, if this goes pear-shaped then I can justify my involvement by saying that I had personally discovered and captured this nest of traitors, and claim the credit - or alternatively I'll just put a bullet in Gregorovitch's thick skull and blame everything on him."*

His unsuspecting and ever faithful Lieutenant, Ivanski Gregorovitch, was hunched in his seat, fingers gripping the chair arms, knuckles white. He was shit scared and his arse was twitching like a rabbit's nose.

The 'Travellator' contraption and the concept of 'Time-Travel' frightened Ivanski. As ever though, he had put his full trust in his beloved Lieutenant Colonel Chelpinski. He knew that Chelpinski would never let him down, but he also knew that if things went wrong it was always easier to pass the blame onto the officer in charge. Such was life.

'Prisoner 888' soon to be 'Ex-Prisoner 888' Colonel Penkovsky sat back and tried his best to relax. He was thrilled just be out of the cell and away from his miserable pain-filled existence there. In truth he didn't really care what happened to him now and recognised that he might just have escaped a gruesome execution by the skin of his teeth, (the few remaining that hadn't been knocked out).

Ж

CHAPTER THIRTEEN

'BEHIND THE HIDDEN WALL'

"OK, that's it, I think we're here lads, 'X' marks the spot!" said Graham. "Well done, Pilot," said Ed, "that was a fancy bit of flying!" Graham smiled and said airily. "A mere bagatelle to a man of my consummate abilities."

Glancing out of the porthole on the side of the 'T3-Travellator' Graham said, "The place is darker than the 'Black Hole of Calcutta.' I hope it's the 'Hidden Library.'"

He continued, " Mike, if you look in the cupboard under your seat you'll find a couple of LED wind-up torches in there. Looks like we'll be needing 'em." Mike rummaged around and said, "There's three here actually."

"Give me one of those torch, instantly!" ordered Chelpinski. Mike turned to Graham and said, "He's very intense, isn't he!" Graham nodded. "Oy, Chelps, just remember that you're part of a team now and not only *that, you're rather low down in the pecking order!"* said Mike. *"And you remember that I have this weapon, Scotchman!"* replied Chelpinski, waving his Makarov pistol threateningly in Mike's face.

"For the last time, Comrade Chelps - it's Scotsman, and get that wee pop-gun oot of ma face!" snarled Mike.

"Don't let him get to you, Mike," said Ed. *"Huh, he'll be getting a Glasgae kiss if he isnae a wee bit more polite,"* said Mike, reaching under his seat to pull out the torches. Begrudgingly he passed one to Chelpinski.

"What is this fancy instrument?" asked Chelpinski. Mike said, *"It's a wind-up torch; it doesnae need batteries."* Begrudgingly he said, *"Here, let me show you how it works,"* then showed Chelpinski how to crank up a charge on the torch. *"Very clever, must have been invented by a Russian,"* said Chelpinski.

"You're wrong there. Actually it was designed by an Englishman called Trevor Bayliss, although I suppose you Russians will eventually claim to have invented it, just like you did with television," said Graham. *"That is because we did,"* said Chelpinsky airily, *"and the telephone."* *"Absolute cobblers!"* replied Mike.

"Now, you, open the cabin door!" Chelpinski said to Graham. *"Say please!"* replied Graham. *"Just do as I say!"* ordered Chelpinski, waving his pistol in Graham's face. Graham sighed, said, *"You try to be nice…"* then reached forward and pressed the button on the T3's

console that operated the door release mechanism. As the door hissed open, they all unbuckled their seat belts and prepared to leave the relatively safety of the 'T3-Travellator.'

"*So,*" said Chelpinsky, stepping out into the room and flashing the beam of his torch around, "*here we are after our magic carpet ride, in the supposed 'Hidden Library.' Now what happens?*" Ed stepped forward then the remainder followed, "*Guess we'd better crank up our torches and have a good look around to see what we can find, eh!*" said Ed.

Turning to Colonel Penkovsky, Ed said, "*Oleg, You go and sit on that box over there my friend, and rest your weary bones. You've had a very rough time and you need to get some of your strength back.*" A relieved Penkovsky nodded his thanks and went to sit on the dusty old box.

Chelpinsky turned to the KGB guard, who was still not fully recovered and said, "*You, go and sit with him!*"

Penkovsky's face was very pasty and his emaciated body was trembling. "*What I really need is some food and a decent sleep,*" he thought, "*then I'll soon be back to my old self.*" In his heart of hearts he was still wondering if what was happening to him was all part of some weird dream that his brain had generated in order to help him through what he was convinced were his last terrible hours on earth.

He pinched his bony thigh to see if he was awake and to prove to himself that all of this wasn't just a fanciful dream. Deciding that it was real, he slumped back against the wall and drifted off to sleep.

The musty, cavernous room that they were in was full of tall well-constructed dust covered wooden shelves and several glass-faced, finely tooled ornate wooden cabinets that reached right up to the top of the high vaulted ceiling, their shelves cram-packed with all sorts of exciting oddments and 'things' that twinkled in the flickering torchlight. It was, much to their delight, something of an 'Aladdin's Cave.'

Everywhere they looked they could see treasure of one sort or another. *"You've gone very quiet, pal,"* Mike said to Chelpinsky. Chelpinsky nodded, *"So, the fairy-tale was true. Look at it all - I can hardly believe my eyes,"* he said quietly. *"Aye, well perhaps now you'll believe that the lassie Anastasia really is a Russian princess then, eh!"* said Mike. Chelpinski chose to ignore him.

Graham gazed around the library then with trembling hand pointed his torch at a large section of nearby racking and gasped, *"Hell fire! Look over there, see that shelving lads, unless my eyes deceive me it's stacked right up to the ceiling with bloody gold bars. I don't know about the 'T3,' we'll need a fleet of Eddie Stobart's trucks to shift that lot."*

"Och, dinnae fuss yourself, Graham. We've got all day - and in case you'd forgotten, we're here in a 'Time-

Machine.' If we have to, we can nip backwards and forwards through time to stash the stuff. The important thing is that we've found it!" said Mike.

'The Gold inside Ivan the Terrible's 'Hidden Library''

"Listen, we need to be both logical and methodical about this, guys," said Ed. *"It would take us far too long to move all of that gold today, so why don't we just select some of the best items of jewellery and a few gold bars each then leave the rest here to be re-discovered by someone else, eh?"*

Mike sighed, *"Aye, you're right, Ed. I was overcome with gold fever for a wee moment there and anyway we can always teleport back here for some more gold if we need to - now that we know where 'here' is."*

A now more amenable Chelpinski said, *"I would prefer to remove the gold rather than too much of the jewellery. It would be much easier for me to dispose of, Comrades."*

"*Ah, so suddenly we're all 'Comrades' now that we've got the chance of a few quid, eh, Chelps!*" said Mike.

"*So, where would you like us to take yours and your friend Ivanski's share of the gold?*" asked Ed. "*I have a contact, ex-KGB naturally, who owns an island just off the coast of Finland, on the outskirts of Helsinki. I would like to stash mine and Ivanski's share right there,*" said Chelpinski.

"*And where, precisely, is this island then?*" asked Graham. "*I doubt very much if you'll have heard of it. I don't suppose you have any maps on board of that infernal contraption of yours, then I could perhaps show you?*" said Chelpinski.

"*We've got 'Google Earth,' that should be more than up to the task,*" said Graham. Chelpinski nodded, "*I don't know what 'Goggle Earth' is, but I'll take your word for it. Anyway, we can sort all that out in a moment or two. Let us have a closer examination of the contents of this room first. Who knows what we are going to stumble across, eh!*"

"*It's 'Google Earth,*" said Graham airily, "*it's an on-board computer system.*" "*I'll have to take your word for that,*" replied Chelpinsky.

As they walked around the room, pausing every now and again to crank their torches, they examined the shelving and opened up the various cupboards, seeing things on display there of such beauty that caused them to gasp with surprise and pleasure. The Library was literally heaving with valuables, from floor to vaulted ceiling.

Graham called out, "*Hey lads, take a look at this!*" holding something in his hand. "*What have you got there?*" asked Chelpinski. "*It's Stalin's bonce I think!*" said Graham, lifting up a crystal skull embedded with glittering diamonds. Chelpinski tutted and continued looking around.

A laughing Mike said, "*You got him going there, G.*" "*Well it's modelled on some poor buggers skull,* " said Graham, "*and these look like real diamonds. I'm claiming this for my sideboard!*"

"*So, gentlemen, this is what happened to everything of value. All of it tucked away down here by the Romanovs, hidden away from the true owners, the Russian people.*" He sneered, " *There's just a few other relatively paltry trinkets placed on display in museums and the like, just to keep the masses happy. Huh, no wonder they got rid of the profligate swine!*" said Chelpinski, gazing around.

"*By the way,*" said Ed, "*What I didn't tell you, Colonel, was that somewhere in e are some of the Russian Crown Jewels. I promised Princess Anastasia that I would 'redeem' one or two of them for her, if we can locate them. I think that's fair enough, considering that in reality they belong to her and not only that, we'd never have found this Aladdin's Cave without her help.*" said Mike.

"If the Crown Jewels are here then they belong to the Russian people!" said Chelpinsky sniffily, pausing for a moment, then continued, *"but I don't suppose they'll miss the odd item."*

Graham said, *"I've never seen as much stuff in my life, there's nearly as much loot in here as there is in the Tower of London and Fort Knox combined. I mean, look at that tray of Fabergé Eggs over there,"* he said, flashing the beam of his torch at a nearby cabinet.

'Fabergé Eggs'

A sneering Chelpinsky said, *"Just look at all of this! It is truly disgusting what those profligate swine had!"*

Mike replied, *"Not too disgusting for you to come and dip your little trotters in the trough though, eh, Chelps. You're a bloody hypocrite!"* *"Once again, you overstep the mark!"* said an enraged Chelpinski as he raised his hand to strike Mike - and then had second thoughts, taking a pace backwards when he saw Mike bunch his meaty fists.

"You ken what, Chelps," said Mike, *"I'm just looking for an itsy-bitsy excuse to give you a damned good seeing to, you pious little get, so dinnae tempt me!"* *"Leave him be, Mike,"* said Graham, placing a restraining hand gently on Mike's hunched shoulder, *"he's not worth bruising your knuckles on, bud!"* *"Knuckles be damned, I was thinking more of a well-placed size nine toe-cap!"* said Mike.

Turning to Chelpinski, Graham said, *"Anyway, you should be looking on the bright side, Colonel Chelpinsky."* *"What do you mean, look on the bright side?"* asked the puzzled Colonel. *"Well, if the Russian Royals hadn't hidden this stuff down here in the first instance, there'd be nowt left for us to half-inch, would there!"*

"Half inch?" asked a puzzled Chelpinski. *"Pinch!"* said Graham, *"Let's face it, if he'd known about all of this, I can guarantee that Comrade Josef Stalin would have purloined most - if not all of it! Am I right or am I right?"* asked Graham. Chelpinski ignored him.

"And anyway, pal, if you think about it, you and your comrade, Lieutenant Gregory Peckski, are Russian people." said Mike. *"It is Lieutenant Gregorovitch - and I fail to understand just what point it is that you are making?"* asked a puzzled Chelpinski.

Mike sighed, *"Jings, it's like farting in a thunderstorm. What I mean is that by extension, some of this stuff in here is rightfully yours, so dinnae be going off on a guilt trip.!"* he said.

Chelpinski shook his head then replied, "*Huh, typical. Trust a Capitalist to be able to justify theft and misappropriation with such unbounded enthusiasm.*" He sighed, "*Having said that, I suppose that in a way you are quite right, Comrade Capitalist, and thinking about it, I do actually feel a certain sense of entitlement and ownership!*"

"*Well there you are, my wee Russian pal. For a man of such high principles, that wasn't too difficult changing tack, was it!*" said Mike. "*One has to go with the flow,*" said Chelpinsky. "*Aye well, you'll be a Capitalist yourself afore ye know it!*" said Mike.

As Chelpinski gazed around, eye-balling the contents of the roomful of cabinets, with voice full of wonderment he said, "*My God, Ivanski, just feast your eyes on all those items in the cabinets - diamond encrusted swords, jewelled ceremonial daggers, crowns, tiaras, gem encrusted ceremonial wear and mountains of antique books – huh, even their covers are laden with gold leaf, pearls and precious stones. How could one family lay claim to all of this? It is an obscenity!*"

Lieutenant Gregorovitch, gesticulated at a large dusty leather-bound book that was resting on a lectern right in front of him, "*Colonel, I've just been leafing through this book. It is some sort of register, listing what appears to be the entire contents of this Library.*" "*Let me see, pass it over here,*" ordered Chelpinski.

"It's rather heavy and fragile, Colonel, might be better if you came over here to read it," said Gregorovitch. "*Oh, very well*," said an impatient Chelpinski, rudely elbowing his way past Mike.

Mike turned to Ed and said, "*I'll tell you what, Ed, if that roaster touches me again I'm going to skelp his wee behind!*" Ed replied, "*I don't know what the expressions 'roaster' or 'skelp' mean. You're speaking in Klingon again!*" said Mike said, "*You mean 'McKlingon!' Well, put it this way, if wee Chelps bumps into me like that again, watch and see what happens, then at least you'll know what 'skelp' means.*"

Chelpinski bent over and began reading the contents of the ledger out loud, "*It says here, gentlemen, 'List of Imperial Valuables found in Tobolsk in 1933,*" continuing, "*and it is dated the 20th of November 1933! We the undersigned appraisers, Zverev and Borovskikh, evaluated the valuables listed below.*"

Chelpinski shone his torch on the pages then called out some of the items from the listings:

Cabinet One

Diamond Brooch - (100 carats)
Diamond Crescent with 5 large diamonds - (up to 70 carats)
Diamond Hairpins - (up to 70 carats)
Diamond Pin - (44 carats)
Diamond Necklace - with Pearls and Ruby Pendants

Chelpinsky tutted, "*There are pages and pages of this stuff, describing the precious items in the Library and annotating their value at the time of writing. It's breathtaking. These things will, of course, be much more valuable now*"

"*Just imagine, the Romanovs had all of these invaluable objects whilst the Russian peasants were cold, starving and living in filth!*" he said bitterly.

'The Russian Royal Family'

(Picture: Hermitage Museum)

(The treasure consisted of some of the personal jewellery and valuables of the Tsar, Empress Alexandra, their four Princess daughters, and son and heir Alexei Nikolayevich, all of whom were claimed to have been executed in Ipatiev House, Yekaterinburg, in July 1918).

Chelpinsky continued:

Cabinet Two

Gold Chain - with Emeralds
Pendant - with Diamond and Double Gems
Watch - with Diamond Studded Bracelet
Gold Pencil - with Pearl
Crosses - with Gems

"*Pah, the list is endless, the profligate swine,*" said Chelpinski, slamming the dusty ledger closed, with a loud bang.

"*Och, somebody's getting their wee galliffets in a right twist,*" Mike whispered to Graham, then turning to Chelpinski he said, "*Profligate those Royals may have been, my friend, but Tsar Nicholas and his family certainly didnae deserve what the Bolsheviks did tae them!*"

"*Absolute nonsense!*" said Chelpinsky, "*they deserved everything they got from the Bolsheviks. Indeed, had they been allowed to survive, we Russians would all still be living like pigs in shit!*" Mike said, "*Oh, right. Is that why they built a wall in East Berlin, to keep you all in then?*"

A sneering Chelpinsky said to Mike "*Maybe you should try it in Great Britain with your Royals!*"

Graham, elbowing his way forward, said, "*Totally different kettle of fish, cock! You see, we love our Royal family and wouldn't see a hair on their heads harmed."*

"*Huh, you British are all brainwashed. One day it will sink in!*" said Chelpinsky.

An affronted Graham, a devout Monarchist, glared at Chelpinski and said, "*You know what pal, I don't know about the others in here, but you're beginning to get right up my sneck! And not only that, you're guilty of double-standards!*"

"*What do mean, double-standards?*" snarled Chelpinski.

"*Well,*" said Graham, "*the profits from your share of the valuables that you'll be filching from here won't be going to the Russian people, will they? They'll be heading straight for your off-shore bank account, you bloody hypocrite!*"

Chelpinski smiled, "*In case you hadn't noticed, I am Russian, as is my comrade here, Gregorovitch.*" "*And your point being?*" said Graham. "*As your Mr De Jong so kindly pointed out, Ivanski and I are both Russian 'people' - so that is justification enough for me!*" replied Chelpinski. "*As Graham said, double standards, you arrogant tit!*" said Mike.

"*He's a right piece of work is that lad!*" said Graham to Mike.

Mike turned to Ed and said, "*I'm telling you, pal, Chelps is going to get such a smack on the beak in a minute, pistol *or not!"* "*Oh, just ignore him Mike, he can't help it, he's been brain-washed.*" said Ed.

"*We'd better start sorting through the mountains of stuff in here,*" said Ed, "*then Chelpinski can load his selection onto the 'T3-Travellator' and we'll whizz it off to Finland or wherever it is he wants us to take it. Once we've kept our half of the bargain we can off-load him and his oppo, then we won't ever have to look at their ugly faces again.*"

Addressing the group, Ed said, "*OK guys, this is what I suggest we do. Graham, you and Colonel Chelpinski can go and have a look on 'Google Earth' and locate the co-ordinate's for the Colonel's Finnish island, whilst the rest of us start selecting batches of precious items to load on board the 'T3-Travellator' ready for transportation.*"

"*OK, you'd better come with me then, Colonel,*" said Graham to Chelpinski.

"*No tricks, Comrade St Anier!*" said Chelpinski, tapping his pistol. Graham sighed, "*You can trust me, old pal, I was a policeman in a previous life. Come on, follow me!*" "*Keep a watchful eye on them, Ivanski!*" ordered Chelpinski. Gregorovitch nodded.

Graham and Chelpinski headed back to the 'T3-Travellator' whilst the others started examining the contents of the cabinets and cases and lifting lids on the various chests and boxes laid out around the 'Hidden Library,' carefully selecting various precious items and piling them onto the floor.

"*The difficulty is,*" said Mike, "*in deciding what to take and what to leave behind. Good gracious, just look at all these Fabergé eggs in here. It's like a chicken farm!*" he said, pointing to a large velvet lined box that he'd opened.

Three hours and several 'T3' journeys later, a substantial amount of the gold bullion and, despite what Chelpinski had said, many items of precious jewellery had been transported to Chelpinski's Finnish island. "*I think that you've got enough now Colonel, eh?*" said Ed, "*It's time we started loading our stuff on board the 'T-3.'*"

Chelpinski said, "*Wait a moment. Whilst we have been travelling back and forth in your 'Time-Machine,' I have had a complete change of heart.*" "*What do you mean you've had a complete change of heart?*" asked Ed. "*Didn't know he had one,*" chipped in Mike.

Ignoring Mike, Chelpinski said, "*I've decided that just a few more 'trinkets' wouldn't go amiss. For instance, I spotted some superb jewellery in that cabinet over there that I would like to have. It's only one more load.*" Ed sighed, "*OK, but make this your last journey. We need to get our stuff moved as well.*"

"*He's a greedy wee scunner is that Chelpinsky, we should bin him!*" Mike whispered to Ed. Ed nodded, "*I don't like Chelpinski's attitude either Mike, nor do I trust him, but much as I agree with you, a deal's a deal,*" said Ed.

After Chelpinski had selected a further large amount of jewels and other precious items, they were loaded onto the

'T3-Travellator' and once again Graham piloted Chelpinsky and his ill-gotten gains off to the Finnish island where his ex-KGB contact was waiting to help him unload and stash the loot.

Whilst they were waiting for him to return, Mike whispered to Ed, "*Ed, call me old-fashioned, but like yourself, I dinnae trust that Chelpinsky geezer one iota. I doubt that he'll be wanting to leave us here in one piece when he gets back. We know too much.*"

Ed nodded, "*I agree and I'll be watching him like a hawk. You just keep an eye on his henchman 'Lurch.'*" Mike nodded, "*Och, the wee clipe, Gregory Peckski. Well if he so much as farts out of tune, I'll just have tae deck him!*"

Mike looked across at Gregorovitch who was watching them from across the room. Mike waved and called out, "*Alright pal! Just grabbing yersel a few diamond are you, eh. Well, you do right!*"

Ed and Mike continued selecting some prime items from the cabinets and laid them out on the floor near to where the 'T3-Travellator' would de-materialise.

"*I think that just about does it,*" said Ed, "*there's more than enough loot here to keep us all happy and we don't want to flood the international markets.*" Mike nodded, "*Aye, I agree, and anyway, we can always nip back here if we want to top-up, eh. We'll be in good odour with the Prime Mister once we've delivered Colonel Penkovsky to* him, so getting authority to 'Time-Travel' back here shouldnae pose a prob."

The 'T3-Travellator' suddenly de-materialised, its door hissed open and both Graham and Chelpinsky stepped out. *"That's it then,"* said Graham cheerfully, *"we can start loading our valuables on board now, chaps."*

"Before we go any further, gentlemen," said Chelpinski, sliding his pistol out of its holster, *"You can all put your hands in the air, then go and stand over there next to the traitor, 'Prisoner 888!'"*

Chelpinski tutted, *"Ivanski, put your hands down please, I don't mean you! You and the guard come over here and stand next to me!"* Lieutenant Gregorovitch dropped his hands then pushed the bewildered KGB guard over to where Chelpinski was standing.

The KGB guard had only just recovered from the blows to his head and still hadn't quite worked out what was happening to him. Not only that, everyone was speaking in a language that he didn't understand, although he thought that it sounded like English. In time honoured fashion, he would just obey orders and wait to see what happened.

"Now just a minute, I thought that we had a gentleman's agreement, Colonel," said a seething Ed. Chelpinski smiled, *"Well, as you have no doubt gathered, I'm no gentleman - and our agreement has just been rescinded!"* he sneered. Mike snorted, *"Och, yer bum's well oot of the*

windae there, pal!" Chelpinski cocked his pistol and snarled, *"I have had just about as much as much…"*

"Er, excuse me Colonel," said Graham, tapping Chelpinski on the shoulder, *"Yes, what is it?"* Chelpinski asked, *"I'd like to give you something?" "Really, what could you possibly have that I would want, you boring little man?"* said Chelpinski. *"This,"* said Graham and promptly hit the Colonel on the jaw with a very swiftly delivered and handy right hook.

A dazed Chelpinsky spun backwards onto the floor, but still managed to hold on to his pistol. Gregorovitch went to help him. *"Oy, leave him, Lurch!"* said Mike.

Rubbing his knuckles, Graham said to Mike, *"I used to use that particular punch on a Saturday night in the Beverley pubs at closing time. Never failed me once. The lucky recipients referred to it as the 'St Anier Streamline Special!"*

"You English swine, you will pay for that." said Chelpinsky, rubbing his jaw.

He pointed the pistol directly at Graham, then pulled the trigger several times. There was just a series of clicks.

"Oh, I forgot to tell you, lad," said Graham, *"when you took your belt and jacket off whilst we were unloading the gold on 'Treasure Island' in Finland, I took the opportunity to unload your pistol. I'm surprised that you*

didn't hear the splashes when I threw the ammo into the water by the log cabin."

Mike threw his head back and laughed, *"Och, you're a wee genius, Graham. I could smother your body with kisses!"* he said. *"I think we'll give that one a miss for now, Mike. We have certain standards in Yorkshire, where it is forbidden to snog with a Jock,"* said a smiling Graham.

Ed turned to Lieutenant Gregorovitch and, gesticulating towards Chelpinski, ordered, *"You, help your boss up off the floor - now!"* Ivanski sidled across the room, helped Chelpinsky up on his feet, brushed him down then stood next to him waving his hands in the air. *"Put your hands down, you look like you're directing traffic, you prat!"* said Graham.

Ed turned to Graham and said, *"We'd better make sure that they can't get up to any mischief behind our backs whilst we're loading the 'T3.' See if you can find something to tie the three of them up with, Graham. A couple of those gold ropes over there should do the trick!"*

"What do you intend doing with us?" snarled Chelpinski. *"Nothing,"* said Ed, *"apart from tying you up whilst we finish loading the 'T3-Travellator' with our share of the valuables. Then, once we've finished, we'll be heading off into the wild blue yonder in the 'T3.'"*

"Aren't you going to execute us?" asked a bewildered Chelpinski. Ed shook his head, *"Don't judge everyone*

else by your own shitty standards, Chelpinski. We've decided to leave you, the guard and your Lieutenant here in the Library when we go."

Chelpinski spluttered, *"But there is no way out of this place. You know full well that the entrance is bricked in! "No sympathy, pal!"* said Mike, *"We kept our part of the bargain, you got your share of the treasure and we offered you a good plan to cover your activities - but you blew it because you are thoughtless and greedy."*

"But how are we to survive?" wailed Gregorovitch. Graham said, *"You'll have to use your initiative, lad."* Pointing at Chelpinski, Graham said to Gregorovitch, *"Looks like you've hitched your horse to the wrong waggon, mucker!"*

"What is happening here, Comrade Colonel?" asked Gregorovitch plaintively. *"These Capitalist swine are going to leave us in here when they go, Ivanski,"* said Chelpinski. *"But there is no food or water in here, we will die, Comrade Colonel,"* said Gregorovitch.

"Well, Chelps" said Mike, *"tell him you'll just have to tuck into one of those gold bars, and you never know, there might be a few bottles of expensive vodka or wine stashed away in here somewhere to wash it down with!"*

The KGB guard, who was still woozy, was stood at the side of the two officers, looking distinctly gormless. He still wasn't quite the full shilling; his ears were ringing and his head was throbbing. He still didn't understand what was going on, so just stood there looking gormless and awaiting further orders.

Using some very substantial gold ropes that they'd found, Graham and Ed began tying Chelpinsky, Gregorovitch and the guard up, *"I'd like to see the curtains these came off,"* said Graham *"The ropes are not ideal,"* said Ed, *"but it'll help delay them until we get out of here. Now, the three of you - sit on the floor, legs crossed, hands behind your backs!"* he ordered.

Chelpinsky and the other two men slumped down onto the floor. The guard still didn't have a clue where he was or what was going on. It was all too much for him so he decided to leave all of the decisions to the two officers and follow their example. After all, officers always knew what they were doing, didn't they, (although he thought that the Lieutenant seemed like a bit of a knob-head).

Graham tied their wrists and ankles securely with the gold rope, looping it around their necks and ankles to make things even more difficult. *"See, Mike, my time in the Boy Scouts wasn't wasted!"* said Graham, pointing proudly at the knots.

Ed called across to Penkovsky, who had woken up and was sat watching the proceedings, *"How you feeling Colonel? Are you ready to make a move yet?"* Colonel Penkovsky nodded, *"Yes, I'm feeling a little bit better thank you, Ed."* *"Come on then,"* said Ed, *"let's get cracking. You go and sit inside the 'T3-Travellator' for now, Colonel, whilst we finish the loading."*

Ed, Mike Graham and a doddery but cheerful Penkovsky headed for the 'T3-Travellator.'

"*I must say, you've been very quiet, whilst all this has been going on, Colonel Penkovsky*" said Graham. "*I caught up on some much needed sleep. Just recharging my batteries, my friend. I cannot begin to tell you just how overjoyed I am at seeing those miserable swine over there getting their just desserts. Had it been up to me I would have shot them. They never showed any mercy whatsoever to me or to any of the other prisoners. I'm more than happy to let the three of them rot in here for all eternity!*" said Penkovsky, unable to hide the bitterness in his voice.

"*Come on then, gentlemen, form a chain and let's get the gold and these jewels and the rest of the stuff inside the 'T3-Travellator' then we can head for the hills.*" said Ed. "*Colonel,*" said Graham to Penkovsky, "*you go inside the 'T-3' and find yourself a seat, then make yourself comfortable whilst we get on with the loading.*"

It took them the best part of an hour to load the remainder of the precious items into the 'T3-Travellator.' Once they'd finished, there wasn't much room left inside for anything else. Ed, Mike and Graham climbed on board.

"*Take your seats and strap in, guys. Time to head for Amsterdam and get all of this this stuff unloaded at Ed's place, then we whizz Oleg over to Hull so that he can be taken down to London.*" said Mike, leaning across and checking that Colonel Penkovsky had managed to fasten his seat-belt properly.

Mike called out to the three Russians, *"Right, Moe, Curly and Larry, we'll be on our way then. We're really going to miss you - TTFN, Comrades!"*

An enraged Chelpinski screamed out, *"You Scotch Svolotch!"*

Mike said, *"Dearie me, I dinnae ken what 'Svolotch' means, but it sounds awfy rude!"* *"Svolotch - it means 'Bastard!'* said Penkovsky. *"Och really, and how did he come by that piece of highly sensitive information?"* asked Mike. *"He must have read your birth certificate?"* said Graham, a mischievous glint in his eye.

"A slur on my dear old Mother's reputation methinks! It's lucky for old Chelpie that we're leaving or I might have to give him the good message!" said Mike.

They all laughed as the 'T3-Travellator' door hissed shut and it began to materialise, then disappeared as it flew off into the ether carrying its precious load.

A few moments after the 'T3-Travellator' had disappeared, the simple KGB guard turned to Lieutenant Colonel Chelpinski and said, *"Comrade Colonel, could you kindly explain what is going on here?"* *"Shut up, you dim-witted toe-rag!"* snarled Chelpinski. *"Yes sir!"* replied the guard, sitting to attention as best he could

The light from the remaining rapidly fading torch cast a mean yellow glow around the Library. Gregorovitch asked, *"Colonel, excuse my ignorance, but what does the* phrase TTFN mean?" Chelpinsky sighed, "*It means 'Goodbye for now,' Ivanski. One of those ridiculous public school expressions that the witless British upper classes use,*" he said.

"*Now, Ivanski, enough of the language lessons, let's try and free ourselves from these rather expensive bindings shall we - and then we can give that torch a good wind. We need to be able to see what we're doing and I need to think of a way of getting us out of here in one piece.*"

"*We will never undo these bindings*," said Gregorovitch, despairingly. "*Well, use your initiative man and have a look around to see if you can spot a ceremonial dagger or a sword or something with a cutting edge to slice them off with. We need to do something before that torch dies out on us.*"

Gregorovitch whispered, "*Comrade Colonel, what are we going to do about the prison guard? He has seen everything that has gone on here, even though he doesn't understand what we've been talking about.*"

"*Once you've found a sharp blade, use it to cut my bindings, then I'll slice through yours, then we simply cut his throat.*" replied Chelpinsky. "*Trust me, Ivanski, I will seek a way out of here for you and I.*" He smiled, "*The guard can remain here and keep an eye on this place for us. Now go and find a suitable implement, a sword or dagger, something like that!*"

Gregorovitch hauled himself to his feet them hopped, kangaroo like, across to the nearby cabinets to try and find something with a sharp edge with which to cut and release them from their bindings.

Whilst Ivanski was hopping about, Chelpinsky looked across at the guard and smiled, "*Your problems will soon be over, Comrade!*" he said. The guard nodded gratefully, "*Thank you, Comrade Colonel!*"

"*There you are,*" thought the guard, "*what a nice man. You can always place your trust in an officer, particularly when he's in a tight spot with you.*"

Ж

CHAPTER FOURTEEN

'AMSTERDAM'

A joyful, out of tune voice rang out, *"Aaaaaah, when it's a-spring again, I'll bring again, a-jewils from H'Amsterdam,* It was Graham St Anier, singing joyfully as he looked at the great stash of very valuable items that they'd unpacked from the 'T3-Travellator' on their return from the 'Hidden Library' in the cellars of the Lubyanka Prison.

"Right guys, that's everything unloaded and about to be safely stashed away. So many beautiful and valuable items. It will break my heart having to part with them when they are sold," said Ed.

Mike, Graham, Ed and Colonel Penkovsky were stood in the closely guarded security compound at the centre of Ed's business offices, which were sited on the edge of the diamond district on the outskirts of Amsterdam.

Looking at his watch, Ed said, *"Hadn't you three better be jumping back on board the 'T3-Travellator' and making your way back to Humberside Travelport asap, otherwise your Prime Minister's security boys will be wondering what's happened to you!"*

Mike nodded, *"Aye, that's right, they're expecting us - and coincidentally, I've just received a text confirming that there's an RAF HS-125 Executive Jet stood by at the Travelport to fly the three of us down to RAF Northolt where there'll be a staff car waiting to drive us straight to Downing Street."*

"It's been a busy old day and it's not over yet," said Graham, adding, *"you know what, it feels like we've spent more time in Downing Street than Theresa May did!"*

Colonel Penkovsky didn't say anything, he was too busy concentrating on munching a hefty bacon, lettuce and tomato sandwich. It had been difficult for him to adjust to all that had happened to him over the last few days, but he was getting there slowly but surely.

"Take it easy with that sandwich, Oleg. No need to rush, there's plenty more where it came from," said Ed.

Penkovsky nodded and smiled, as a dribble of delicious dark brown HP sauce dripped down his chin. He was in seventh heaven. Graham handed him a serviette, *"Here, wipe you chin, you little muck-bin!"* Shaking his head, Penkovsky said, *"I would never have thought that such a strange combination of food could be so delicious. The Russian 'Mushka Yulia' pales into insignificance by comparison."*

"'Mushka Yulia,' even the name sounds vaguely disgusting. What is it?" asked Graham. *"Salted Herrings and Onions,"* replied Penkovsky. *"Mmm, I think I'll be giving that one a body swerve,"* said Graham, *"it sounds as inviting as Sheepshead Broth!"*

Ed remarked, *"I'll be in touch with you three guys once I've had this Russian stuff valued and sold on. Just give me a couple of weeks, then I'll get your share of the profits transferred to your off-shore accounts - usual procedure."*

"Oleg, once we find out what's happening to you and where you're likely to be, Mike and Graham will let me know about that, then I'll make all of the necessary financial arrangements on your behalf. You'll just have to trust me until then." he said smiling.

Placing his freshly bandaged hand on Ed's shoulder, Penkovsky replied, *"I trust all of you gentlemen with my life, after all - it was you three that saved it!"* ' *"Come on then, let's get the old girl cranked up and head off into the wild blue yonder,"* said Graham. They all shook hands then Mike, Graham and Colonel Penkovsky headed off towards the 'T3-Travellator.

Penkovsky, pausing mid-stride, turned to Ed and said, *"Before we leave here, Ed, I would just like to have a few private words with you."*

"Oh, that sounds a bit serious, Oleg," said Ed.

Penkovsky continued, *"I would like to thank you most sincerely for coming to Moscow and saving me from a fate worse than death. I know now that I was only a few hours away from the horror of the furnace, courtesy of those 'govno-doms' – sorry, that's shit-houses, Lieutenant Colonel Chelpinsky and Lieutenant Gregorovitch. Huh, at least they got what they deserved!"*

"It was a great pleasure being a part of all this my friend," said Ed, *"and one of life's little joys leaving Chelpinski and his partner in crime tucked away behind a bricked wall in the Lubyanka Prison. Shame about the KGB guard, but it was no more than the three of them deserved. I would have quite happily put a bullet in the back of their heads there and then but that would make me as bad as them."*

"I agree, much better that they are left there to rot," said Penkovsky.

Ed continued, *"Now, Oleg, might I suggest that you head off to your security de-briefing, make whatever deals and promises you have to with the Prime Minister, then get on with the rest of your 'new' life. As I said, I'll arrange it with Mike and Graham for your share from the sale of the Russian treasure trove to be forwarded on to your off-shore account, which I'll be opening on your behalf later today. It'll help you considerably with your new life."*

"The lads will explain how you will be able to gain access to the off-shore account - and I can assure you that no-one, not even the FSB, will be able to trace it back to you."

"*The FSB?*" asked Oleg. "*That's the new name for the KGB,*" said Ed.

"*That is so very kind of you, my friend,*" said a grateful Penkovsky, shaking Ed's hand enthusiastically, "*because I doubt very much that the Russian government will be forwarding my military pension on to me!*"

Mike called out, "*Graham's got the 'T3-Travellator' cranked up, and our PM doesn't like to be kept waiting. He'll have us all sent to the Tower of London if we're not careful, so come on Colonel, get your Russian arse in gear!*"

"*Ah, you English fellows, you employ such colourful phrases,*" said Penkovsky. "*How very dare you! I heard that! I'm Scottish, I'm not a Sassenach!*" said a smiling Mike, bunching his fists jokingly, "*Now come on, Oleg, my porridge is getting cold!*"

Ж

CHAPTER FIFTEEN

'NUMBER 10 DOWNING STREET'

It never ceased to surprise the constant stream of visitors to Number 10 Downing Street, situated right in the heart of London, just how serene it was inside the world-famous building that housed the Prime Minister, the Chancellor of the Exchequer and their staffs, sat there as it was right in the centre of what was usually the eye of the storm, with a bustling Trafalgar Square just down the road.

At the Cenotaph end of Downing Street, just a few yards away from Number 10, were crowds of cheerful rubber-neckers, jostling with the various groups of political activists waving placards and shouting furious abuse down the street, (hoping that the PM might hear them, which of course he couldn't). The patience of the policemen and women guarding the entrance was often sorely tested, but they inevitably treated everyone with impeccable politeness, apart from the odd pompous politician.

'Security gates at Downing Street, London'

An endless stream of traffic, mainly London black cabs, drove past the huge metal gates that protected Downing Street, their horns blaring impatiently, interspersed with queues of bright red 'Boris' buses chugging along at regular intervals, pausing occasionally outside 'Horse Guards' to disgorge even more enthusiastic camera-clicking tourists.

The man selling 'Brexit' flags, Union Jacks and suchlike from his little stall at the side of the pavement was doing a roaring trade in traditional tat.

On that particular morning, at the rear garden side of Number 10, the PM had his sash windows flung wide open and was stood tapping his foot and listening to the music of the Band of the Coldstream Guards, his old military outfit, as they bounced along Pall Mall from

Buckingham Palace heading for Horseguards Parade, where they would then practise their marching display under the eagle eye of their Musical Director and the Garrison Sergeant Major, for the forthcoming state visit of the President of the United States of America.

"*Bloody fun and games we'll be having there*," thought the PM "*I suppose he'll be expecting another medal or some other sort of decoration!*"

In the distance he could hear the band striking up the popular military tune, 'Colonel Bogey' - which brought back many fond memories of the time when he was a young subaltern in the Coldstream Guards and long before he went into politics.

The smiling PM joined in with the band, tapping the window ledge with his hand and singing the very rude accompanying words to the music that he'd often bellowed out enthusiastically at Regimental Dinner Nights, along with his brother officers:

'Hitler has only got one ball,
Göring has two but very small,
Himmler is rather similar,
But poor old Goebbels has no balls at all!'

There was a knock on the office door, disturbing his reveries.

Disappointed, he slid the window closed and called out, "*Enter!*" "*Sorry to bother you, Prime Minister,*" said the

P.M's Chief of Staff, Gregory Waterhouse, *"but Colonel Penkovsky, Mr Fraser and Mr St Anier have arrived from RAF Northolt. They're waiting in the outer office."* The PM smiled, *"Oh, good show Greg, bring them straight in would you please."*

As the three visitors filed into the P.M's office, he smiled and shook hands with each of them then said, *"Kindly take a seat gentlemen, make yourselves comfortable. Er, can Greg get you something to drink before we begin, tea, coffee, water?"* *"No thank you, sir, we've been fed and watered already,"* said Mike, *"the RAF catered to our every whim on the flight down here."*

"Excellent!" said the PM *"they always do a first-class job, the 'Brylcreem Boys.' You know, I have quite a penchant for their corned-beef and onion sandwiches, delicious, although they do tend to make one rift for hours afterwards, what!"* His visitors smiled politely and nodded in agreement.

When flying down to London from Humberside Travelport on board the luxurious RAF HS-125 Executive Jet, the flight attendant had asked Colonel Penkovsky what his favourite meal was, to everyone's hilarity he'd replied, *"The next one, Comrade!"* Penkovsky was obviously beginning to regain some of his old self-confidence, despite all of the traumas he'd recently undergone.

After his Chief of Staff, Gregory Waterhouse, had left the office, the PM turned to Colonel Penkovsky, (who had managed to have a shower and shave - and change into some suitable clothing,) and said, *"Well, Colonel, quite a memorable few days you've had, what! The exfiltration operation went remarkably smoothly, I thought."*

Penkovsky returned the P.M's smile, *"That is an understatement, sir. A few 'memorable' days indeed. It is a great pleasure and relief for me to have been rescued from the Lubyanka Prison by my brave comrades, and it is a distinct honour to be accepted here in a free and democratic country. I am eternally grateful, sir."*

The PM smiled, *"Yes indeed, well you're more than welcome here, old boy. I hear that you had a bit of a close call with that Chelpinski fellow though, eh!"*

"A close call indeed, sir, but your '7th Cavalry' in the shape of these two gentlemen and their friend Ed De Jong arrived just in the nick of time to save my bacon, which was very nearly grilled bacon!" said Penkovsky, gesticulating at Mike and Graham.

The PM nodded, *"Nick of time indeed, Colonel. Still, you're safe and sound now. So, that's the niceties out of the way, so let's get down to business shall we. Incidentally, after we've had our little chatette here, you Colonel will be escorted over to that strange looking cream and emerald edifice at Vauxhall Cross - er, that's the Headquarters of our Secret Intelligence Service, for a couple of days."*

Penkovsky's face fell. *"You needn't worry old chap"* said the PM, *"there's nothing sordid planned for you, just a comprehensive debrief and then you'll be told precisely what we've got planned for you regarding a change of identity and relocation."*

"A little dicky-bird tells me that you'll be heading off to Canada shortly after your debrief, but you'll get to know all about that sort of thing later. Hope that's OK?" he said, as if Penkovsky had any choice in the matter.

Penkovsky smiled, *"It is more than I could ever have hoped for, sir."*

The PM turned to Mike and Graham, and doing his best to sound Churchillian, he said *"Gentlemen, once again you have helped our country to resolve a most difficult problem and I personally am extremely grateful. You have carried out some most invaluable work which regrettably, for security reasons, you can expect no public recognition. Your reward is in knowing that the information that Colonel Penkovsky will be providing us with, although somewhat historical in nature, will be of immense value."*

"Not half as valuable as the loot we lifted from the 'Hidden Library. Wonder what the PM would say if he knew about that,'" thought Graham.

The PM addressed Mike and Graham, *" Now, gentlemen, if you don't mind, I need to speak to Colonel Penkovsky privately, so I would be immensely grateful if you could make your final farewells now. Unfortunately you won't be meeting him again."*

"That's what you think, Sir Rog!" thought Mike.

Graham and Mike stood up to shake hands with Penkovsky, "*Good luck Oleg, mate,*" said Graham, "*I'm sure that everything'll be tickety-boo for you from now on.*" "*Thank you Graham, my friend. I cannot begin to tell you how grateful I am,*" said Penkovsky.

Then turning to Mike he said, "*And as for you, Scottish Mike, my admiration knows no bounds. I can never repay the pair of you - and of course, Ed - for what you have done for me, right from my 'surgical' extraction from the Lubyanka Prison to bringing me here to begin my new life.*"

"*Och, think nothing of it my dear fellow, it's been a great adventure and, I have to say, it was really nice meeting you and getting to know you. You've proved to us that some Russians can be quite nice. Good luck for the future, eh.*" said Mike, winking.

Penkovsky had been warned by the lads beforehand not to mention their trip to the 'Hidden Library' so had remained resolutely silent on that subject.

Graham went to shake Penkovsky's hand but the Colonel brushed his hand aside, grabbed him by the shoulders and kissed him heartily on both cheeks, "*That's the Russian way,*" said Penkovsky. He turned to Mike and did the same.

"*I'll tell you what, you're not a bad kisser Oleg, but I think that you need a closer shave,*" said Mike laughing,

A grinning Penkovsky replied, "*I've had enough close shaves of late, my friend. You know, there is a Russian saying - 'an old friend is better than three new friends, but in the case of you, Graham and Ed, I make an exception!*"

"*Look, I hate to break this 'snog-fest' up, chaps,*" said the PM "*but we really must crack on.*" Mike and Graham shook hands with the PM then left the room laughing. They'd both be heading straight back to RAF Northolt for their return flight to Humberside Travelport.

After they'd gone, the PM invited Penkovsky to move his chair closer to the desk. "*Colonel, there's just one more thing that I would like you to do for me before you leave here and head on up the Albert Embankment to Vauxhall Cross for your debrief,*" he said quietly, sliding a pen and a notepad across the desk towards Penkovsky.

"*What do you wish me to do, sir?*" asked Penkovsky. "*I would like you to write down the name of the KGB's contact in MI6 who was supplying Moscow with classified and sensitive information way back in the year 1962. Purely for the record you understand,*" said Sir Roger.

"*Ah,*" said Penkovsky, smiling wryly, "*so the KGB's 'deep-throat' was rumbled then?*" The PM nodded, "*Oh yes, we'd been playing him for quite some time. I just need confirmation from you that he was who we thought he was, that's all.*" said the PM confidently, but who in reality was being economical with the truth, in fact he was lying through his teeth.

Neither the PM nor the Security Services had got an inkling who'd been passing highly sensitive and classified information to the Russians over the years. The return of Penkovsky was a heaven sent opportunity to find out just who the cuckoo in the nest was and, in essence, that's what his rescue had been all about.

Penkovsky took a deep breath, "*I have no difficulty with that, Prime Minister, I owe no allegiance to Russia.*" He paused for a moment then continued, " *In fact, I can provide you with two names!*" he said.

The P.M's eyebrow shot up, "*Really! Two names you say?*" Penkovsky nodded and started scribbling on the notepad. When he'd finished writing the two names he pushed the notepad back across the desk to the PM

"*Please excuse my poor handwriting, sir, you can see what the KGB torturers have done to my hands!*" said Penkovsky, showing his badly crushed fingers. The PM nodded sympathetically, "*Yes, quite shocking. Not to worry, we'll get our medical chaps to have a look at your pinkies and sort them out for you, they can work miracles these days,*" he said.

"*Will I still be able to play the piano?*" asked Penkovsky. The PM nodded, "*Oh, I should think so.*" Penkovsky smiled, "*It will be a miracle then, because I couldn't play the piano before they took the pliers to my hands!*" The PM looked puzzled. "*A little Russian joke, sir,*" said Penkovsky. "*Quite,*" said the PM.

The PM slowly ripped the sheet of paper off the notepad and read it. As he was doing so, he went as white as the sheet of paper he was holding and murmured, "*Are you certain about these two names?*"

Penkovsky nodded, "*Absolutely, sir. I give you my solemn word. They were both relatively young men at the time they were recruited, in the late 1950's early 1960's. The KGB had assessed that they both had good careers ahead of them within your Security Services, which regrettably, judging by your reaction, seems to have been proven to be correct.*"

"*Unfortunately it was relatively easy to entrap them both, because one was a closet cross-dresser who frequented the night-clubs in Soho, and the other was an inveterate womaniser and gambler. Both easy targets for the KGB.*"

"*Good God, I can hardly believe my eyes. This one's a member of my bloody club!*" thought the PM glancing down at the top name on the piece of paper.

"*Are you certain about this?*" he asked Penkovsky. "*It is absolutely true, let me assure you, sir. Why would I need to lie to you?*" said Penkovsky, shrugging his shoulders,

"*I can give all of the other important details, dates, times, information that changed hands and so forth during my debriefing if you wish. Incidentally, I also know the names of a few Americans who were working in the CIA under deep cover over in Washington at the time, if that would be of any use to you?*"

"*Good gracious me!*" said an astounded PM, "*Yes, you'd better add their names to this list.*"

He passed the piece of paper and pen back to Penkovsky, who wrote the additional names down. When the PM read the additional names, he shook his head and said, "*Buggeration, they'll never believe this.*" He pointed to one of the names, "*I've played golf with this bounder!*" then hurriedly folded the piece of incriminating paper and placed it in his jacket pocket.

The PM exhaled and nodded, "*Thank you for that invaluable information, Colonel. However, I would like you to do me a personal favour. You see, just at this precise moment I do not wish anyone else to know about those names,*" he said, tapping his jacket pocket with a well-manicured finger, "*I need a little time to cogitate, so would much prefer that we keep it between ourselves just for now.*"

Penkovsky nodded, although he would have to ask someone what 'cogitate' meant.

Sir Roger continued, "*Please, at all costs, avoid making any mention of the names that you have written on this piece of paper whilst undergoing your debriefing - at least until late tomorrow anyway."*

Penkovsky nodded, *"I give you my word, and you can rely on me, sir. I received a great deal of training regarding interrogation techniques and know how to resist torture."*

"Oh, we don't employ those sort of extreme techniques here," said the PM his fingers crossed behind his back. *"I assure you that I will do whatever I can to assist. My lips are sealed,"* said Penkovsky. *"Good,"* said the PM *"then let us shake on it."* They shook hands and Penkovsky winced. *"Whoops, sorry about that old chap. Forgot about your pinkies,"* said the PM.

The PM reached forward and pressed the buzzer on his desk to summon Chief of Staff. The PM could feel the piece of incriminating paper burning a hole in his inside pocket. *"The shit will definitely hit the fan when I reveal these names to 'M.' He'll go ballistic,"'* thought the PM.

His Chief of Staff came into the study, *"Ah, Greg,"* said the PM, *"can you let the security escort know that Colonel Penkovsky is ready to leave now."* The Chief of Staff nodded, *"He's waiting just outside the door, Prime Minster."*

Gregory beckoned Colonel Penkovsky, *"This way if you please, Colonel."* Penkovsky stood up, shook hands with the PM again, more carefully this time, then moved towards the study door.

The PM suddenly smacked his forehead head with the palm of his hand, "*Oh how foolish of me! I've just had a brain fart! There's just one more thing, Colonel. I forgot to mention to you that sometime over the next week or so we'll be sending your three new friends back in time to Moscow to collect your wife Olga and daughter, Maria Gapanovitch, for you - although we haven't told the 'Time-Travel' lads about it yet. I'm sure that they won't mind though.*"

Penkovsky, face wreathed in smiles, said, "*Sir, I am virtually speechless with gratitude. My sincere thanks.*" "*Oh, a mere bagatelle, think nothing of it. It's the very least we could do for you,*" said the PM "*and all in a day's work, what!*"

"*Ebat kopat!*" *(Oh Shit*!) thought Penkovsky, as what the PM had just told him sank in. He thought that he'd finally gotten rid of Olga and had been hoping to replace her with a new, improved model. Still, at least he would be seeing his beloved daughter again. As for his wife, he'd just have to bite the bullet and welcome Olga back into his arms. The last thing he wanted to do was upset his new masters by appearing to be ungrateful.

Once Penkovsky had departed, the PM picked up his private scrambler telephone and dialled a number, known and used by only a very select few. After a few seconds it was answered, "*Prime Minister here. Put me through to 'M' would you please.*" ordered the PM.

After a very short delay, 'M' answered, "*Hello Prime Minister?*" "*Switch to Scrambler 'M'!*" ordered the PM and then pressed the scrambler button on his own 'phone.

"*Now, 'M', I'd like you to drop whatever it is that you're doing and pop across to Number 10 immediately. Oh, and you'd better bring the National Security Advisor with you as well. The Foreign Secretary will also be here waiting in my office.*"

"*I have some important news that concerns you all. Penkovsky has come up with the goods.*" "*I'm on my way, sir!*" said 'M.'

The PM then rang off, leaving an intrigued 'M' at the other end of the line.

The PM pressed the buzzer on his desk and asked his Chief of Staff to come back into the office.

"*You buzzed, Prime Minister?*" "*Ah, Greg, get onto the Head of Special Branch will you. Ask her to drop whatever it is she's doing and pop over here straight away. I have a very delicate task for her.*"

"*Tell her that she'll need to bring a people carrier with darkened windows and several armed escorts. They are all to wear civilian clothing - no uniforms! I'll explain everything to her myself once she gets here.*" Gregory nodded and left the P.M's. office.

Once outside the office, Gregory threw himself into his desk chair, beads of sweat breaking out on his top lip, *"Bloody hell, I've finally been rumbled. Oh, my wife's going to slaughter me when she finds out about the 'Hell Fire and Damnation Club' and my gambling debts. Then there's the photo's! Oh My God - I'm doomed!"*
Greg gave his secretary a buzz and asked her politely to bring him a cup of tea then, with quivering hands, he put in the call to the Head of Special Branch.

After he'd finished his telephone call to the Head of Special Branch, Greg lolled back in his chair, deep in thought.

After a few minutes, he slowly slid his desk drawer open and glanced at the small pistol that was tucked away in there, hidden underneath a file cover. He reached for the pistol with trembling fingers, then hearing his secretary tapping on the door, quickly slid the drawer closed.

His secretary, the delightful Amanda, came in carrying the cup of tea. She looked at him and said, *"Are you OK, Chief of Staff, you look a bit green about the gills if you don't mind me saying so. PM not been playing up has he?"*
Gregory shook his head, *"No."*

"You're not sickening for something are you?" she asked. Greg smiled wanly, *"No, I've just had a bit of bad news that's all, Mandy."* *"Anything I can help you with?"* she asked. *"Fraid not, it's just something that's finally caught up with me,"* he replied.

"*I'm sure it's not that bad,*" she said and smiled at him as she left his office.

As she closed the office door, Amanda thought, "*Now what's the little sod been up to?*"

Not too long afterwards the Chief of Staff's outer office door swung open and both the Head of MI6 and the National Security Advisor strode manfully in.

The Chief of Staff stood up and shook hands with them both, "*Ah, gentlemen, the PM is waiting for you, I'll take you both straight in. The Foreign Secretary's already gone through,*" said Gregory. "*Thanks,*" said the Head of MI6, "*oh, and by the way Greg, we'd both like a quick word with you when the P.M's finished with us, if we may?*"

Greg nodded and smiled, his top lip sticking to his teeth, thinking, "*Oh my God, that's it, it's definitely me they've come for, I'm doomed!*" "*You look a bit wan, Greg, are you OK?*" asked the National Security Advisor. Greg shook his head and gave a nervous smile, "*Yes, yes, I'm fine thanks, just another rough day at the office, that's all,*" he replied.

"*Well you should try and get out into the fresh air a bit more,*" advised the Head of MI6, "*this place will drive you into the ground if you let it!*"

A short time later, inside the PM's study, there was a palpable tension and an atmosphere that you could have cut with a knife. Two immaculately suited and booted, late middle-aged men stood before the Prime Minster, heads bowed, both looking like naughty schoolboys who had been summoned by the Headmaster and were waiting to be caned.

"*So that's it, gentlemen,*" said the PM, "*I'll cut straight to the chase. The game's well and truly up for the pair of you - and I use the term 'gentlemen' advisedly*" He passed them both a sheet of paper each, "*Now, I require you both to read and sign these typed confessions before you leave my office.*"

One of the men started to protest and was stopped in his tracks by the PM "*The subject is not up for discussion!*" he said, "*You both know what you've done wrong, I have the proof, now you must accept the inevitable consequences! Sign those documents, immediately!*"

The two men gazed at each other as the PM continued, "*To be perfectly frank, you've both had a jolly good run for your money and I can't for the life of me think why you haven't been collared before now. Naturally that will be the subject of a further investigation. Heads and Deputy Heads will roll!*"

"*You know, if I had my way neither of you would ever see the light of day again, but of course that's not how we do things these days, is it! We'll leave that sordid side of things to your Russian colleagues, what! However, we'll start to drain the swamp today by getting rid of you two!*" he said, voice dripping with sarcasm.

"*Now, sign those pre-prepared statements of confession, then you can get out of my sight. The Head of Special Branch and an armed police escort are waiting for you in the outer office. They'll take you back to your respective offices where you will clear your desks of all personal effects - which will be checked, then hand over your security passes, passports and oyster cards, after which you'll be escorted out of the building and taken away for a full de-briefing, then that's it. Game over.*"

"*I've instructed the Head of Special Branch to spare you the embarrassment of being handcuffed. I do not wish to either see or hear from either of you ever again. If I do, you will be arrested immediately and will be sent down for a very long time. Is that perfectly clear?*"

The two shocked men both nodded. "*You have been well and truly snared, gentlemen, and I have the evidence to prove it!*" added the PM tapping a folder on the desk in front of him, "*I cannot even begin to imagine the damage that you have both caused to the nation by your disloyal and treacherous activities,*" he snorted.

"*Might I just say something, Prime Minister?*" said the more effete of the two. "*No, you may not! I'm having a very fraught day as it is. Now, sign those statements and then piss off out of my sight, you pair of tossers!*" ordered the PM

Realising that the game was well and truly up, the two unmasked traitors signed the statements of confession and

then slunk out of the PM's office without further ado, shutting the door quietly behind them. T
The Head of Special Branch and escorts stood waiting for them and manhandled them straight out of the building without a word being spoken. The Chief of Staff was sat at his desk, giddy with panic, convinced that they'd come for him.

The PM turned to the other men sat in his office, the Foreign Secretary, the Head of MI6 and the National Security Adviser, and said, *"Bit of a relief that, chaps. Neither of them denied it!"* The Head of MI6 nodded, *"Considering that we didn't have any evidence other than Penkovsky's statement, that file was a very clever move, sir!"* *"Yes, bloody good show, Prime Minister!"* said the Foreign Secretary.

"More luck than judgement," said the PM pretending to be modest.

The PM handed the signed confessions to the National Security Advisor, *"Those two confessions are never to see the light of day, is that clear!"* The National Security Advisor nodded, *"They'll be tucked away in the same place as the UFO files, sir, and will not resurface in our life-time,"* he said. The PM nodded his approval.

The PM continued, *"Gentlemen, and this is off the record, I would like a few months to pass then those two scumbags are to meet with very unfortunate and very different fatal accidents. Get your heads together and organise something, please."* The men said nothing, but it was taken as read that they would comply.

After a few moments the Foreign Secretary asked, *"Are they going to be permitted to hang on to their knighthoods until then, Prime Minister?"* *"Yes, because if their knighthoods were to be rescinded it would attract too much attention and bring unwanted queries from the Media."*

"Undoubtedly that would lead to embarrassing questions being raised in the House and then the cat would be out of the bag, so we'll keep a lid on everything and just let 'nature' take its course shall we?" said the PM.

The men nodded. The PM continued, *"Huh, I can still remember all of the kerfuffle when Sir Anthony Blunt was unmasked as being a spy and then stripped of his knighthood. Bloody newspapers loved it and Her Majesty was spitting feathers for months!"* said the Sir Roger.

"I'll give the C.O. of the SAS a call and ask him to make the necessary arrangements for their 'disposal' Prime Minister. Let me assure you that it will all be nice and neat." said the Foreign Secretary.

The PM nodded his approval again, *"Keep me in the loop will you,"* said the PM *"and, gentlemen, nothing about this is to be written down, word of mouth only. This is just between our three selves and the Head of Special Branch."*

"I don't suppose that we could consider 'turning' them and getting them to act as double-agents?" asked the National Security Adviser. *"Absolutely not, old bean. They're two mean spirited, self-centred, traitorous reptiles!"* replied the PM, *"They're categorically out of the running - and that's that! Now, if you'll excuse me gentlemen, I have an appointment at the Palace in half an hour or so and need to prepare myself for that."*

"Her Majesty will want putting in the picture about all of this sordid business. She always wants to know the far end of a fart. God alone knows what she'll have say about two of her knights dropping off the perch. I dread to think."

The men stood up, shook hands with the PM and then left his office.

When the Head of MI6 and the National Security Advisor had walked through into his office after seeing the PM, the Chief of Staff very nearly shat himself. He couldn't believe it when all they wanted him to do was to obtain a couple of tickets for the next Queen's Garden Party at Buckingham Palace. They shook hands with him and left.

On his way out the Head of MI6 turned and said, *"Don't forget now, Greg - fresh air!"* Greg gave him a rictus grin and nodded, *"Yes, yes, quite - 'M' - fresh air."*

A short time later the PM was busy jotting down some of the more salient points that he would be discussing with the Queen, when there was the unmistakeable crack of a pistol shot from the P.M's outer office. The PM jumped up from his desk, pulled his office door open and saw, to his horror, the Chief of Staff slumped across his desk, groaning, a smoking pistol in his hand.

There was a very small amount of blood dripping onto the Chief of Staff's blotting pad, emanating from a small wound on his temple. It had all been too much for Gregory and he'd decided to put himself out of his misery once and for all.

At the other side of the office, directly opposite the Chief of Staff's desk, there were several large chunks of a colourful and irreplaceable Ming vase spread across the Axminster carpet. The vase had been shattered by the bullet from the Chief of Staff's pistol.

Because his hands had been shaking so badly, Gregory had failed to shoot himself properly, merely scraping his temple with the bullet. The bullet had then sped across the office and hit the vase. Seeing his own blood dripping onto the blotting pad, the Chief of Staff had promptly fainted.

The PM gasped, "*Gregory - what in God's name is going on here?*" Before the dazed Chief of Staff could reply, the outer office door opened and Mandy popped her head in, "*Did I hear something going orft?*" she asked. "*Bugger off!*" commanded the PM.

Mandy swiftly exited, easing the door closed behind her. She couldn't wait to get down to the typing pool to tell the girls what she'd seen. Meanwhile, the glassy eyed Chief of Staff sat up and looked around the office vacantly.

"Look!" said the PM pointing at the pile of broken china with a trembling forefinger, *"you've ruined that bloody Ming vase! It was a gift to the nation from the President of North Korea! One of a pair! What's the 's.p.' eh?" "It was only a fake, Prime Minister,"* mumbled Greg. *"It's the principle!"* roared the PM - *"What happened?"* he demanded.

"I, er, I was just cleaning my pistol and unfortunately I had a negligent discharge, sir." gasped the Chief of Staff, dabbing at his bleeding temple with a handkerchief. It was the best excuse he could come up with on the spur of the moment. *"Unload the bloody pistol and put it in your drawer, then come into my office this instant!"* said a furious PM.

"Oh no, he's going to sharpen my feet now, that's all I need," thought the Chief of Staff, his head wound now reduced to a dull throbbing. He unloaded the pistol and threw it into his desk drawer as ordered.

Completely wrong-footing him, the PM said, *"Sit down, Greg, there's a good chap."* and handed him a sticking plaster for his small head wound. *"Oh Christ, he's in the Mother Theresa mode,"* though the Chief of Staff, *"this will be more excruciating than a bollocking."*

The PM looked at him and said, *"Now then, Greg, would you like to explain to me why 'a' you have a loaded* weapon in the office and 'b' why you thought it necessary to fire a shot off at the faux Ming vase?"

"As I said, it was purely a silly and unfortunate accident on my part, sir," stuttered the Chief of Staff. "*I must have left a round up the spout when I was last at the shooting gallery.*"

"*Well, old boy, you really need to be a bit more careful, someone could easily have been injured - and someone i.e. you, will have to pay for a replacement vase you know. We're not covered by insurance for that sort of thing*" said the PM.

"*Can't I just try and stick it back together?*" asked the Chief of Staff, plaintively, "*They tell me that 'Uhu Glue' works a treat?*"

"*Don't be a blithering idiot, man!*" said the PM.

Ж

CHAPTER SIXTEEN

'NEWSFLASH'

Graham and Mike were sat lounging in the 'Dog and Duck' Inn at Beverley, East Yorkshire, one of the town's quaint old coaching inns. They were passing the odd comment whilst scanning the Sunday newspapers, and quaffing pints of Taylors 'Boltmakers Ale' and were both replete after having scoffed a fine traditional roast beef Sunday lunch, closely followed by a steaming sticky-treacle pudding with lashings of thick, creamy custard.

"*I am well and truly stuffed,*" said Graham. "*Aye, we're living the dream, my friend,*" said Mike, patting his tummy. Graham looked at the buttons straining on Mike's shirt, nodded and smiled.

Over in the far corner of the thankfully music-free pub, four ancient 'coffin-dodgers' were noisily slamming their dominoes onto the table and hurtling friendly abuse at each other. There was lots of "*Ey Up! Cop for that one, numpty!"* and *"Sither, I think tha's gorra double-six there! Are you knocking or what?"*

"Ah, just another day in paradise," said Mike.

As Graham leafed through the pages of his newspaper, he peered at the top of one page, paused then gasped, *"Hey Mike, you're never gonna believe this!"* Mike smiled, *"What is it, G, are you volunteering to get the next round in?"*

"No, it's more serious than that," said Graham, *"there's an article here by their Foreign Correspondent in Moscow about those who've been appointed to various senior security posts after surviving the recent overthrow of President Putin - and get this - the new 1st Chairman of the Committee for State Security and Leader of Soviet Security and Intelligence Services is none other than a certain 'General' Igor Bloody Chelpinski - and his Chief of Staff is no less than his sidekick - the now Colonel 'Doom-brain' Ivanski Gregorovitch!"*

"God save us!" said Mike, *"So, they both must have managed to escape from the 'Hidden Library' then; wonder how they managed that? He's a sleekit swine is that Chelpinski!"*

Graham nodded in agreement, *"Well, he's certainly a survivor. He probably battered his way out of the 'Hidden Library' using some of those gold bars that we left in there. You know, I wouldn't be surprised if he didn't become President himself eventually!"* *"Well, he wouldn't be the first KGB operative to have done that, would he,"* said Mike.

Mike continued, *"You ken, Graham, we should have suspected something when those three Fabergé eggs came onto the market in New York last month. Remember - on his last run from the 'Hidden Library' in the 'T3-Travellator' as well as Finland, you transported Chelpinski to his Mother's house in St Petersburg and deposited some of the booty there. As I recall, he had several of those Fabergé eggs with him the."*

Graham nodded, *"Yes, that's right, he did – and he had that beautiful jewel encrusted sword with him."*

Mike shook his head, *"And we thought that Chelpinsky and his mate Gregorski would be trapped in the 'Hidden Library' for ever and ever, amen. Wonder what happened to the dozy KGB guard that we left in there with them?"* said Mike.

"Those two probably ate him!" replied Graham. *"Aye, well I suppose anything's better than Mushka Yulia!"* said Mike. *"You can never underestimate people like that brute Chelpinski. Psychopaths like him always seem to float to the surface of a very murky pond,"* said Mike, *"and he must have done some pretty fast talking to his bosses to explain the disappearance of Penkovski."*

"I would imagine that like you advised him at the time," said Graham,*"he probably just told them that Penkovsky*

departed this life via the furnace room. It wouldn't have been questioned."

Mike nodded, *"Yes, suppose so, but what about us getting Penkovsky's family out of Moscow. That must have raised a few suspicious eyebrows. Wonder how Chelpinski slithered out of that one?"* said Graham. *"He'll just have blamed the Brits or the Americans for looking after one of their spies families,"* said Mike. Graham nodded and said, *"He's obviously one of life's survivors is old Chelps."*

Mike said, *"You know, the more I think about it, the more I agree with you, he'll have done exactly as we suggested and pretended that Penkovsky had been been put in the furnace then his ashes disposed of, like the rest of his victims,"* said Mike, *"I mean, how could they check that out, eh!"* Graham nodded in agreement.

Graham said, *"Hey, I wonder if Ed De Jong knows that Chelpinski's still kicking about?"* Mike nodded, "*Good point, Graham. I'd better give him a bell when I get home. We don't want him nipping over to Russia to do a bit of ducking and diving and falling headlong into the clutches of the KGB, or the FSB as they call themselves now."*

"*I would imagine that Chelpinsky will have our three names at the top of an 'undesireable aliens' list."* said Graham. Mike nodded in agreement, "*Yes, I'm sure you're right there, pal.*"

"By the way, Mr St Anier, what size shoes do you take?" asked Mike. Graham sighed, *"I'm not falling for that old chestnut again. I'll go and get the beers in!"*

A smiling Mike said, *"Could you bring me a nippy sweetie as well, Graham. I need a wee bit of a jolt to get over the shock of Chelpinski and his evil henchman Gregory Peckovitch resurfacing."*

"You know what, I think I'll join you in that wee dram, purely for medicinal purposes you understand!" said Graham. *"Good man! You can beat an egg, you can beat a drum - but you cannae beat a pint of Timmy Taylors reinforced with a wee nip!"* said a grinning Mike.

Whilst Graham queued patiently at the crowded bar, waiting to be served, Mike sat in the corner of the barroom smiling to himself and thinking about Oleg Penkovsky and his family, who were now 'living the dream' tucked away in a far corner of Canada.

Both Oleg and his wife Olga had undergone comprehensive plastic surgery and were enjoying their new lives, in the lap of luxury - courtesy of the British Government's generous pension, along with the huge amount of money that had been generated from the sale of the 'Russian Stash.' As long as the Russian Security Service didn't locate them then they'd all live happily ever after.

Mike, Ed and Graham had popped across to Canada a couple of times in the 'T3-Travellator' just to see how they were getting on.

Penkovsky had put a bit of weight on, had grown a luxuriant moustache and was looking very prosperous, which of course he now was. He'd even developed a Canadian accent. Olga had lost several stone, had unbdergone a breast enhancement and gone blond. Oleg and Olga were both now good friends again and were rubbing along nicely.

Mike had left an emergency contact number with Penkovsky so that he could nip over to Canada to collect him and his family at short notice if ever Oleg felt under threat from the Russian bad boys. Happy days.

The precious items that they'd taken from the 'Hidden Library' had gradually been sold for very profitable amounts and the three lads would never have to work again if they didn't want to. Ed had also made sure that Princess Anastasia had not been left wanting and she was also living in the lap of luxury, as befitted a Royal Princess, money was now no object. Everything had turned out very well.

Once Graham returned with their drinks, Mike had a proposition to put to him that he knew would thrill him to bits. This one was as a result of a very recent 'phone call he'd received from Ed De Jong in Amsterdam, confirming precisely how much profit they'd made from the sale of the Russian 'treasure' the amount of which had definitely put a smile on their off-shore bank manager's face.

Much more interestingly, though, was Ed's proposal in relation to locating and recovering some of the many millions of dollars that had been stashed away in Russia, Moscow to be precise, by President Saddam Hussein, prior to his downfall.

Ed had assured Mike that there was more than enough dollars to go around and that it would be a bit of fun trying to get some of them! Mike had promised to discuss it with Graham and then get back to Ed. They didn't need the money, but getting it would be a bit of a wheeze.

"Mike Fraser! You look like the cat that got the cream. What are you grinning at?" asked Graham as he sat down. *"Well, Graham, funnily enough, Ed De Jong rang me the other day and he's stumbled across some information that he thought we might be interested in,"* said Mike. *"Come on then,"* said Graham eagerly, *"spill the beans!"*

Mike said, *"Just let me have a wee swig of this beer, then I'll tell you all about it."* He took a hefty swig of his Timothy Taylor's 'Boltmakers' Ale, wiped the foam off his top lip with the back of his hand, then sighed and said, *"Life just can't get any better. I'm in seventh heaven!"* *"And I'm still sat here waiting!"* said Graham.

"Och, sorry Graham. Well, according to Ed, there's a security compound in Moscow that is ripe for our specific attention," said Mike. *"Oh yes, and what's so 'special'*

about it?" asked Graham. "*It would appear that it is packed from floor to ceiling with crates and crates of crisp American dollars, stashed there by Saddam Hussein before he took the long leap. In essence, or should I say in a 'T3-Travellator' - Ed wants us all to pop across to Moscow and reduce the pile a bit.*"

"*When?*" asked Graham. "*Oh, he said that there's no rush, the money's not going anywhere, and could we both pop across to Amsterdam next week to discuss how we'd go about doing it. Are you up for a slice of the action?*" asked Mike.

Graham smiled, "*Does a chicken have lips!*" he said. Mike sighed, and said, "*Ah, Time-Travel, it's the gift that just keeps on giving.*" Graham looked at him and winked. He knew that they were both well and truly hooked.

Ж

THE END

(EXTRACT FROM THE NEXT BOOK)

'SADDAM'S MISSING MILLIONS'

'President Saddam Hussein Abd al-Majid al-Tikriti'
High Excellency, Field Marshal
& Commander of all Iraq

Introduction:

Saddam Hussein Abd al-Majid al-Tikriti was the President of Iraq - from July 1979 until April 2003, when his time expired and he was dangled from the end of a rope. For several years before his elevation to President, Saddam had already been the 'de facto' head of Iraq. He had been a very brutal dictator and it is believed that the total number of Iraqis slaughtered by his government during various purges and genocides was somewhere in the region of a quarter of a million innocent souls. His invasions of Iran and Kuwait also resulted in many thousands of deaths. Saddam Hussein's power throughout his reign was absolute.

Things came to a head for Saddam, however, in 2003 when a mighty coalition, led by the USA, invaded Iraq and toppled both him and his Ba'ath Party. The Ba'ath Party was disbanded and 'free' elections were then held. Saddam, who had slunk off into hiding, was eventually captured on the 13th of December 2003, after being discovered skulking in a hidden underground pit outside the town of ad-Dawr, near Tikrit, as a result of an American military security operation, 'OPERATION RED DAWN.'

An exhausted and frightened Saddam captiulated without a fight.

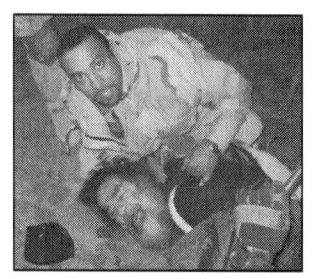

The capture of
'President Saddam Hussein Abd al-Majid al-Tikriti'
High Excellency, Field Marshal & Commander of all Iraq

(US Army photo)

Towards the end of the invasion, when American bombs began falling on the Iraqi capital, the President's son, Qusay Hussein and Abid al-Hamid Mahmood, Saddam's personal assistant, along with five other 'officials' removed nearly $1 billion dollars from the Nation's Central Bank, using two or three flat-bed trucks to transport the money to a secret location.

The removal had been authorised by President Saddam personally, prior to his downfall. Only a few key people were told where the money was being taken. It is believed that the money was to be used to fund the President's escape and also to help him and his family survive once he'd been removed from power.

The money amounted to roughly a quarter of the Iraqi Central Bank's hard currency reserves. In addition to that, about $400 million American dollars and a huge amount of Iraqi currency was also taken by looters from banks across the country, most of which disappeared into thin air.

Saddam was duly placed on trial front of an Iraqi Special Tribunal where he was found guilty of crimes against humanity and sentenced to death by hanging. Like one of his hero's, Germany's Hermann Gőering, Saddam requested that he be executed by firing squad, which, like Gőering, was denied. He was to be hanged and that was the end of it.

Saddam ate his last meal, his favourite - chicken and rice, washed down with a cup of hot water and honey, before being executed early one morning at the joint Iraqi-American base, Camp Justice, in Iraq on the 30th of December 2006.

It has long been rumoured that a fortune in unclaimed cash is tucked away in a high security area at Moscow's Sheremetyevo Airport. It is believed to have been stashed there by Saddam Hussein whilst he was in power.

Upon investigation, the money appeared to have been transported to Moscow from the Arab Emirates.

'Sheremetyevo Airport, Moscow'

It is also claimed that there are some 200 one-ton wooden pallets containing a total of up to $26 Billion American dollars stacked up in Sheremetyevo Airport's closely guarded high security compound and that it belongs to a so far untraceable individual called 'Ferzan Mollags.'

The Russian Intelligence Agencies took control of and responsibility for the shipment and so there it sits gathering dust in the compound - which is purportedly as safe as Fort Knox, waiting to be collected - when the time is ripe.

FERZAN	MOLLAGS	SADDAM	HUSSEIN
6 letters	7 letters	6 letters	7 letters

(Just saying – Author)

Ж

CHAPTER ONE

'MOVING ON!'

A totally relaxed, unconcerned and thoroughly bored looking President Saddam Hussein was sat back lounging in a finely tooled leather desk chair in his lush, windowless personal bunker at the Presidential Palace, his feet on the desk and idly twirling a gold plated 9mm Glock 18c pistol around his forefinger, rather like a cowboy in a 'B' western movie. The gold pistol was one of several such weapons that had been presented to him by various feather-bedding heads of State wishing to curry favour with the President, back when Saddam was still a forced to be reckoned with

Mounted on the wall behind the Dictator's desk was also an eye-catching, glittering gold-plated AK-47 rifle, one of several that Saddam had scattered around his palaces. Stood directly opposite Saddam and direct line of fire was his 'body-double,' an apprehensive Akram Shamoon. Akram was praying that the safety catch on the President's pistol was switched onto the safe mode.

The resemblance between Saddam Hussein and Akram Shamoon was startling and it was said that the only time anyone, even some of Saddam's close family members, could tell the difference between the two of them was when the Presidential Bodyguards accompanying the President were seen to be relaxed, laughing and joking.

That indicated to those in the know that it was Akram and not Saddam that they were there protecting. The Presidential Bodyguard would not have dared to laugh and joke in the presence of the real, murderous and vindictive President. He would have had them shot out of hand.

The double, Akram Shamoon, purported, in public anyway, to worship and adore his President and had publicly sworn to willingly lay down his life for him if necessary. In reality though, it was just a way for Akram to earn a good living and one for which he was paid handsomely.

Unbeknown to Akram, the option of sacrificing himself was now out of his hands because Saddam had arranged for precisely that to happen to him. Akram Shamoon was destined to be the 'sacrificial lamb.' The date for Akram Shamoon's 'voluntary' suicide had already been decided and pencilled in.

The Presidential intention was that Akram would go on the run and would not under any circumstances allow himself to be captured alive by the enemy forces. His body would then be 'found' and the enemy, wrongly, would assume that it was Saddam Hussein. Were Akram to attempt to change his mind and not want to commit suicide, those members of the Presidential Bodyguard that would always be accompanying him would ensure his swift demise.

It had to look as though Saddam Hussein had been defiant and fought the enemy bravely to the very end, but under no circumstances was Akram to be captured alive.

Unusually for him, Saddam was dressed in civilian clothing and not wearing one of the many splendid, colourful well-tailored military uniforms that he favoured. To all intents and purposes it could have just been another day at the office.

As the President was speaking to Akram they could both clearly hear the sound of enemy jet engines screaming across down-town Baghdad as they flew over, dropping their deadly loads on various key military targets. Every few minutes there was the thunderous sound of yet more bombs exploding, followed by the blood-chilling whooshing of rockets being fired from coalition air force jets at anything that moved on the ground.

The cacophony of sound was interspersed with the Iraqi Ground Defence Forces pounding anti-aircraft cannons and heavy machine guns, their gun-crews frantically firing at the incoming aircraft with, apparently, very little demonstrable effect. If anything, despite the Iraqi forces desperate efforts, the volume of incoming destructive ordnance was increasing.

It didn't take the brains of an Archbishop to work out that it was rapidly becoming a downhill battle and one that Saddam and his General's knew they couldn't and wouldn't win.

Unlike another one of his all-time heroes, Adolf Hitler, Saddam had decided, despite all of his speeches to the contrary, that he wasn't prepared to make a final heroic stand against the coalition forces from the Presidential 'bunker' inside which he was currently skulking and sulking. Saddam knew full well what would happen to him and his family if they fell into enemy hands - and that it wouldn't be a pretty sight.

He recalled what had happened to the Italian Dictator, Benito Mussolini, when he and his mistress Claretta Petacci had been captured by Italian partisans – and it hadn't been a pretty sight.

'Mussolini'

He wasn't particularly worried about the coalition forces, but he knew that there were many of his own people thirsting for revenge for the outrages that had been committed against them and who were determined to get their hands on him. He would be torn limb from limb.

With animal cunning, which he possessed in barrow-loads, Saddam had recognised that he had, for the moment, overstayed his welcome in Iraq. In view of which, he had decided to grab whatever riches he could and make a swift, covert exit when the right moment came.

Determined to live on to fight another day, he had planned to temporarily leave his beloved Iraq but would return in due course and resume what he considered to be his rightful position as Head of State. He would then wreak a terrible revenge upon those who he considered had brought about his downfall.

Just as Saddam began speaking to Akram there was a particularly thunderous explosion. The walls of the room shook and a layer of fine white dust floated down from the ceiling onto the President's desk.

The ostentatious Swarovsky chrystal chandelier that lit the room rattled, flickered and then suddenly went out, leaving Saddam's desk lamp as the only source of light. Akram visibly flinched, but Saddam didn't bat an eyelid, still convinced that he was invincible.

"*Fear not, my brother, no harm will come to us*" said Saddam, "*we have several feet of reinforced concrete above our heads protecting us. We are perfectly safe in here.*" Saddam looked at the badly frightened Akram and thought, uncharitably, "*Huh, look at him, trembling like a jelly! Cowards die many times before their death. The valiant never taste death but once.*"

Pointing to an ornate throne-like chair directly opposite him, Saddam waved his hand towards it and said, "*Rest your bones and be seated, Akram, you are making me nervous!*" Akram sat down and waited patiently for the pearls of wisdom that he was sure were about to drip from his beloved President's mouth.

Akram wished that the President would get a move on, he wanted to get out of the palace, desert his post and scuttle off back home to his family. Akram had already decided that the first thing he was going to do once he got home was to shave off his bushy moustache and rinse the black dye out of his hair. Even he could see that the body-double game was well and truly up.

Unfortunately for Akram, President Saddam had made other plans for him.

Saddam took a deep breath, then began speaking. "*I have summoned you here today, Akram Shamoon, because I wish to discuss something of great importance with you!*" he said, "*We have, you and I, attended many secret briefings in the past regarding the implementation of* **'OPERATION DOUBLE-DIAMOND'** - *is that not the* *case?"* Akram nodded respectfully and replied, *"That is correct, Your Excellency."*

The President continued, *"Good. Well, the time has now come for the operation to be activated. You know precisely what is required of you and I am relying upon you to carry out your duty to the letter. You will be well rewarded for your efforts and in the unlikely event that things should go amiss, then you have my sworn word that your family will never want for anything again, ever."*

"They and indeed you will be well taken care of, I personally guarantee that."

Wringing his hands, Akram, who was starting to sweat, replied, ingratiatingly, *"Mister President, please permit me to assure you that my life is yours to do with as you wish ..."* Saddam held his hand up, *"My brother, I appreciate that you are dedicated to making the ultimate sacrifice - if it ever becomes necessary, but I don't believe that is likely to happen."*

Saddam smiled, causing Akram to sweat even more, *"Fortunately we are always one step ahead of those who wish to do us harm and in particular those stupid Americans who don't know their arses from their elbows."*

"It has been and always will be a great honour to serve you, in whatever capacity, and I have every faith in you, Your Excellency," said the fawning look-alike, Akram.

Saddam Hussein nodded and smiled again, his hooded eyes looking for all the world like those of a fearsome crocodile surfacing from the murky depths, its jaws about to snap shut on the juicy and unsuspecting body of an innocent swimmer.

Pausing momentarily, Saddam sucked on his gleaming white teeth then said to Akram, "*Once I have finished speaking with you, you will be escorted from the palace by members of my Presidential Bodyguard and taken to the 'Domes Palace' where you are to remain for one evening only. After that you will switch alternatively between the 'Domes' and the 'Victory over America' Palaces for the forseeable future. That is a course of action that would be expected of me and will continue to confuse the enemy. Is that clearly understood?*"

Akram nodded, "*I am yours to command, Your Excellency.*"

Akram knew that Saddam had always preferred the Domes Palace to any of his several other palaces simply because it had a fully equipped 'en-suite' torture chamber, situated immediately adjacent to his personal suite. The well used torture facility was, like a bathroom, simply a matter of convenience as far as Saddam was concerned and he'd spent many happy hours in there watching the cruel and horrific proceedings.

Akram could never understand how the President could fornicate and sleep comfortably in a bedroom where there was nothing but a thin wall separating him from the blood-stained hell on earth that was a torture chamber; one that was equipped with several fearsome wall-mounted surgical instruments, the mere sight of which would turn a victims bowels to ice.

Saddam hardly ever 'bloodied' his hands, but in the main took great enjoyment from watching the proceedings, that was until he got sometimes got bored and ordered that the poor unfortunate victim was to be 'despatched.'

Giving Akram a lop-sided grin, Saddam said, *"You had better be on your way, my brother. My Chief of Staff will contact you in the very near future with further instructions. Obey only him, no-one else. In the highly unlikely event that you do fall into enemy hands and are taken prisoner, you know precisely what is required of you!"*

A trembling Akram said, *"I will willingly lay my life down for you, Your Excellency."* Akram leapt to his feet and begged, *"May I have the honour of kissing your hand, Mister President?"* Saddam thought, *"Akram, you imbecile, you can kiss my arse for all I care. Your days on this earth are numbered."*

Saddam nodded and held out his hand, Akram then lightly kissed the back of it. Akram noticed that despite his stoic demeanour, the President's nicotine stained fingers were trembling slightly. *"Ultimate victory will be yours, Excellency, you are a God amongst lesser men,"* said Akram. An expressionless Saddam nodded in agreement, thinking, *"Ah, Akram, will you never learn. It is better to remain silent and be thought a fool than to open your mouth and remove all doubt.*"

"*You may leave me now!*" said Saddam, waving Akram away. A relieved Akram bowed, turned and walked out of the Presidential office and away from the evil presence of his glorious leader for what was to be the very last time, although he didn't know that.

On his way out of the palace, Akram met Saddam's malevolent number two son, Qusay Hussein. Akram sidestepped Qusay, saluted then bowed his head respectfully as Qusay strode past. "*Good morning, Your Excellency!*" said Akram.

The vile Qusay had been known to execute people for not paying him the requisite amount of respect and the expected obeisance, (as one unfortunate Army officer had discovered when he failed to salute him and was beatern to death on the spot).

That unfortunate officer had also been shot in the head by an enraged and murderous Qusay. When his doting father, the President had heard about it, he'd just tutted and laughed and put it down to Qusay being a little over-enthusiastic in his duties.

Qusay glanced at his father's double and half-heartedly returned Akram's salute. Then, much to Akram's relief, Qusay continued on his way. A much relieved Akram, glad to be away from Qusay's evil and pervading presence, scuttled off to find the Presidential Bodyguard, as instructed. The sound of explosions outside the palace seemed to be getting more frequent.

Without being invited to, Qusay sat down in the chair in front of his Father, one of a very few who would dare to do that. *"Well, what news have you, my son?"* asked Saddam. *"Your aircraft is fully fuelled and waiting for your arrival at Saddam International Airport, as per your instructions, father. It has had it's livery totally altered and now looks exactly like a Red Cross aircraft, as does the second aircraft that we are also using for the escape and evasion."*

He continued, *"Your wife Samaira, my sisters Raghad, Hala and Rana, accompanied by their families, are on board the first aircraft waiting for your arrival. The remainder of our family, including myself and Uday, will follow on in the second aircraft, shortly after you have departed."*

"Where is that rascal Uday at the moment?" asked Saddam. *"He's out settling a few old scores before we leave here, Father,"* said Qusay. Saddam shook his head sorrowfully, *"That boy will be the death of me!"* he said.

Saddam continued, *"And my Parisoula?"* (Parisoula Lamapsos was Saddam's long-time mistress). *"After we were informed by the Mukhabarat* (Jihaz Al-Mukhabarat Al-Amma, the General Directorate of Iraqi Intelligence) *that her movements were being closely monitored by enemies of the State, father, I had her moved by road to the safe house in Al Aubar. She will be well guarded there.*

She was accompanied by a small but very efficient armed escort at dark o'clock this morning. I have informed them that their own lives depend upon her continued safety."

Qusay glanced down at his ulktra-expensive Rolex Daytona jewel encrusted, solid gold watch, (rumoured to have been once owned by the American actor Paul Newman), and said, *"Later on today your Parisoula will be moved safely across the Iraq border. I will then get a confirmatory 'phone call to that effect and will let you know at the earliest opportunity."*

Saddam nodded, *"Yes, you must let me know immediately. As you are aware, I am very fond of Parisoula, Qusay, and would not like to see any harm befall her."*

"She will not come to any harm, Father, you have my word on that," said a confident Qusay. *"Well, in the unlikely event that it does, then it will be your cock that is on the block, as the vulgar Amercans say!"* said Saddam. Qusay smiled at his father's veiled threat but could never work out if he meant it or not. The odds were that he did.

Qusay had larded many palms with a great amount of (other people's) money to ensure that Parisoula would get out of Iraq and reach Moscow safely. Moscow was where the President and his crew were heading for once they 'abandoned ship.'

Qusay had also made all of the necessary arrangements with the Russian SFB and would be doling out even more money to them once he arrived in Moscow himself.

Money was the very least of the Hussein family problems. They'd been stashing vast amounts away in various safe places for many years in the event that they had to cut and run.

'FSB - The Russian Federal Security Services'

"Parisoula will catch up with you in Moscow in a few days, father," said Qusay confidently, *"I personally guarantee that."* Patting Qusay on the shoulder, Saddam said, *"Congratulations, my dear son. I know that I can totally rely upon you to get the job done."*

Sighing contentedly, Saddam continued, *" How I love it when a good plan comes together. Now, my son, tell me about the money. Is everything in order there?"*

Qusay nodded, *"Yes father. I will be leaving for the State Bank very shortly, accompanied by Abid al-Hamid Mahmood and a small escort of the Presidential Bodyguard. Abid has already arranged for the 'withdrawal' of the final one billion dollars, American, and for it to be trucked away to the secret location, precisely as we agreed."*

"*Excellent,*" said Saddam. Qusay continued, "*Once the money has been cross-loaded and is ready to be moved onto the next location, as per standard procedure - the bodyguards and drivers will be executed, thus removing that link in the chain.*"

"*And the onwards transmission of the money to Moscow?*" asked Saddam.

"*All in hand, Father. As you directed, it will be taken by container ship to Saint Petersburg where it will then be unloaded and moved overland to the secure location in Moscow. As agreed with the SFB, it will be disguised throughout as medical supplies. The Russian President's staff could not have been more helpful. It's as if they've done this sort of thing before,*" said Qusay.

Saddam smiled knowingly and tapped his bulbulous, red veined nose with a well manicured forefinger, "*They have, my son, many times and for many people. They are not to be trusted though, they are attracted to money like iron filings to a magnet!*"

"*Very well, in view of what you have just told me,*" Saddam continued, "*let* **'OPERATION DOUBLE-DIAMOND'** *begin!*"

Qusay nodded, "*Everything is ready, Father. Your armoured Mercedes has been fuelled up and is waiting at the secret exit at the rear of the palace to take you straight to the airport. We have ensured that no-one will see you leaving here.*"

He continued, *"Once you have left the airport and the second aircraft has taken off, those men that escorted us to the airport and those in the aircraft tower monitoring our departure will be removed immediately and executed. There will be no witnesses left to let the cat out of the bag,"* said Qusay. Saddam nodded his approval. *"We must keep our enemies guessing,"* said Saddam.

Saddam was inordinately proud of Qusay, who was a most reliable son, the complete opposite of his totally unpredictable and lunatic brother, Uday. Uday was a different kettle of fish and was, alas, more like his father in temperament and needed to be handled with kid gloves. He had an incredibly short fuse.

Saddam had realised long ago that Uday was a suitable case for treatment and had arranged to have him admitted to one of the best psychiatric hospitals in Moscow at the earliest opportunity after their arrival there. Uday had never been the same since the assassination attempt when he had been badly wounded. It had tipped him completely over the edge.

As Qusay stood up to leave, Saddam said, *"Oh, there is just one other small matter, Qusay!"* *"There is something I have forgotten to do, father?"* asked Qusay. Pointing towards the door, Saddam asked, *"Has the family of my body-double, Akram Shamoon, been dealt with in accordance with my instructions?"* Qusay nodded, *"Yes indeed, father, they were executed and disposed of late last night, as per your wishes."*

Saddam nodded approvingly and smiled. *"Good boy, well done. You have an excellent eye for detail!"* he said, *"It's the little things that matter."*

After Qusay had departed, Saddam stood up, stretched then confidently holstered his pistol. He, more than anyone else, knew full well that the time had come for him to step off the international stage - just for the moment anyway. It was beyond doubt that the hated coalition forces would do their utmost to try to capture him alive and place him on trial, and that's where his body-double Akram Shamoon would come into the picture. The real Saddam would be long gone and skulking in Moscow.

Akram Shamoon had been well briefed regarding the Presidential deception and would continue with it for as long as humanly possible and if captured he was instructed to crunch down on the cyanide capsule that had been hidden inside one of his molars by Saddam's personal Dentist.

Despite his never-ending protestations of undying loyalty, Akram had already decided that if he was captured by the enemy he would immediately confess to being a 'body-double' and then eventually, when everything had quietened down, he would hopefully be returned unharmed to the bosom of his family. After all, he personally hadn't committed any crimes other than acting as a body-double for the President and where was the harm in that? He was also confident that there would be a good living to be made in the theatre and possibly in movies as a double for Saddam after the war.

Akram had absolutely no intention of committing suicide and had secretly arranged for his own dentist to remove the cyanide capsule from his tooth and replace it with a dummy one. Why should he take the fall, he'd thought. All he'd done was play a part - and he'd had no choice in the matter.

Meanwhile, as Akram headed for the 'Domes Palace' the elaborate security precautions that had been made for Saddam Hussein and his cohorts to fly out of the beleaguered Saddam International Airport kicked in and the two illegally disguised private jets that were waiting to take off and then fly on to the safety of Moscow by a circuitous route, well away from prying eyes, had their engines fired up and ready.

Both jets, as his son Qusay had informed him, had received expert paint jobs to disguise their original Iraqi Air Force livery so that they now resembled International Red Cross aircraft. Needless to say, the workmen who had carried out the respraying jobs would not be using paint sprayers ever again. As soon as their work had been completed they had been taken away and executed.

As planned, Saddam's airliner would be the first to leave, then the second similarly disguised aircraft would follow half an hour or so later, carrying the remainder of Saddam's close relatives and a few key Generals. Like the first aircraft, it was cram-packed with gold, jewellery and other such valuables that had been pilfered over the years.

Once he had boarded his aircraft and it had taken off, Saddam turned to a very pretty, leggy French stewardess and ordered, *"Bring me some iced champagne, then instruct the pilot to get me the Russian President on the 'phone!"*

The Stewardess nodded, *"Immediately, Your Excellency."*

The stewardess returned with the champagne, the President's favourite, a bottle of Brunello Di Montalcino Reserve 1950 Biondi Santigh (a snip at at £10,500 a bottle). She carefully poured a glass of the sparkling champagne, not daring to spill a drop, and placed it on the table in front of Saddam, just as the small red light on the 'phone in front of Saddam started to flash.

"Is there anything else you require, Your Excellency?" she asked. He leered at her and said, *"Perhaps later,"* then waved her away.

He picked up the telephone and said to his Russian counterpart, *"Mister President, how are you, my dear comrade. I thought you'd like to know that I have now left Iraq and am on my way to Russia."* He listened for a few moments as the Russian President replied, *"I look forward to meeting you again, my brother. All of the arrangements are in hand."*

On arrrival in Moscow, it was planned that Saddam would be met at the airport by his dear and close friend, the Russian President himself, then be swept off under heavily armed guard to a pre-prepared huge and luxurious dacha where he would eventually be reunited with key members of his own staff and family at a sumptuous welcoming party.

Both of the Iraqi aircraft would then be unloaded, refuelled and flown out of Russia to Kazakhstan where arrangements had been made for them to be destroyed and their crews executed.

The Russian had also arranged for Saddam's mistress, the glamorous Parisoula Lamapsos, to be provided with a luxury apartment in central Moscow, hidden well away from the eyes of Saddam's fiery wife. The FSB would ensure that never the twain would meet.

It was taken as read that once Saddam had become bored with his mistress Parisoula, she would either be paid off or more than lilely disposed of, probably to a brothel.

Once he had settled in and got his metaphoric breath back, Saddam would then begin making plans with his team and the Russians for his eventual return to power. Then, he vowed, he would make his enemies tremble and sweat with fear. Saddam was not a man to be crossed. He had a long memory, was extremely vindictive and would have his revenge.

Ж

ABOUT THE AUTHOR
TERRY CAVENDER

After a 30-year career in the British Army, Terry retired as a Major, then took up an appointment with the Ministry of Defence for a further 18 years, latterly as a Media Operations Officer, until finally retiring. He has written, produced and directed several stage plays, pantomimes, films and radio plays but now concentrates on writing fiction/faction.

Born in Keighley, West Yorkshire, Terry and his wife Maggie now live in faded gentility in the delightful market town of Beverley, East Yorkshire.

Printed in Poland
by Amazon Fulfillment
Poland Sp. z o.o., Wrocław